START AGAIN

J. SAMAN

1

ate

THIS IS the moment I've been dreading. Then again, it can't get any worse for me, so what the hell do I have left to lose? Absolutely nothing.

Freshly baked zucchini bread infuses the air with cinnamon and chocolate, which would usually be comforting. But it's not. Partially because comfort and I haven't been on speaking terms for quite a while, and partially because I have the unhappy task of trying to speak to my mother about something important this morning.

Never a pleasant thing.

The couch cushion sinks beneath me as I shift my position to cross my legs, taking my can of Diet Coke with me. I haven't slept much this week. Not that I've been sleeping all that great over the last two years, but it had been better until now. My fingers go up to the pendant hanging off my neck, touching it gently, a reflex when I think about them.

I should be in a better place than I am.

At least that's what my therapist says. She hasn't been too pleased with my progress to date. Every time she mentions something along those lines in her perfectly crafted, psychobabble way, I remind her —far less subtly—that I lost my reason for living, so she should just back the fuck off.

I made the changes I had to, and the rest is just a matter of getting through each day.

But now those changes are no longer enough.

I see them everywhere.

I see them in the grocery store, at the movies, in the coffee shop, and walking around town. Everywhere. And it's killing me. Little by little. Day by day.

It's killing me.

I can feel it, and I need to do something. I need to get out of here. Away from the place that I spent my entire life with Eric, and then the last few years with Maggie.

So I'm sitting on my mother's couch, nursing my Diet Coke and avoiding the guilt zucchini bread in front of me. Her small frame is sitting across from me in her hideous floral chair, patiently waiting for me to say something.

Here goes.

"I'm leaving, Mom."

"Leaving?" she asks, her dark blonde eyebrows raising up to her hairline. "But you just got here."

I sigh. This isn't going to be fun. "No, Mom. I mean, I'm moving away. Leaving town."

She leans forward with a scowl etched on her wrinkle-free surgically enhanced face. "Moving? Oh, goodness, Kate. Don't be ridiculous. You know your problems will follow you wherever you go."

Right. And *that's* why I hate talking to my mother.

"This is happening, Mom. Can't you just wish me well?"

"Of course I wish you well, Kate. I hope things go well for you in... Where did you say you're going?"

"I didn't say," I mutter, ignoring her jab. "I haven't decided yet."

"Well." She leans back, crossing her arms and legs, essentially dismissing the idea. "Be sure to let me know when you figure it out. We'll have to get together to see you off on your little trip."

Now it's my turn to lean forward. "It's not a trip. And I'm leaving in a few days. I'm gonna drive around the country until I find a place that speaks to me."

"That's absurd." She purses her lips off to the side. "You can't just drive across the country—" Her arm sweeps out in front of her toward the window, before folding it across her chest again. "—by yourself, until something *speaks* to you." Her head shakes back and forth, her blonde bob swinging around her shoulders. "It's not safe for a young woman to go off on her own with no plan or agenda. No, Kate." She points her finger at me as if that makes it final. "No."

"I wasn't asking permission. I'm twenty-seven years old and am perfectly capable of making my own decisions."

Yeah, I'm trying to hold firm, but this woman has always had a way of reducing me to a weak puddle of coward.

"I'm going," I huff out, setting my can on the coaster and rubbing my hands up and down my face. "I need this, Mom," I confess, my hands still covering my eyes. I hate speaking to my mother this way. She's never been loving or nurturing, which makes emotional confessions that much harder. "I'm drowning here, and I can't find my way back."

She scoffs. Actually freaking scoffs at me. "That's ridiculous. You'll be fine. You just need to get yourself back out there."

I suck in a deep breath, holding it tight in my lungs before I let it out and explode at her. Because I'm *this* close.

Instead, I sit back, squaring my shoulders and looking her dead in the eyes. The same blue as mine.

"I'm going, Mom. In two days. I've given up my apartment, packed my things, and that's it." I stand, glaring back at her narrowed eyes, wishing I had her love and support because I desperately need both right now. "I was just letting you know."

I take two steps toward the front door before she calls out to me.

"Wait." She sighs, sounding just a little defeated and a lot annoyed. "Fine."

I turn back to her, but don't bother to sit again.

"I get it. You're a grown woman and you're leaving." She waves a dismissive hand. "I can't stop you." She stands now, walking toward me and placing her hands on my shoulders. "If I suggest something, will you listen?"

"Maybe," I reply hesitantly. I can see the wheels spinning in her eyes, and that's hardly ever a good thing.

"Well." She laughs lightly. "This is just too darling for words." She giggles like she's just had the most brilliant idea. "So I was talking to Jessica Grant this morning. You remember her."

I shake my head, but she just continues.

"You met her when you were six, at their house outside of Philadelphia. She was my sorority sister in college." Another head shake. "Whatever." She waves me off like it's not important. "She was telling me how her son is moving across the country to Seattle for a new job that he starts next month."

I tilt my head at her because I have a bad feeling about where this is headed. "And your point is?"

"My point is—" she's smiling huge now, "—that he doesn't like to fly and was debating renting a car to drive out there. Jessica was against this, naturally, but now that I know you're going off into the wind—," she points at me, "—*you* can take him."

"Um. No."

"Katherine, he's a nice young man, and since you don't have a destination picked out, this is perfect."

"Mom, I'm not driving a stranger across the country." I'm trying to be firm here, but she's not listening. She's already decided on this, and I can feel her itching to run over to the phone to tell this Jessica woman—whom I'm certain I've never met—about the ride I'm giving her son.

"You know him. I just told you." She huffs, as if annoyed that she has to repeat herself. "You met him when you were six."

"Right. Let me amend that then. I'm not driving across the country with a man I don't *remember*." I widen my eyes for emphasis.

"You are. It's the friendly thing to do, and if you're going to be traveling in a car across this godforsaken country, it's much safer if you do it with a man. I won't take no for an answer, young lady."

"Mom. No."

"It's done." She's smiling like she just won. "I'm calling Jessica now and telling her that you'll pick him up in three days. His name is Ryan and he's a very nice young man. A computer whiz or something."

Have I mentioned that my mother is mad old-school? Like she thinks that this is the 1950s or something. Even her furnishings are reminiscent of that era, and not in a cool mid-century modern way, but in a very floral, ugly, grandmotherly way.

"Mom. I don't feel comfortable driving with a man I don't know for several weeks." It's my last ditch effort. "Please understand that I can't take him."

"Katherine." She grabs my shoulders again, leveling me with her most serious motherly expression. "If you don't travel with him, then I will be calling you eight times a day *at least* to make sure you're safe." She means it. *Shit.* She just got me, and judging by her smug expression, she knows it.

"Fine," I huff out, feeling like such an epic failure. If this were a few years ago, she never would have won. Losing Eric and Maggie has taken all the fight out of me.

Now I'm a spineless zombie.

"I have to go finish packing. Text me his info." I lean forward to kiss her cheek, which she accepts stiffly. Maybe this guy won't want to drive with me any more than I want to drive with him.

"I'm going to call Jessica now." She's bubbly sunshine, and now all I want to do is go home and crawl back into bed for the rest of the day.

And that's exactly what I do. I go home, shut off all the lights and close the curtains, making the small apartment as dark as it's going to get for this time of day. I hate this bed. I hate this apartment. I hate this life. So I sleep, ignoring the phone calls and chimes to indicate voicemails and text messages.

I wake an untold amount of time later to the familiar feeling of a vise wrapped around my chest.

That's why I need to get out of here.

I will never be able to move forward if my grief is constantly holding me back—at least that's what my therapist says. In my gut, I know I'm running away. I know this, but I have to.

I miss them too much. I can't take it anymore.

Instead of getting easier, it's getting harder, and I find I have to remind myself of my morning promise more and more throughout the day.

I don't want to die. I just don't want to live without them.

I don't know *how* to live without them.

Rolling over, I grab my phone and see I have missed text messages and one missed call, with a voicemail from an unknown number. I check the text first and see it's from Ellie.

Ellie and I used to be best friends, and then the accident happened. She couldn't handle my grief. I think it made her uncomfortable. And I get that. Grief makes people uncomfortable.

But it's not exactly like I'm having the fucking time of my life.

She completely bailed on me without a word, and any time I run into her, I get the pity eyes.

Let me tell you, there isn't much worse than those, because no one wants pity. Someone to listen? Sure. A shoulder to cry on? Absolutely. But pity is the worst, and that's all I get from her. That and her talking about me behind my back. So when her text says, *Heard you're moving away. I think that's a smart idea. Good luck with your life,* I don't respond. I mean, what can I say to that anyway? Thanks? Yeah, no.

Finally, I get to the missed call. I hit the button to listen to the voice message and put the phone on speaker so I don't have to move my position to hear it. An unknown male voice comes out of the speaker.

"Hi, I hope this is Katie Taylor—" No one has called me Katie since I was a child. Which suddenly gets me thinking. "My mother,

Jessica Grant, gave me your number. She said that according to your mother, you offered to drive me out to Seattle. I have no idea if my mother was fucking with me or not—she can be a bitch like that—but if she wasn't, please give me a ring back. If she was, then I'm sorry to have bothered you. Later."

And then he hangs up, and I have to just laugh at that.

This guy actually called his mother a bitch. Who says that on a voice message to a complete stranger? Then there's the fact he wants me to call him back if I'm willing to drive him. That means he's interested in riding with me.

I don't exactly know what to do with that.

I was sorta banking on him not being into it.

The way I see it, I have two choices.

Choice one: Call this guy back, offer him a ride, and give it a shot.

Choice two: Don't call him back and deal with my mother incessantly calling me all the time—which she will.

My fingers drag up to the pendant resting flat against my sternum. I really don't have a choice, do I? I'll go insane with my mother calling me, and maybe I can just drop this guy off in Seattle and then be off on my own way. Or maybe I'll make him crazy after a day and he'll run for the hills.

Crap.

I hit his number before I can talk myself out of it, and the phone rings exactly three times before his voice fills my ear. "Katie," he says like we're old friends.

"Yeah, um. Is this Ryan?"

He chuckles softly into the phone. "Obviously it is, since you called me and I picked up using your name."

"Right." I close my eyes feeling just a little stupid and annoyed. *So not digging the sarcasm.* "And it's just Kate. I haven't been Katie since I was a child."

"Sure. So was my mother fucking with me or what? I don't mean to come off as gruff, it's just been a hellishly long week and my mother is pressing my last nerve."

Boy do I get that one.

He continues before I can reply. "I moved out of my place last week and have been staying with my folks since, so you can imagine my mood at this moment."

"Yeah, I think I can. And you're moving to Seattle?"

"Yup. The land of gray skies and rainy days. Actually I moved my business out there so it's either we do this together or I have to drive myself. I won't fly."

I'm not going ask why that is since I don't know him, though I am exceedingly curious. "Can I ask you something?" I throw my arm over my eyes because this has to be the oddest conversation of my life, and we're only a few minutes into it.

"Shoot."

"Is driving across the country with a complete stranger something you're actually interested in doing?"

Another chuckle rumbles through the phone. "You're not a stranger, Katie. We met once before. I was ten, and you were six."

I sigh. "It's Kate, and I realize that, according to my mother, we've met before, but that was twenty-one years ago, and I have no memory of you."

He's silent for a beat, and something about that makes me hold my breath. "Given the situation, it's a shame you don't remember me. But I definitely remember you, so to me that doesn't make you a stranger."

Okay, we're going in circles here. This guy is already pissing me off; no way I could tolerate being in a car with him for several days on end.

"Is that your way of saying yes?" I ask.

"Sure," he replies this like it's the easiest thing in the world. "Why the hell not? Beats the shit out of renting a car and going solo."

"But you don't even know me." I'm practically pleading now. Why am I the only one who thinks that this idea is insanity?

"That doesn't make much of a difference to me at this point. I need to drive, and I think it would be fun to do that with someone else. My mother mentioned you don't have a set designation in mind so we can explore around a bit if you're interested."

"But. I just... I don't know, Ryan. This all feels..." *Insane.*

"My mother told me a little about you, but she got that from your mother, so I'm going to reserve judgment since my mother is who she is, and I'm assuming yours is as well, if you know what I mean."

I have no response for that.

"I swear," he says. "I'm a totally normal guy."

"That's what all the crazies say."

He laughs. Kinda loud. "I guess you're right. Listen. I don't have to be in Seattle for another four weeks. I'm up for a road trip if you are. Come to Philadelphia and meet me. If you can't stand me, then no hard feelings and we'll go our own way. Sound like a plan?"

I sigh. It's at least a better plan than hopping in a car without meeting him first.

"Come on, Katie. Take a chance on me."

The way he says that sends a strange flutter through me.

"Okay. Text me your address, and I'll be there in three days."

"Awesome. I'm hanging up now before you can change your mind. See you soon." He hangs up, and I toss my phone on the bed beside me, wondering what the hell I just got myself into.

2

K *ate*

I HAVE no recollection of ever stepping foot in this city. Though according to my mother and Ryan, I was here when I was six. Great. That means nothing to me.

Ryan texted me his address two days ago and said he was up for an adventure. Adventure wasn't really part of my plan. This was more about escape, followed by trying to find a place that seemed like a good fit where people won't stare at me like I am some horrifying creature.

So I'm sitting in my hotel room, chomping my nails to the quick as I debate whether or not I'm going to drive to his house or just go on my own.

All you have to do is meet him, Kate.

Right. That's not exactly helping.

The idea of traveling across the country and having to share my time with another human isn't appealing.

I need this time. I need this space, and I don't want to answer or have to listen to another's opinions on shit.

And he seems like the type of guy who has opinions.

I look over at the clock on the bedside table. 8:47. I'm supposed to be there at nine. I need to leave now if I'm not going to be late. I hate being late, even for strangers that I don't want to meet. A frustrated crazed huff leaves my mouth before I grab the suitcase I brought up and head out the door.

I'm pulling up in front of a moderately sized house in a decent neighborhood exactly twelve minutes later, but I sit in the car just staring at the house for another five. Finally, the front door opens, and a woman with very dark brown hair stands there and stares at me.

Shit.

I'm creeping people out, and the last thing I want is for someone to call the cops on me for sitting in my car.

The door shuts behind me with a quiet click, and I find myself trying to smile for this woman who is practically beaming at me like we're long-lost friends.

Her dark, almost black hair is cut very short and styled perfectly. Not even the strong wind is able to blow a hair out of place. As I get closer, I see her eyes are an intensely bright, vivid jade. They're stunning, and she's an exceedingly attractive woman, but her face rings zero bells in my head.

"Hello," she coos, her arms outstretched like I should embrace her. I do, but awkwardly and with as much distance between us as I can manage.

She's the opposite of my mother it's not even funny. How these two are friends, I'll never know.

"I'm Jessica Grant," she says, holding me at arms-length and examining me up and down. "My god," she shakes her head, her hair unmoving. "You're just darling."

I smile. "Thank you."

"You've grown into such a beautiful young woman." Her smile drops into a knowing frown, and I don't want to hear the next words that I know are coming out of her mouth. "It's such a shame about your family," she says with no remorse in her voice. She may as well have been lamenting about the weather. I don't respond. Anything I say will not be polite, and I'm not usually in the habit of being a bitch to elderly strangers.

"Mom. Back off." A male voice startles our little moment, causing my eyes to flash over to the front porch. A guy who can only be this woman's son is standing there with his arms crossed over his chest, and an annoyed expression marring his face.

He's tall. Like giant tall. Well over six feet. Broad shoulders slope into a perfectly muscular physique—not too bulky—barely hidden beneath his fitted T-shirt and designer jeans. His hair is as dark as his mother's, and sort of all over the place in a way that says he just rolled out of bed and didn't bother to brush it into submission. His eyes are also the same jade green, but his are encased in dark-framed glasses. A moderately thick beard lines his jaw, but not in an unkempt way.

Unfortunately he's gorgeous, no denying that. The kind of gorgeous that's almost too much to look at.

"No one is in the mood for your bullshit platitudes." Well, shit. I've *never* heard anyone speak to their parent like that. Ever.

I absolutely cannot help the small smile pulling at the corners of my mouth. "It's fine," I say, waving off her feigned look of horror. Whether it's directed at me or her son, whom I assume is Ryan, I have no idea.

"I meant no harm, dear," his mother snaps, still looking at me. I smile, because this is just getting worse by the minute. "Please come in and meet my son," her voice drops with obvious aggravation when she says the word son. Would it be too weird if I just ran for my car and fled?

"Thank you."

Ryan is standing there with his large arms crossed over his larger chest, eyeing me like I'm either the answer to his prayers or the reason for his eternal damnation. Hard to gauge, actually.

"I'm Ryan," he says as I approach the porch, his hand outstretched now to shake mine.

"Kate," I say, slipping my much smaller one into his and allowing his entire hand to engulf mine. A strange kinetic pulse hums across my skin, raising the hair on my arms. I pull back instantly.

He smirks almost like he felt whatever that was too. "Nice to see you again, Katie. Come in, and I'll grab my stuff." He opens the screen door and I freeze. I thought he said he were going to talk about this first?

"Um." He doesn't stop walking so I'm forced to follow. "Ryan?" I call out because suddenly he's gone. Like, nowhere to be seen, gone. There is an older man sitting on a recliner in front of the television, watching college football and completely ignoring me. "Hello," I say hesitantly, looking around hoping to be rescued, but by what I'm not entirely sure.

"Oh, don't mind him dear," Jessica says, waving him away like he doesn't exist. "Ryan will be out in a moment. Can I get you a drink? I have vodka, gin," she starts to list on her fingers. "Oh, I can make Bloody Marys."

"No thanks. I have to drive." *And it's nine in the morning*, I don't add.

"Another time then." She walks away from me into what I assume is the kitchen area, and I'm left standing in the middle of the room with a mute watching television and waiting on a guy who assumes he's already traveling with me.

How did I get here?

And the worst part?

My first reaction is that I'd love to tell Eric all about this because he'd get the biggest kick out of it. My fingers go up to my necklace, rubbing it gently, hoping for some comfort to ebb the familiar empty twist of pain.

"All right, Katie. I'm good to go," Ryan says, walking back into the room with a large suitcase. That's it. The guy is moving across the country and only has one suitcase. I guess I can't talk since I only have two boxes and two suitcases, but still.

"I thought we were going to talk about this first?" I hedge, stare down at the dark green carpet before craning my neck to meet his eyes. "You know, to see if we're on the same page with this trip and everything?"

"Look," he sighs, running a hand through his messy hair. "I need to get to Seattle in around four weeks, and I don't fly," he says that last part firmly. "You're driving around the country. I've always wanted to do that, and you seem like a nice chick." His arms cross against his chest again. "I'm not overly chatty, open to pretty much anything except country music, and have enough money that this could be a lot of fun. You in or out?"

I cross my arms to match his stance. "What's your opinion on classic rock?"

"Could take it or leave it."

"Do you smoke?"

"No. Do you drink?"

"Anything except beer and gin."

He tilts his head, considering my answer. "I guess I can live with that."

"I have a list of places I want to visit, and I don't do nasty-ass motels that never wash the linens."

He nods in agreement. "I'm cool with both of those stipulations, as long as they include DC, New Orleans, Vegas, and SoCal."

All seem reasonable and were already on my list.

And he's tall and foreboding.

He could kick the ass of anyone we come across. As much as I hate to admit it, traveling across the country by myself is not the safest. I sigh internally, because I have no idea what I'm in for with this guy.

"All right. Let's go." I can't believe I'm doing this. Getting in a car with a hot stranger.

"Awesome," he grins. "I won't even complain about the Prius."

I raise an eyebrow. "Smart move."

"Yeah. Though I'm sure it's super fun to drive and all, I guess the whole saving on gas thing is a good idea."

"It's not bad. You'll be pleasantly surprised," I grin back.

"Katie." He tilts his head like I'm crazy. "I'm six-foot-three. Something tells me that pleasantly surprised with regards to riding in a Prius across the country is not what I'll be feeling."

I shrug. "Yeah. Maybe not. But that's the situation so...," I trail off, turning away from him and heading toward the door past the strange, mute, football-watching, older man.

"Bye, darlings," Jessica calls out from the doorway of the kitchen, with what I assume is a Bloody Mary in hand.

"Bye, Mrs. Grant," I smile at her, and she holds her drink up to me in salute.

"Later, Mom. I'll call." I get the feeling he doesn't mean it. He said it like it was a blanket statement instead of a promise. "Bye, Dad." No response, so I don't say anything because I was never introduced. "At least you got dark gray instead of some bitch color like powder blue or red." He's referring to my car, so I ignore him.

"We should probably discuss a flight plan."

"Nope." He shakes his head. "Not my style, Katie." He tosses his suitcase in the trunk next to mine and slams the hatch closed. "Though I will recommend going to D.C. tonight, because it's close and I have a friend there who will spend a lot of money and take us out."

He settles into the passenger seat, sliding it back as far as it can go so his ridiculously long legs stretch as best they can.

"I'm good with DC I haven't been since I was a child." My hands grip the wheel. "What's your timetable like for this trip?"

He shrugs absently, buckling his seat belt and checking his phone. "Like I said, I've got to be there in a little under four weeks."

"Okay," I nod, but I still haven't started the car yet. I feel like I need to come clean with the guy a little. "My plan with this whole thing is to drive around the country and find a place where I eventually want to live." He looks over at me with interest. "I'm...done with Boston, and don't really know where I want to go yet." He's staring at me, and I feel like a strange specimen on display, but I hold his eyes as I continue. "I'll get you to Seattle, but I may want to spend more or less time in a particular place. Are you cool with that?"

His green eyes bore into mine for a minute, and for a moment, I can't look away. It's their color, or perhaps their intensity. Whatever it is, it makes my belly flutter nervously.

Then the severity in them lightens as he shrugs. "Katie, I'm down for whatever you have planned. I promise. I've always wanted to travel the country, and unless you turn into a psycho crazy girl, or super clingy in love, then I think we'll have some fun together."

"Well, I'm a little psycho crazy," I admit with some degree of honesty. "But it will never be directed at you specifically, and you do not need to worry about me ever being super clingy in love with you. That certainly won't happen." I tilt my head. "Can I expect the same from you? No craziness or falling in love with me?" I tease.

"I'm a little crazy, though definitely not psycho." He pauses here, his eyes dancing about my face. "And as for falling in love with you... well, I think you're probably safe. But I make no guarantees." He winks, teasing me back.

I smile so wide I can't help it. "Then I guess we're good."

"I guess we are."

I'm finally getting the excited butterflies because I feel like, for the first time in two years, I'm taking my life back into my hands. I'm practically vibrating with it.

"Driver picks the music, and as a rule, since it's my car," I turn to look at him intently, "no classic rock."

He stares at me for a minute, but doesn't ask why. I'm sure he can guess. It's not a hard one to make.

"You got it."

I nod and start the car. It's already set up for my phone to come through the Bluetooth, so when Silversun Pickups blares out, Ryan nods his head approvingly.

"We'll get along just fine, Katie. Just fine."

We'll see.

3

ate

I'VE BEEN ACUTELY aware of the large man beside me since we started driving with only music to fill the miles. It's unnerving being this close to someone I know so little about. The scent of him, of whatever amazing cologne he wears, permeates the air along with his size, making me jittery. Anxious.

"Why do you call me Katie?" I ask after half an hour of silence. Ryan had been tapping away on his phone, and I didn't want to interrupt, but I've been curious about this, especially since he hasn't stopped, even when prompted.

He doesn't pull his eyes away from the passing landscape out the window. "Because that's how I remember you. That was your name when we were introduced," he says like it's really just that simple.

"Ryan, you were only ten when we met. That was a long time ago. I doubt you even remember much about me from that one visit."

He shakes his head, finally turning to look at me.

"You're wrong, *Katie*," he emphasizes my name. "I have an amazing memory, and I remember everything about that visit."

I scrunch my nose. "Really?"

He nods once. "Yup," he says, popping the p sound.

"All right. Lay it on me then, and maybe it will spark something, because I don't remember *anything* about that visit."

His face breaks out into a crooked smile that's a little unnerving. "Well, within the first five minutes of coming to my house, you stripped down to your days-of-the-week panties and ran through my sprinklers." My eyes widen, and he nods. "It was awesome," he chuckles. "Your mother started freaking out, but your father pulled her back, telling her you were just being a kid."

I smile at that. "My dad was super cool like that."

"He seemed like a good guy," Ryan agrees. "So after you were done with your wet strip-show, you ate everything in our house, lost three games of checkers to me, refused to learn chess, did some other stuff and then passed out in my bed."

"Seriously?" Wow.

"Yes, your mom said that you were a bit of a wild child. I think everyone agreed with her assessment." He's still smiling, the memory amusing him.

"I was," I laugh. "I never listened, always did my own thing, or annoyed everyone until I got what I wanted. Maggie was just like that." I shake my head, but then my smile drops when I think about what I just said, and the lump forms in my throat that I have to swallow past. "Where did you sleep that night if I commandeered your bed?" I ask, needing to change the subject quickly.

"I slept in Kyle's room. He had a bunk bed, which incidentally worked out in your favor; otherwise, I would have shoved your cute ass to the floor."

I chuckle lightly, but it still feels forced. "Who's Kyle?"

Ryan looks over at me like I'm a moron. "My brother."

I shrug sheepishly. "I didn't realize you had a brother. Sorry."

"It's fine. He's younger than me. He was only three when you came to visit that time. He lives in New York now, finishing up law school."

"That's pretty cool." Ryan gives a strong nod like he agrees whole-heartedly, and I can tell just by that small gesture that they're close. "So how come you guys never returned the favor and came to visit us?"

Ryan runs a hand through his hair and stays silent for a moment, his eyes going back to the window as I-95 south breezes past. "Kyle was diagnosed with leukemia when he was five, so we didn't travel and didn't have people over either. My mom was really paranoid about him being exposed to germs."

"I can see that." Ryan doesn't turn, just stays focused out the window. "But he's doing well now?"

He nods. "Yes. He underwent chemo on and off for years, but eventually I donated marrow and platelets, and everything else I could give, and he got better."

"Wow," I gasp in awe, because I know that what he did for his brother had to have been hard and very painful. "That's incredible you did that for him."

He shrugs one shoulder like it's not.

"He's my brother."

And I get that. Not exactly the brother part, but definitely the doing whatever it takes to save your loved one part.

We both fall silent, sliding into our own introspection. But it's not awkward or uncomfortable. It's companionable and easy, and for the first time since this whole thing with Ryan started three days ago, I'm happy he's along with me.

After navigating our way through DC traffic, we finally make it into the city limits. "Where should we go?" I ask, looking around for a hotel. "Should we try and find a hotel or something?"

"Nope. My friend made reservations for us at the JW. I know where we're going, just continue down Pennsylvania Ave."

"Who is this *friend* of yours, and why would he make us hotel reservations?"

"I went to college with him and have done some work with him since." He looks over to me. "And he owes me, so this whole night or however long we stay is on him."

My eyes widen. "For real? I can't accept that."

"You can. Trust me. He could pay for everything, and it still wouldn't cover the debt." Ryan points for me to take a right turn, so I do, and then I see the hotel's valet area coming up.

"Do I even want to know?"

"It's nothing crazy or scandalous. I just saved his stupid ass from getting hacked, and made it so he got to market with his app sooner than he would have. Instead of payment for my endeavors, I asked to be repaid in favors. This is one such favor," he explains simply.

We get out of the car, and I grab my suitcase with my spring/summer stuff in it, because even though it's the end of September, it's hot here. At least in the eighties.

The valet takes my car with the rest of my stuff in it. Ryan and I walk into the large, open, elegant lobby appointed with marble floors and crystal chandeliers and head toward check-in.

"Why did you ask to be paid in favors?" I question as we're waiting in line.

"Because favors are worth more to me than money."

Okay, sort of cryptic, but whatever. "And this favor was worth a lot I take it?" Gesturing around the expensive-appearing hotel.

Ryan turns his gaze down to me just as we're being called up. "Because of me his app didn't get hacked and it came out ahead of any competition. That app made him well over a hundred million dollars."

My eyes widen and my mouth pops open, but Ryan doesn't say anything further as he steps up to the counter.

"Good afternoon and welcome to the JW. Do you have reservations with us?"

"We do," Ryan speaks for us because I'm still in a bit of shock over what he just told me. I have no idea what Ryan does for work. All I know is that it has something to do with computers, but guessing by what he just told me, I'd say he's very good at whatever it is. "One is under Katie Taylor and the other is under Ryan Grant."

I'm relieved we're not sharing a room. I didn't want to ask since this is free and all, but still.

"Excellent." The guy types away for a moment. "Ah, yes, I have you in our large concierge-level king rooms, both with excellent views of Pennsylvania Avenue." The guy continues with his whole speech about the benefits of the concierge room and what our suites—yes, I said suites—have for amenities, and that anything we should require has already been taken care of, and blah, blah, blah. I'm overwhelmed. It's a nice way to start the trip, don't get me wrong, but it all feels like too much.

The guy directs us toward the elevators, and we ride up in silence. Our rooms are next to each other, but Ryan walks me into mine since he's rolling my suitcase for me, despite my protests.

"Wow," I exclaim as we enter. The room is large and very nice with white linens and gray floors, but the best part is the large wraparound windows that show Pennsylvania Avenue all the way up to the Capitol. "This place is awesome. Thanks so much to your friend." I spin around to look at him. "Or should I say you?"

"I'm going next door to settle in," he ignores my comment. "We're meeting him out for dinner and drinks around eight. That work for you?"

"Sounds great. Thanks, Ryan." I smile huge, and it feels a little foreign on my face, but I go with it.

He nods once. His eyes remain focused on me for a moment, and then he turns and heads for the door. "Oh, Katie?" he calls out over his shoulder. "You should smile like that more. It looks really good on you." And then the door clicks behind him, leaving me alone with his words lingering in the air.

Of course, my smile slips, leaving me with the inevitable feelings of guilt and pain that sweep through me. I take a deep breath and do my best to push them aside before walking over to my purse that I had set down on the desk. I text my mother to let her know that I'm in DC with Ryan and that everything is going well thus far. She doesn't respond and I'm glad about that because I'm not in the mood to chat with her.

Opening up my suitcase, I set out what I want to wear that night when we go out, use the massive bathroom, and then walk over to the window. It's only a little after one in the afternoon, and I haven't had anything to eat, so I'm hungry. Plus, I have the whole day and I don't want to waste it sitting in a hotel room.

I debate texting Ryan to see if he wants to go on an adventure around the city with me. He didn't indicate that he wanted to hang out anymore until tonight, but I feel sort of weird about going off and not letting him know. I stand here, holding my phone two minutes longer than I should before I shoot off a quick text that says I'm going in search of lunch and sites, and if he wants to join me, that would be cool.

I quickly change into a pair of shorts and a loose pink tee before grabbing my purse and room key and heading toward the door. The heavy door swings open, and I nearly jump two feet in the air when I see Ryan standing on the other side with his hand raised about to knock.

"Shit," I pant out, grabbing my chest. "You scared the hell out of me."

"Sorry. I just figured I'd come by instead of texting back." His mouth quirks up into a playful grin, his eyes flittering down my body in a quick sweep before returning to mine. My heart begins to shift its rhythm as we stand here, staring at each other, something unfamiliar and tight strangles my stomach. I clear my throat and shift my gaze, unable to maintain his.

"It's fine," I laugh lightly, trying to calm my heart rate back to its regular beat. "You want to come with?"

"Sure. What did you have in mind?"

We step into the waiting elevator. "I'm hungry, so I'd like to eat something, but after that, are you opposed to taking in some of the sites?"

"That's fine. Are you thinking a museum, or walking, or one of those bus things?"

I laugh, nudging his arm with my shoulder and marveling at how...normal it feels to do so. To touch him like that. "Hadn't given it that much thought yet, Ryan. I thought you weren't a planner?" I tease.

He smiles crookedly down at me. "Fine. You got me. Lead on then, little Katie. I'm at your disposal today."

We end up finding a place to eat, where we can sit outside, and after scarfing down an entire salad filled with yummy things, we start to walk toward the White House, which is only a few blocks down.

"It's such a pretty city," I say, holding my arms out wide. "I mean, I always knew it was designed and built like this on purpose, but you just don't expect this sort of cleanliness and charm in such a large city, ya know?"

"Yeah," he agrees. "I come down here with some frequency for work, but I rarely walk around or take in the architecture."

"Do you think you'll miss the East Coast?" I ask, genuinely curious for my own reasons as much as his. I've lived in the Boston area my entire life. I even went to college there, so the idea of leaving is hard, since it's all I've known.

But I'm looking forward to the change just as much.

"Maybe some parts of it," he says, giving my question some genuine thought.

That's actually a nice thing I've noticed about Ryan. He listens to you when you speak. Not only that, he makes it seem like everything you're saying or asking is important. That's such a rare thing. I feel like people are always talking over each other, interjecting their thoughts and opinions without really taking in what the other person is saying. I didn't think it would be this easy to talk to Ryan. That I'd like it as much I do. He's... different than I expected him to be.

"Not enough to stay, though."

"Must be a good job for you to move so far away from your family. Especially when you don't fly." We're walking toward the Capitol Building now, away from The White House. The wide berth of Pennsylvania Avenue flanked by the eighteenth-century whitewash buildings provides the perfect amount of eye candy to keep me enthralled.

"The flying thing is relatively new, not that I enjoyed it so much before. My family will come visit me if they want. Kyle has already promised to come skiing in December."

I smile. "It's nice that you're so close. Where did you go to school?"

"MIT."

I look up at him in surprise. "Really? How did I never meet you again if you were in Boston when I was?"

He shrugs, looking down at me quickly before turning his eyes back up to the buildings.

"You weren't available."

"Huh?" I have no idea what that means.

"I'm four years older than you, Katie, so when I was in college, you were still in high school."

"Oh. Right."

That makes sense, I guess. I mean, what college kid wants to meet a high school kid? Can you say jailbait? Not that anything would have ever happened between us. I was with Eric, and like Ryan said, he's four years older than me.

I was fourteen when he was eighteen. Gross.

It's funny how age can go from meaning so much to so little. Four years doesn't seem like much of a difference anymore now that I'm in my late twenties. I have friends who married men five and six years older than them.

The thought that Ryan is not so much older than me now, that he's actually the perfect age for me, suddenly makes me blush furiously. I turn away from him, hoping he doesn't catch it, as I pretend to take in the city around us. I'm not oblivious to how good looking he is. Tall, muscular, piercing green eyes that feel like they can see through me. Not that I'm interested. I'm not.

But four years. That age difference means very little now.

4

R *yan*

I HAVEN'T BEEN able to stop staring. Not once. Even when she thinks I'm looking at other things, I'm looking at her. So insanely fascinated by all things Katie when she is the last person on the planet I should be fascinated by. We spent all afternoon walking around the city, and by the time we make it back to the hotel, we are both exhausted.

"I'm going to take a nap, I think," Katie says as she leans her tiny body against the back wall of the elevator. "You said we're not going out until eight, right?"

"Yes." I check my watch. "It's almost five now. Is that okay?"

"Perfect," she says through a yawn. "Sorry." She covers her mouth. "All the driving and walking wore me out, plus I didn't sleep well last night." She looks up at me with a smirk. "I was a little nervous about meeting you this morning."

I laugh lightly. "Me too," I lie, and she knows it, because she snorts out a laugh.

"Don't tease me." She nudges me as we step off the elevator and walk toward our rooms at the end of the hall. The plastic keycard swipes along the outside of her door and the mechanical lock disengages, allowing her to open it up. "I'll see you at eight. Thanks for today. I had fun." She gives me a sleepy smile before shutting the door behind her.

I enter my room, dropping down onto my bed face-first with a heavy bounce, sinking contentedly into the plush bedding. Katie. What a wild day. I can't believe I'm here with her.

My eyes shut instantly only to open again what feels like two minutes later to a pounding on my door. A groan slips from my lips as I pry myself out of bed slowly before putting my glasses back on. The bright red numbers of the bedside clock tell me that it's 7:14.

Shit. How did that happen?

It's still too early for that to be Katie, but I'm not surprised when I open the door to see Tommy on the other side. "What's up, dude? You look like shit." His standard greeting.

"You too, asshat." Tommy brushes past me, dropping himself into a chair and kicking his feet up on the desk. "Make yourself at home," I say dryly.

"Hey, I got you these nice digs." I throw him a look, and he holds his hands up in surrender. "Which you more than deserve," he amends quickly.

"What are you doing here, man?" I yawn, rubbing my hands up and down my face under my glasses, trying to wipe the sleep away. "I thought we said eight?"

"We did, but I wanted to get here early to talk some business, and to find out about the lady you're traveling with." He bounces his eyebrows at me suggestively.

"What business?" I ask, ignoring the comment about Katie. I'm just not ready to share her with this douchebag yet.

"It's about a new app I'm developing." His fingers intertwine behind his head as he leans back casually in the chair. "I'd like you to take a look for me. Do all the usual checks, and when it hits the market, I'll give you fifteen percent."

"Twenty," I respond in a bored tone like it doesn't matter much to me either way, because even though I'm curious about what he's got going on, the money doesn't drive me anymore.

He pretends to think this over for a minute, his dark eyes slightly narrowed at me. "All right. Twenty." This must be important to him otherwise he never would have caved that easily. "I'll send it over to you later."

"Sure," I walk over to my suitcase and pull out a t-shirt and jeans for me to change into after I shower. My hand comes up to scratch my beard, which has gotten way out of control. I should trim it, but I don't have the energy to do it tonight.

"So, this girl?" he starts, and I should have known he wouldn't let it go. "Katie Taylor is it?"

"It's Kate to you, dicklick."

He smiles that wide, greasy smile I hate. "But she's *Katie* to you?"

"Don't start," I warn, because Katie is different, and I don't want him making her uncomfortable. "She's been through more than you can imagine, so none of the usual slimy bullshit you like to pull with women."

"Slimy bullshit?" Tommy says with mock indignation. "I'm always a perfect gentleman." He smiles again, and it sort of makes me want to punch in his perfect teeth. "So she's hot, huh? Smoking body?"

I do my best to hide my frustration and anger, because he'll just feed off of it. The idea of Tommy looking at her, thinking about her makes my jaw tic.

"Tommy, I'm not messing with you on this. She's been through the deepest levels of hell, man. I'm not gonna say it again. *Don't.*"

I sit on the edge of the bed and level him with my eyes. It's not my place to tell Katie's story, and from what I can decipher about her in the brief time we've spent together, she doesn't like to talk about herself. So I won't do that, but Tommy needs to know she's off the market all the same.

He examines the deliberate and weighted look I'm giving him. Ever so slowly, his arrogant, cocky grin slips, and he nods. "I'll be good," he promises.

"Thanks, man. I'm going to go grab a quick shower. I'll meet you down in the bar."

"You kicking me out?"

"Absolutely." I stand up and head to the bathroom. "As much as I love you, I'd rather not have you in my room when I come out of the shower naked. See you at eight."

I shut the bathroom door, effectively dismissing him, and start the shower. In the back of my mind, I know that once Tommy sees Katie, he'll push the limit with her. Katie is tenacious, and I have a feeling she can hold her own, but the thought of him hitting on her and making her uncomfortable grates on me.

I feel protective over her for some reason.

Maybe it's what I know she's been through, or that I know she's in search of a new life.

I don't want a piece of shit like Tommy to hinder any progress she's making with it. Whatever the hell it is, I want to see that smile she showed me earlier on her sweet face again, and I'll do what I have to do to make that happen.

By the time I shower, throw on my clothes, and run a brush through my hair it's almost eight, so I check my phone and write out a few emails before I need to grab Katie.

When the knock on my door comes, it surprises me.

Girls are always late, and I figured Katie was no different. When I open the door, my fucking breath catches in my damn lungs as I take her in.

Katie is stunning.

She's wearing a dark pink halter neck dress that looks like it's made out of the softest cotton, hugging her curves and stopping just above her knees. Matching strappy wedge sandals adorn her adorable feet. Her long, platinum blonde hair is piled on top of her head in a messy bun and she's wearing just enough makeup to make her golden skin look sun-kissed and radiant. Her lips are a glossy raspberry and her eyes sparkle with a hint of something silvery. She's a princess. A fantasy.

"You look beautiful," I say before I can stop myself.

She smiles sweetly. "You look good yourself," she nods at my graphic tee, and for once, I wish I were wearing something nice. I look down with a slight scowl. "No," she says quickly, obviously noting my expression. "I'm serious." I look up at her and she's nodding in approval.

"You ready?" I ask, and she nods, taking a step back to allow me to walk out. "You're taller," I comment, staring down at her, unable to drag my eyes away.

"Four inches, but I'll take what I can get. You make me feel like a Lilliputian," she laughs. "I needed to help that out a bit."

"Does that make me Gulliver?" I laugh.

"Yeah. Sorry," she peeks up at me with wide blue eyes. Blue eyes that are the most intense blue I've ever seen. Like the sky before it storms. "You are sort of a giant next to me."

We step off the elevator, and I point in the direction of the bar where we're meeting Tommy. "How tall are you?"

"Five foot one and a half," she mutters, and I laugh out.

"That half an inch makes all the difference, huh?"

"You bet your ass it does. Us little people need those precious half inches."

We enter the well-lit bar, and I spot Tommy nursing a beer down at the end of it under one of the televisions. "Well, tonight you're five foot five and a half."

She nods, smiling big like that was the best compliment anyone has ever given her.

Damn... this girl. She hits me on a different level. On a level I wish I didn't have with her since she absolutely does not look at or think of me the same way.

Tommy spots us, holding a finger up in the air before tossing some money on the counter as he downs the rest of his beer, then heads in our direction. His eyes widen as he takes in Katie, and then a slow, easy smile spreads across his face.

I know that look.

And it pisses me the fuck off.

Tommy stops in front of us, staring right at Katie and waiting patiently for an introduction I now don't want to make.

"Katie, this is Tommy Madigan," I say to her before looking at Tommy. "Tommy, this is *Kate*," I emphasize her name to him.

Tommy sticks out his hand and she places hers into his. "A pleasure," he says in a sultry tone, and instead of shaking her hand, he kisses the back of it. Douchebag.

Katie doesn't fall for it. "You too." She gently pulls her hand out of his grasp. "Thank you for the room; it's very nice."

"It's my pleasure," he purrs, taking a small step into her personal space. "I would have offered for you to stay with me in my apartment. It's so big and I rarely have people to share it with—" I roll my eyes. "—but Ryan here," Tommy juts his thumb in my direction, "insisted on a hotel," he says this like it's the most selfish thing in the world. *Dick.*

"That's so kind of you to have offered your home to us, but Ryan knows how much I love hotels, so he was doing me a favor with that," she smiles sweetly, and inside I'm half-shocked and half-smug. She just fucking nailed him, and we all know it.

"Well, I'm glad you're enjoying it then," he looks to me. "We should go."

We walk into The Hamilton and are seated quickly in one of the livelier bar areas. This place is big and crowded and loud, and Katie has gone quiet since we entered.

The waitress comes over, and after Tommy flirts with her for a few minutes, he orders us a round of tequila shots and margaritas. I have no idea what kind of drinker Katie is, but I don't want her getting sick so when the waitress comes back with our drinks, I suggest that we order some food.

After we place our order, the waitress leaves and Tommy raises his shot glass after he and I both salt-up our hands. Katie doesn't, I note.

"To nights we'll never remember, shared with friends we'll never forget." It's the same toast he's been using since college, but I don't comment, and neither does Katie.

I lick my salty hand, smashing the granules between the roof of my mouth and my tongue before tossing back the clear liquid. It burns all the way down my throat and I quickly take the lime into my mouth, sucking out the juice to ease it.

Tequila has never been my favorite. I'll do it because it's there, but I don't order it for myself.

Katie closes her eyes as she drinks hers down, lowering her glass back to the table and licking her lips like she's savoring the flavor.

I stare, mesmerized, and I can feel Tommy doing the same, because damn that's sexy as hell. Her eyes open and she picks up a lime wedge, sucking on it once before dropping it into her glass and licking the remaining juice off her fingers. I'd give anything to know what that tastes like on her. My cock twitches at the thought.

"Jesus, Kate, if I knew you took shots like that, I wouldn't have ordered anything else." I'm not really disagreeing with him on this, but I still throw him a look that says be careful.

Katie blushes, clearing her throat.

"How long have you lived in DC, Tommy?" she asks, changing the subject away from herself.

"I moved here after I graduated MIT." He pretends to think about this, but I know he's hoping that Katie will remark on where he went to school. She won't. She's not impressed by bullshit like that. "Nine years, I guess," he finishes when she doesn't indulge him.

Katie nods, pulling the elastic from her hair and letting her long blonde mane tumble down her back as her fingers massage her scalp. Does she have to do that? Be the sexiest woman I've ever seen?

"Look, Mommy." A little girl's voice startles us, our heads turning in unison to the sound. "It's Rapunzel," the little girl with brown hair and eyes says, pointing at Katie.

The mother looks mortified and bends down to her daughter. "No, sweetie. That's not Rapunzel." She looks up at Katie. "Sorry."

Katie waves her away like it's nothing before she looks at the little girl with a soft smile that lights up her eyes.

"Is Rapunzel your favorite princess?" she asks, and the little girl nods enthusiastically. "Mine too," she winks conspiratorially. The little girl, who can't be any older than five, giggles.

"Mommy and Daddy are taking me to Disney World to meet her next week."

"You're such a lucky girl. I'm jealous," Katie smiles, and the mother thanks her with her eyes before leading her daughter away from us.

The second they're gone, Katie's smile falls and her expression morphs into utter devastation.

"Excuse me," she whispers, getting up and walking in the direction of the bathroom.

Tommy throws me a look that asks, *what just happened*, but doesn't say anything. She's gone a good five minutes, and I'm stuck here listening to Tommy blather on about bullshit I could care less about.

My mind is stuck on Katie.

When she returns, our food has arrived, but she just picks at her burger, hardly eating a bite. The difference in her is extreme, and I feel terrible for it, considering I know the cause.

Only someone who has experienced that kind of loss can understand what she's feeling, but that doesn't mean I don't sympathize.

Tommy prattles on the entire time, and either he's completely oblivious to the shift in her demeanor, or he's trying to compensate. Regardless of the reason, I'm grateful for it because I find myself at a loss for words as well.

After dinner, Katie says she's tired and wants to head back to the hotel. I insist on walking her, despite her protests, with the promise of meeting Tommy back at the bar.

Katie's reticent the entire walk back, completely lost in her thoughts. When we get to her door, she turns and looks at me, and the despair I see cuts me to the quick.

I want to reach out and hug her. I want to hold her in my arms and take away every ounce of pain I see leaching from her gorgeous eyes. But I can't do any of that with her, so I just stand here like a chump instead.

"I'm sorry about how I acted at dinner," she laughs nervously. "I swear I'll be better company tomorrow."

"You were perfect." She's staring at the carpet. "Do you want me to stay with you?" I offer, not really knowing what else to do at this point.

Her eyes fly up to mine, and a small smile touches her lips, which I take as a personal victory.

"No. I'm just going to go sleep this off. Thank you, though. That's..." she looks over toward the wall like she's searching for the right words before turning her attention back to me, "really great of you. Go have fun. I'm fine. Good night, Ryan. It's been an interesting first day with you."

And with that, she walks into her room and shuts the door, leaving me feeling a little lost and a lot out of sorts. Wanting to comfort the girl who will never want you back is proving harder than I thought.

5

K *ate*

RYAN DIDN'T MENTION my mini mental-freak-out and I was grateful for that. Some moments I'm okay. Then something hits me and it's all I can do to breathe.

I had woken up the next morning early as hell, hit the gym, ate breakfast in the concierge lounge and was done before eight. But when I got back to my room, I saw a text from Ryan asking if I was up for breakfast. I was surprised that he was awake early since I assumed he had stayed out late drinking with his friend Tommy.

Ryan ate without me since I already had, and then we mutually agreed to move on from DC. We decide to haul it down to Nags Head, North Carolina, which is freaking beautiful.

The sand dunes and the waves are so captivating that we sit on the beach together for a few hours just staring out at the Atlantic. We end up only staying one night and don't do much with it other than dinner and sleep, mostly because I told Ryan I really want to go to Charleston, which is a long drive.

He was fine with that. Ryan seems to be fine with everything.

I like that about him.

How easy he is to be around. How comfortable I already am with him. That is until I catch myself stealing peeks of him. Peeks that make my chest flutter.

Ryan is driving, and we're listening to Cold War Kids—a band I really enjoy, but haven't heard all that much.

"What's your favorite band, Ryan?" I ask, needing something to talk about since we've got a seven-hour drive ahead of us.

"Hmmm."

He looks out his window briefly before turning his eyes back to the road. He looks so giant driving my little car, though I imagine he'd look big driving almost anything. I shift in my seat so I'm facing him, drawing my knees up and tucking them under me.

"Honestly, I don't know if I have a *favorite*," he emphasizes the word. "I like a lot of different music, and find myself listening to different things depending on my mood or where I'm at in my life." I secretly love that answer. A lot actually.

"But you tend to listen to more indie stuff?"

It's not really a question. Thus far, every time he's driven, it's been music on his phone, and it's ranged from Arctic Monkeys, to Taking Back Sunday, to Cage the Elephant, and now Cold War Kids.

"I guess," he shrugs before catching my eye quickly with a smirk attached to his lips. "We seem to have that in common."

"We do," I nod in agreement and then laugh out suddenly. "Eric used to complain every time he was in the car with me."

Ryan tenses up, and I suddenly feel bad about bringing Eric up. I'm sure my talking about him makes Ryan apprehensive. Or uncomfortable even. People never know what to say when you talk about loved ones who are dead. Especially when they died so young and tragically, but suddenly I'm in the mood to talk about him.

I *need* to talk about him.

"He used to listen to only classic rock, which was okay, just not my favorite," I smile, staring out the window at the beautiful scenery we're passing because, damn, it's so pretty here. My fingers play with my necklace. "That is until we had Maggie, and all she liked to hear was Radio Disney."

"Radio Disney?"

"Yup," I nod with wide eyes to show my suffering. "It was terrible, but she loved it and would sing along to everything, butchering the words the way only a two-year-old can." I grin to let him know that it's okay and that I won't shut down on him.

"How did you meet Eric?" he asks softly, hesitantly, like just saying his name could set me off, and I feel bad about that.

I hate making people diffident with my misery, and that's clearly what I've done. I make a note to suffer in silence a bit more around Ryan, who's been nothing but nice and easygoing since we started on this strange venture together.

"His family moved down the street from me when we were twelve. My mom and I went over to welcome them to the neighborhood, and Eric and I ended up playing together all day." I smile, thinking back on that day. He was so damn cute. So sweet and funny and perfect. "Two weeks later he asked me out for ice cream," I shrug, because I don't want to think about the ice cream.

"For real?" He glances over at me quickly before looking back out to the road. "You're telling me you were with him since you were *twelve*?" His tone is completely incredulous, and I can understand why. Everyone I've ever told reacts this way.

"Yes." I scrunch my nose. "Crazy, right?"

"Um." He looks like he's deciding how to respond. "A little maybe," he chuckles uncomfortably, running a hand through his thick inky hair. "Did you ever break up?"

"Nope," I laugh at his expression. "And yes, before you ask, he's the only man I've ever slept with."

"Fuck." His hand meets his bearded jaw, and I try to picture him with smooth skin. I can't decide which version of Ryan I'd like better. Clean-cut Superman or this sexy brooding Batman. *Sexy? Shit, did I just call him sexy?* I don't realize I'm staring until he catches me, and I quickly look away. "I've never heard of anything like that."

"I know, right?" I muse, hitting Ryan in the arm playfully. "We just worked, you know? It never even occurred to me to break up or date someone else."

He smiles a crooked smile. "That's actually pretty sweet. Innocent and a little twisted maybe, but sweet."

I laugh, smacking him again, and he feigns injury, rubbing his arm like I hurt him. Pussy.

"Can I ask...," he trails off, shifting uncomfortably, like he's afraid to push his luck. "What was your daughter like?"

"Perfection personified," I reply automatically, and he nods once as if he's not surprised by my easy response. My hand clasps my pendant. "She had hair like mine and eyes like Eric's. Sort of a perfect mixture of both of us, but totally tenacious. At the age of two, she had mastered the art of manipulating her parents. Especially Eric. He gave her whatever she asked for. He could never say no to her."

I swallow down the burn in the back of my throat as I think on that. I don't want to think on that or I'll cry. I know I will.

So I continue, and he lets me, staying silent while I work through this.

I haven't spoken about either of them really, and I don't know why I'm doing it now with a virtual stranger, but I am. It's Ryan, I realize. There's something freeing, almost familiar about talking to him, and I'm taking full advantage.

"She was smart," I tell him reverently. "I mean," I laugh a little self-consciously, "I know all parents say that about their kids, but she totally was. She had the ABCs down after me singing it to her twice and could count to twenty at the age of two."

His gaze shifts over to me with a warm smile. "Smart like her mommy." I smile back at the compliment, ignoring the burn in my chest at the word *mommy*.

I keep going. I can't seem to stop myself.

"Eric really wanted a boy." Ryan's eyes go wide, and I think I've officially stunned him with my candor. "He wouldn't even discuss girls' names."

"You didn't find out ahead of time?" I love that he asked me that question.

I shake my head no. "There are few really good surprises in life, and finding out the gender of your baby upon delivery is one of them."

Ryan nods like he can understand that logic. "So was Eric really upset when you had a girl?"

I shake my head again, thrilled that Ryan is playing along in this conversation. The man sets me at ease in a way I haven't experienced since Eric. And maybe that should scare me, but it doesn't for some reason. There is something about Ryan. More than just his handsome face and perfect body.

"No. When Maggie came out, they placed her on my stomach, and he began to weep with the biggest grin on his face. Said he couldn't imagine anything more perfect than our little girl, and if he died that moment, he'd die happy." I smile, but it's so freaking sad that it turns into a frown and tears begin to roll down my cheeks.

"Shit," Ryan says, glancing over to me and reaching out like he's about to grab my hand. A rush slams through me at the thought of him touching me. I can't decide if I'd welcome his touch or not. If it would be comforting or... something else entirely. Luckily, he doesn't touch me, his hand goes back to the wheel instead. He's stricken. "I'm sorry. I shouldn't have asked anything."

"No," I shake my head, trying to smile through my tears. "Thank you for asking me about them."

He's baffled. "How can you say that? You're crying."

"I am," I nod in agreement. "But no one ever asks me about them. Probably because I don't usually want to talk about them, and they're afraid of this," I point to my tears. "But today I did want to talk about them, and you asked, and it was exactly what I needed, so thank you."

He sighs out, running a hand through his hair. "I'm just going to say this, and I'm sure you've already heard it a million times over, but whatever. I mean it, so I'm going to say it." I look at him with bated breath because I have no idea where he's going with this. "You're the strongest person I've ever met, Katie." My breath stalls. "Thank you for sharing all of that with me."

I grin, but it's weak. "Thank you for listening, Ryan. You're an amazing man." He chuckles lightly, and I suddenly wonder. "Do you have a girlfriend?"

He laughs out at my random change of topic, his eyes skirting to mine for the briefest of seconds, before he replies, "No." There is something in his tone I don't quite get.

"No, as in not right now, or no, as in never?" Some guys are just players and don't do the girlfriend thing. That could be Ryan. I highly doubt that he would have trouble getting a woman if he wanted one, so it has to be something else. As far as I can tell, he's pretty much perfect. A woman would have to be insane to not want him.

"I've had girlfriends."

He's being intentionally vague, and I'm about to pounce on that, because I don't do particularly well with that. "Tell me about your last one then."

He shifts uncomfortably, and I wonder if I'm overstepping, but just when I'm about to retract my question, he answers.

"Her name is Francesca. We were together for two years, and she was my world." Shit. This isn't going to end well, and I wish I hadn't gone there with him. I feel like such a bitch right now. "I found out about eight months ago that she was cheating on me with someone I worked with." I gasp. I can't help it. "I think they're engaged now." My eyes bug out of my head, and he nods. "It hurt. I won't lie about that. I loved her and thought she could be the one, but she's not." He shrugs like it's that simple, but I can't imagine it being so. "Stop looking at me like that, Katie. It's fine. I'm relieved not to be with her anymore. She wasn't who I thought she was, and I was blind to the rest. I'm headed out to Seattle, and I've met you, and I'm looking forward, not back. It's the way it's meant to be."

"Jesus, I wish I had your mindset on things," I blurt out, but I realize just how much I mean it once I've said it. "Sorry, I just can't imagine anyone choosing some other guy over you." And now I'm blushing because I know how that sounded. But like I said, a woman would have to be insane.

He grins widely, his expression slightly mischievous. "Maybe we're both headed for better things then."

"Maybe," I agree, and something warm stirs inside of me. Something I have no name for, and yet instinctively recognize all the same.

"Hey, Ryan?" I ask after a few minutes of silence.

"Yes?"

I smirk. "I bet he has a really small dick and sucks in bed."

His smile is huge and breathtaking. "I bet he does too." Then he winks at me conspiratorially. "Can we stop soon for food? I'm getting hungry and need to stretch a bit."

"Definitely. You know me, I never turn down food."

He looks to me with the most serious of expressions. "Yes. I do know you."

Our eyes lock for another moment before he turns back to the road. That warmth from minutes ago turns hotter, swarming everywhere. A tingly bubbly sensation rises over me like I drank a glass of champagne too quickly. I've known this guy less than a week, but I think he may be right.

He does know me. And I think I may know him too.

And that's okay, I tell myself. He's a friend. That's what this feeling is all about. Friendship. It couldn't possibly be anything more.

By the time we pull into Charleston, it's late and we're both fried. We had stopped for a little while in Myrtle Beach and almost stayed the night, but then we decided to just finish the drive here. The hotel we picked is right on the ocean and looks big and beautiful. I drove the last part from Myrtle Beach, and we got stuck in traffic, so what should have been a two-hour drive, ended up being more like three and a half.

Ryan is a good sport, and kept my frustration to a minimum by playing stupid games like *would you rather*. I now know a lot more about Ryan than I thought I would, let me just say that.

Speaking of Ryan, he's walking toward me with an uneasy expression. He had gone to check in for both of us while I watched our stuff and stretched my legs a bit in the lobby.

"So um, bad news."

"What?" I groan, sagging a bit. I'm so not in the mood for bad news.

"They only have one room left. It has two queen beds, but that's it." He's trying to spin this with a brighter tone, and it's absolutely for my benefit. Now I feel like a snobby bitch for my attiude. "It's just one night or we could try to find a different hotel."

I walk over and throw my arms around his neck, hugging him fiercely because he really is so wonderful. This man. All he's done is try to keep me happy when I imagine he's just as spent as I am. Ryan's arms sweep around me and he presses me into his warm, hard chest. He smells like clean laundry and whatever heavenly cologne he wears. I didn't expect this. For a simple hug to feel so... *good*.

"No," I shake my head as I pull back. "It's just one night. I'm sorry if I'm being bratty."

His eyes track me, his typical bright emerald green just a touch darker. "You're not being bratty." I cock an eyebrow, and he smiles big. "Maybe a bit, but I get it. You're tired." He's teasing me now, and I playfully smack his arm, making him laugh. "So you're good with the shared room? They said they'll have two rooms tomorrow should we stay."

"Yes, Ryan Grant, I'm good. Let's get me to bed."

His expression shifts to something I can't quite figure out. He stares me down for another moment, and I can feel my heart beating. Not faster. Not necessarily that. Just... beating. *He's making my heart beat.* Before I can dwell on any meaning behind that, he grabs both of our suitcases, walking toward the elevator. I've stopped fighting him when it comes to carrying my luggage; the crazy gentleman has been insistent on doing it.

The room is large with a pretty bathroom, two beds and even a balcony that faces the ocean. Bonus.

"This is fantastic."

He nods once, staring at the beds and then me. "You can use the restroom first if you'd like?"

"Thanks," I grin, trying to ease the awkward discomfort I can feel rolling off of him.

He's wary, and I get that.

We don't know each other that well and spending the night in the same room is a bit...delicate.

I take what I need out of my suitcase, use the bathroom, brush my teeth, and change into what I plan to wear to bed. I can't exactly call them pajamas because they're not. Normally, I don't wear anything to sleep, other than my panties. Eric loved it, but something tells me that wouldn't be appropriate for Ryan. So I'm wearing a thin white tank top and boy shorts. I'd go baggier, but then I'd be tossing and turning from the discomfort of the extra material against me.

Ryan's eyes dodge me as he grabs his stuff and walks right into the bathroom. I crawl into the bed closest to the bathroom and roll on my side away from his bed. I figure he'll want as much privacy as I can give him. I hear the shower start and the sound of water running through the pipes.

I don't think about the man on the other side of the wall in the shower. I don't think about him once as I fall asleep. Nope. Not even a little.

6

ate

I WAKE EARLY—MUCH the way I do every morning—but on this particular morning, I am instantly aware of the large body in the next bed. His soft, steady breathing fills the otherwise quiet room, making me hyperaware of every move and sound I make so I don't wake him.

I grab my running stuff, bringing it into the bathroom with me and shut the door behind me as softly as I can. I haven't had to deal with sneaking around in the predawn hours in quite some time, and it is a strange feeling. A sad one too, so I'm trying not to think too deeply on it right now.

Once I'm finished, I shut off the lights before opening the door to the restroom and sneak out with exaggerated tiptoe movements.

"Katie?" Ryan calls out, his voice raspy with sleep.

"Crap. Sorry." I take a few steps into the main room. "I didn't mean to wake you."

"What time is it?" Even though the room is still pretty dark, I can make him out as he rubs his hands up and down his face, rolling over to check the clock.

"It's early. Go back to sleep," I whisper.

"Why are you up?" He flops down onto his back again, the blanket only covering him from the waist down, giving me a decent view of his chest.

A chest I should not be looking at.

"I was going to go for an early run on the beach."

"Okay." He sits up, and holy shit, his chest is large and muscular, and did I mention holy shit? His chest leads down into the hard ridges that line his stomach. And lord, he has that V thing. I think I'm drooling an embarrassingly large puddle on the floor. My face is hot, and my body is tingly, and I need to look away.

Look away, Kate!

"What are you doing?" I whisper-shriek, though I have no idea why I'm bothering to whisper, or shriek for that matter. "Go back to bed." Whatever you do, don't get out of bed. Don't sit up and clench those abdominal muscles.

"Nah. I'll come with you for the run, if that's all right?" He's rubbing up and down his face again, scratching his beard and reaching for his glasses on the nightstand.

"Oh. Um. Sure," I shrug, my voice sounding a bit hyper, even to me. I think he's oblivious to it, though, because he's not looking at me. His back is to me now and it's just as amazing as his chest. I really need to look away. He's turning me into some kind of creeper.

I pivot to the door, giving him privacy, as he stands up wearing only his boxer briefs. Thank God it's dark in here or he'd see my very obvious blush.

"Great. Just give me a few minutes." I hear him rustling through his suitcase, and then he walks past me into the bathroom. I take the extra time to stretch out and clear him from my head. A few minutes later, he walks out wearing a sleeveless Eagles football tee, running shorts and sneakers. His inky hair is a mess and he still looks half-awake. "You ready?"

"Yes, are you?" I jest, and he throws me a wink that makes me laugh. "Eagles, huh?" I mutter, eyeing his shirt, making him chuckle lightly. He knows I'm a huge Patriots fan. We talked sports yesterday during our drive.

As we find our way outside, the morning is cool, but not cold, and the sun is just starting to make itself known on the horizon. It's glorious.

"Do you always run this early?"

"Usually, if I can," I tell him as we start down the beach and set off at a decent pace. Running on the beach is super freaking hard if you're not used to it, so after a minute or two, I can really feel my heart going and the familiar trickle of sweat on the back of my neck and in my cleavage. "I didn't know you ran."

"When I can, I try to," he looks down at me with a smirk. "The hotel has laundry service, so I was thinking of sending some out today if you need anything done," he pants out, but doesn't sound overly winded, and from what I saw briefly this morning, Ryan is in good shape.

"Yes. I could use some clean stuff."

We run in silence, enjoying the sunrise over the ocean, and I swear there are few things more beautiful than this. Pinks and purples and yellows fill the sky, bathing us in light. The salty breeze brushes my skin, sticking to my moistened flesh.

I think that wherever I end up deciding to move, the ocean has to be a part of it. The south, not so much because as the sun rises, so does the muggy humidity. Yuck. Not my thing. I prefer cooler weather.

We finish our run, and after walking another hundred or so yards, we both sink into the cool sand, watching the waves crash onto the shore as we catch our breath.

"I'm not going to kill myself today," I whisper, grasping my pendant.

"What?" Ryan snaps, his head whipping toward me and I realize I just said that out loud. I blanch, biting my lip because I don't know what to say. I'm mortified. "Did you just say that you weren't going to *kill* yourself today?" He's angry. No wait, he's *furious*. His face is getting redder by the moment, his eyes blazing. "Was that a fucking possibility?"

"N-No," I stutter. "Not really."

"What the hell does that mean, Katie?" I don't know what to say. "Answer me," he bites out, and I stand up, because I suddenly can't sit anymore.

I've never been so humiliated in my life, and right now, I just want to run away from the glare he's giving me.

"It's not really. Not anymore," I answer, my voice shaking. "It's just something I say now. Sort of like a daily affirmation or something."

He stands now too, walking in the direction of the water with his back to me, his hands on his hips and his chin to his chest.

"But it was, right? Did you ever try to hurt yourself?" He's maybe a little less angry, *maybe*.

"I didn't because I made myself promise not to every morning, and occasionally at other times during the day. But lately, it's only been in the morning." I'm being honest with him on this, for the most part. The week before I moved was tough, but he doesn't need to know that.

"Fuck," he barks out, running his hands through his sweat-dampened hair. "That's bullshit, Katie."

And now it's my turn to get angry.

"Don't you dare judge me, Ryan," I snap, putting my hands on my hips and glowering into his back. "Don't you dare. You have no *idea* what I went through. What I've *gone* through over the last two years. No. Fucking. Idea."

His back is rising and falling, heavy with his breaths. He looks like he's trying to calm himself down and is failing miserably at it.

"I not only lost my husband—the love of my entire life—but I had to watch my baby girl die in front of me knowing I could not save her." His head snaps up, looking out toward the water, his shoulders tense. "She was brought to *my* hospital, and I was down in the room while they worked on her. While they pushed on her chest and defibrillated and stuck her full of medicines and tubes. I was there!" I yell, and it feels so fucking good to do that, rage and adrenaline coursing through me. "I watched as the monitor flatlined and her life slipped away. Then I held her small, lifeless body, knowing it was going to be for the last time." Now the tears are coming in full force like I just opened the dam. "That it was going to be the last time I smelled her hair or kissed her soft skin or whispered that I loved her in her ear. That the second I left her body, I'd never see her again," I sob out. "You have no idea what that kind of pain is like. You can get over losing your spouse. It's agony and impossible, but that sort of loss happens and people move on." He turns to look at me now with an unreadable expression, the sun surrounding his body making him glow and leaving his face cast in a shadow. "But losing your child like that?" I shake my head. "There are no words to describe the utter devastation." I drop my face into my hands. "You're not supposed to bury your child," I cry out, feeling the grief sweep over me like a suffocating wave, taking away my ability to move or breathe.

His arms are around me now, pulling me into his sweat-soaked shirt.

"I'm sorry, Katie. I'm so sorry," he says into the top of my hair as he holds me tighter and tighter. "I was wrong. I was so fucking wrong, and I'm sorry. Please forgive me, Katie. *Please*," he begs, and I can hear the anguish in his voice. "I didn't mean to judge you. I just...," he pauses, pulling me back so I have to look up at him. "I care about you, okay?" His thumbs wipe away the tears that have started to slow. "I get that we've only known each other less than a week, but when you spend this kind of time with someone, it becomes inevitable."

I nod my head, understanding what he means.

"I'm sorry if I freaked you out by saying that. It's just something I say now, I swear." A shudder wracks my body, and he pulls me in closer to his warm chest. "I didn't mean to unload all of that on you."

"Don't apologize to me about that, ever. I'm glad you shared it with me. I like knowing about you, Katie. The good and the bad, and losing your family like that is a large part of who you are." I nod, not able to say anything because I'm suddenly so overwhelmed by this new friendship. "Just promise me that you'll never hurt yourself."

I look directly into his eyes. "I promise."

And I mean it. I won't.

If I were going to, I would have done it twenty-six months ago when I lost them. He stares into my eyes for another moment, maybe searching for evidence of a lie, and when he finds none, he steps back, releasing me from his embrace.

Ryan lets out a slow, heavy breath.

"I was thinking of spending another night here in Charleston. Is that all right with you?"

I almost want to laugh at the subject change, because it's just so perfect. "I'm one hundred percent good with that."

"Awesome. Then let's go get some breakfast and play on the beach while the hotel does our laundry. If we're going to be spoiled, might as well do it up right."

Now I do laugh. "I'm all for being spoiled and playing on the beach and eating breakfast."

And we do just that.

Ryan thinks it's hilarious to pick me up and toss me in the ocean since I'm so small compared to him, and I think it's hilarious to splash him with water. He's not wearing his glasses while we're in the ocean, and it is the first time I've ever really seen him without them. I can't seem to decide which way I like him better, though the jade of his eyes is easier to see without them on.

After a late lunch, Ryan takes a nap since I got him up early.

I head down to the lobby to call my mother, when I notice a flyer taped to an outside pole. It's an ad for a band I've heard of, playing at a place called Music Farm. I'm so in, and I bet Ryan will be too. After I hang up with my mother, I run back upstairs and tell Ryan about my findings and just as I suspected, he's in.

I sort of love how much Ryan is into music and how similar our tastes are.

By the time we walk into Music Farm, it is standing room only.

I don't care because it is packed and loud and fun. The band is just making its way on stage, and the crowd is hollering out their excitement. I'm driving tonight so I'll just be sticking with water, but Ryan goes straight to the bar and procures himself a beer. The music starts with a heavy bass beat and I'm bouncing on my toes before I even think about it.

"Come dance with me," I shout up to Ryan, who nods his head and lets me pull him by the hand into the fray.

The lead singer is killing it, really amping up the good-sized crowd. I'm jumping and dancing around, and so is Ryan, and we're having fun. Pure fucking fun, and I feel it. I'm reveling in it and allowing it to flow over me because I know for a fact that I haven't smiled or danced or laughed this much in over two years.

The crowd is over the top, and Ryan and I have to maintain points of contact; otherwise, we'll lose each other in no time. After about forty-five minutes, I'm dying and do the universal sign to Ryan to indicate that I need something to drink.

He nods, points to himself, and holds up one finger indicating he wants one too. I nod and leave him there to continue his enjoyment.

The oval-shaped bar is pretty packed, but I manage to squeeze my way through and get up to the counter to place my order, when I feel someone looming next to me.

"Hey, pretty lady, can I buy you a drink?" I look over to see a big dude, with sandy-colored hair, dark eyes and multicolored tattoos everywhere.

I smile at him and shake my head. "No, thanks. I'm all set."

He steps in closer, and I wonder how long this bartender is going to take to get me a bottle of water and a damn beer.

"Oh, don't be like that. Let me buy your drink. You're the best-looking woman I've seen all night, maybe even all year," he grins and instantly, I'm uneasy.

Despite that, he's being nice, so I don't really want to be rude, though I definitely don't love the fact that he's up in my personal space. There is no place for me to go because there is someone standing directly behind me. So I try a different approach.

"I'm actually here with someone, but really, thanks." I give him a closed-mouth grin.

The guy doesn't give up though, he leans into my ear, forcing my head back as far as I can manage. "I could make that sexy body of yours feel really good." And shit. We've officially gone to the next level.

"Not interested," I tell him with a firmer tone that lets him know I mean it. A strong hand slides onto my waist accompanied by a slightly sweaty body, smelling like the embodiment of masculine perfection, pressing against me from behind. It's a possessive gesture, one I'm sure this guy doesn't miss.

"Everything alright here?" Ryan growls with an acerbic edge. There is no missing the fuck off hostile vibe he's shooting this guy, and any uneasiness I had moments ago evaporates.

The guy stands to his full height—Ryan has a good four inches on him at least—and squares his shoulders, leaning in ever so slightly.

"I was just offering to buy the beautiful woman here a drink and maybe get a back room fuck."

Holy shit! This guy is brazen. I'm trying to hold my cool, but I think my eyes just popped out of my head. I've never heard anyone speak like this. Especially to a woman who is obviously taken. I mean, not that I'm taken by Ryan. But this guy doesn't know that! Ryan's hand tenses on my hip as he adjusts me closer. I sink into him, allowing my head to press into his firm chest. I can feel his heart racing. Feel the anger starting to build within him. I have to do something quickly before this gets out of hand.

I look the guy directly in the eyes. "And I told him that although it's a generous offer, there is no way I can accept since I'm here with my boyfriend." I spin around in Ryan's arms, snaking my hands up behind his neck until his narrowed eyes pull down to me. Something passes between us as I silently plead with Ryan. "Come on, baby; we should get going anyway." He leans down and plants the softest of kisses right beside my mouth. My breath hitches and my grip on the back of his neck tightens. Flutters of butterflies leap to life in the pit of my stomach at the unexpected touch, but I quickly push them down, knowing the gesture was all for show.

Ryan blinks once, his jaw clenched tightly as are the fists I feel on my back. I begin to walk forward, essentially pushing Ryan back, before I look toward to the guy. "Have a good night," I smile, and he doesn't say anything else.

He'd be stupid to start a fight, and he knows it.

I don't let go of Ryan until we're outside and next to my car.

"You okay?" I ask since he doesn't seem to be relaxing his tense stance and hasn't spoken a word since I pushed him out of the bar.

"Yes," he bites out. He's not okay, and I don't know why. Walking over to him, I reach up, brushing my fingers across his soft dark beard. He trimmed it, so it's not so mountain man anymore. My hand skims the bristles, admiring the way they feel against my palm.

"Hey," I whisper. He looks down at me, but his eyes are blank and distant, his jaw is still wound tight. "Talk to me. What's going through your head?"

He finally blows out a long steady breath, and I can feel his body relaxing beneath my touch.

"I'm sorry, I don't know what came over me. I just..." He stares up to the starry sky like it has the answer before lowering his furrowed brow back to me. My hand drops to my side. "I got so fucking pissed when I heard him talking to you like that. I knew you didn't want it and I was so close to losing my shit on him, Katie. *So close.*"

"It's fine. *I'm* fine. No harm, no foul."

I wrap my arms around him, holding him close, my ear pressing into his chest directly above his heart. It's still pounding. That guy must have really worked him up. Ryan's hand cascades down the back of my hair as he holds me back. Leaning back, I meet his eyes. I can tell he is softening, because a small smirk is bouncing on his lips. His knuckles brush my cheek as we stare into each other in the dark night. I step away from him, needing space and fresh air that doesn't smell like him.

"How did you do that back there? Normally when a guy says something like that, he's looking for a fight. Either from you or from me."

"He was after sex, and when I wasn't interested, his pride was wounded. Especially when a taller and better-looking guy staked his claim on what he wanted." His mouth quirks up further when I say better-looking, but I'm not here to stroke his ego, so I continue. "The best way is to let guys like that believe that the rejection is not about them specifically." I shrug. "Plus, he knew you were bigger than him and he's not totally stupid."

Ryan shakes his head. "Where did you come from?"

I toss him a wink. "Boston, remember?"

He laughs and pulls me back to him, hugging me again. I try to hold firm. I try to hold back and resist the urge to sink into him. Into his warmth and comfort. I try really hard.

"I'm glad you're okay. I've never been the possessive caveman type, but apparently you bring that out of me. I was ready to beat that guy's ass."

"And I'm glad you didn't. I'd hate to have to deal with the cops."

He chuckles against my cheek before pulling back.

"Let's go back to the hotel. I think we've had enough excitement for one night." I agree with him. Only, Ryan is the one who really got my heart racing tonight. Not the dancing, not the guy hitting on me. No. It's all Ryan. Now I just have to figure out a way to shut that off.

7

R *yan*

Two days later we're hanging out at the pool of our hotel in Miami Beach. I'm sipping on a beer and Katie went straight for a vodka tonic with lemon instead of lime. She's resting on a lounge chair with her shades on and her knees bent up, and I can't seem to pull my eyes off of her. Thank god I have reflective sunglasses and she can't see where I'm looking, otherwise I'd have a lot of explaining to do.

But I'm not the only one staring.

And though that shouldn't piss me off, it does.

She's wearing the smallest white bikini that struggles to hold in her gorgeous curves. Her golden skin is toned yet soft looking.

I'm in trouble.

I know this and I've officially admitted it to myself.

I should have known better before this whole trip even started. Screw that, I *did* know better and chose to do this anyway. I tried to resist. I had been fighting it, but those two nights in Charleston changed everything, and I don't know what to do about it.

Ignore it.

Right.

That's the only thing I *can* do.

But the truth is, I have no idea how I'm going to get through the next few weeks traveling in a car and being with her constantly. Last night we stopped somewhere in northern Florida and she asked if I wanted to go out and get dinner, but I declined saying I was tired and opted for room service.

So when I woke up this morning, I resolved myself to the fact that nothing can or will ever happen. That helped until I saw her in that damn bikini.

She's fiddling with the pendant on her neck that I assume is a mindless habit or something, because she does it all the time.

"What are you up for tonight?" I ask, forcing my eyes back to the beautiful blue water of the pool in front of me.

The same shade as her eyes. *Shit.*

"Well," she rolls on her side to face me. *Fuck.* Not helping me with that view, Katie. "I sort of made a reservation for dinner at a steak place."

My eyes widen. "Really?"

That was so thoughtful of her. We had talked about favorite foods the other day and I mentioned steak, though I did not mention my affinity for Thai—my other favorite—for some reason. We'd talked about so many things that day, and I can't believe she actually remembered.

"That sounds great, thanks." I can't help the smile I feel spreading across my face.

"Of course," she waves me away like it's nothing. "I heard there is a really hot club in our hotel, so I thought, if you're into that sort of thing, we could check it out. If not, I'm open to whatever."

"A club?" I would not have pegged her as the clubbing type.

"Sure," she rolls back, propping her arm behind her head, and I'm grateful that she's not facing me anymore. "I like dancing, but if you'd rather do something else or nothing at all...," she trails off.

"Uh."

I have to think on this.

Going to a club with her could be a bad idea. Dancing with her like that is very tempting in more ways than one. But it's what she wants to do, and she has been in a really good, happy mood today, and I want to keep her that way. I can suck it up and deal. I mean, I know nothing will happen, so what does it matter if I dance with her?

"Sure. The club sounds fun."

She smiles wide, but doesn't say anything else.

After a few more minutes of silence, she turns her head to look at me. "Ryan?" she asks softly, almost like she's not sure if she wants to ask me her question.

"Yeah?"

"Do you think you're over Francesca? I mean, do you think you ever get over someone you loved and lost?" She's hesitant, and I can't tell if she's asking out of curiosity or for herself.

"I am over Francesca," I tell her with assurance, turning to face her and propping my head up with my hand. "I thought I loved her, but in retrospect, I'm not sure if I actually did, or if it was the idea of her.

"What do you mean?"

"Francesca was very shallow. She enjoyed my money and the life-style it provided her. She was selfish. *Very* selfish. And the things that were important to me, that mattered to me, were not important to her. That's not love."

She nods like she understands this. "I know she hurt you, but if she truly is the way you describe her, then I'm happy you're not with her anymore."

"Me too, Katie, me too," I smile over at her. "But in answer to your other question, I think the people we truly love are always a part of us. That said, we can move on and find someone else to love. Maybe we even love that new person as much as the one we lost, but that doesn't mean we have to forget them. Moving on doesn't make the love we have for the person who is gone any less real."

She swallows hard and nods at me.

"I'm going to go back to my room to take a nap," she puts on her best fake smile. I hope my words didn't hurt her or make her feel bad.

"Dinner is at eight, cowboy," she winks, getting up and leaving me here without another word.

I know she's struggling, coming to terms with her loss, and I wish she didn't have to go through that alone.

But she does, to a certain extent, because only she can find peace in her situation.

I'm showered, my beard is trimmed up, and I feel like I look good. I'm wearing a black button-down with the sleeves rolled up, my dark gray pants that sit a little low on my hips, and my black dress shoes. I managed to tame my hair by brushing it back, and tonight I'm rocking my contacts that I rarely wear—mostly because they bother me after extended use.

I knock on her door at seven forty-five, and when the door swings open, I gasp, making her smile and laugh a little.

"Is that a *you look hot* gasp or a *you look terrible go change now* gasp?" She cocks her head to the side, and her long blonde hair falls over her bare shoulder.

"Hot." I look her up and down because I feel like I have permission to do so. "Definitely hot."

She smiles, liking my answer.

"Give me a sec. I just have to grab my bag."

She turns, and I watch her fantastic ass as she walks back into her room. She's wearing a dark-red halter top that is very low cut, showing off her ample cleavage as well as her entire back. It stops just at the top of her tiny skirt, so when she moves, I get glimpses of her toned stomach. Her thighs are on full display, and she's paired the whole death-of-me ensemble with sky-high red stilettos.

Oh, and did I mention the fuck-me red of her lips? Yeah, she's got that going too. She's a siren, and I'm screwed.

"Ready," she announces with a proud smile.

"Can you actually walk in those shoes?" I gesture at her crazy hooker heels.

"Short women get used to wearing psychotic heels. It's the only way we feel tall." She looks up at me. "See, I'm almost cheek height."

"Not exactly, but we'll go with it for now."

She smacks my arm, then loops hers through mine.

"Dick," she mutters playfully. "We can't all be blessed with good looks and height. Some of us have to work for it."

"Uh. Other than the height, you don't have to work for anything. You're the most naturally beautiful woman I've ever seen." The second the words are out of my mouth, I regret them, but she just nuzzles her head on my arm for a second instead of giving me a look that says I crossed the line.

"Thanks. That's one of the nicest things anyone has ever said to me," she looks up at me with her light-blue eyes that I could happily get lost in. "You look great by the way. Totally hot. I'm digging the whole dark and mysterious thing you're rocking tonight." Her hand waves up and down my body, and I laugh at her description. I want to scoop her up in my arms and press my lips to hers. Devour every perfect inch.

This unrequited stuff sucks.

The restaurant is big and trendy, and we both drink more than our weight in alcohol. Hers in apple martinis and mine in whiskey, so by the time we make it back to our hotel and into the line for the club, we're drunk. We're smiling and laughing and touching, and generally having a great fucking time.

We get in about twenty minutes later and she immediately drags me over to a dark sitting area with short white couches and purple mood lighting. Multicolored laser beams of light streak across the room to a synchronized rhythm.

The music in this section is a steady beat of heavy house bass and we have to shout at each other to hear anything. I think she gets frustrated with the whole talking thing because she eventually rolls her es and grabs my hand, pulling me onto the dance floor full of gyrating bodies.

And then she begins to dance.

Rolling her hips and raising her arms above her head and closing her eyes, and I can't stop watching her move, because it's the sexiest thing I've ever seen.

Did I mention how drunk we are?

Because I do something I know I shouldn't, but can't for the life of me talk myself out of. I reach out and put my hands on her hips, pulling her into me and moving my body with hers.

Her glassy eyes open to my touch, and a big beautiful smile lights up her face.

She's into this. Us dancing together. So that's exactly what we do.

We dance and move and even grind a little. My hands roam all over her hips, her ribs, the skin of her stomach and back. Anywhere I feel like I can get away with touching her, I do.

And she touches me too.

My arms, my back, my chest, and when her fingers glide into my hair, I have to stifle my moan. That's always been a weakness of mine, and it feels unbelievable.

We're both sweaty when the song morphs into a slower more hypnotic beat. I think she's going to ask to sit down, given the seductive nature of the music, but she shocks the shit out of me by resting her head on my chest and snaking her arms around my lower back. Her hips are moving, and my hands automatically glide down the exposed silky skin of her back until they stop just above her ass.

I'm holding her in the dark, surrounded by strangers who are practically dry fucking all around us.

My heart rate starts to climb, and I know she can feel it because her ear is pressed right above it. Katie's hand glides up my chest, resting next to her head on my peck, and I reach up with one of my hands to hold it. She lets me. I know it's just because she is drunk, but I can't help the goddamn want that is swirling around inside of me.

Katie is like a drug I can't seem to get enough of, and even though

I know I need to quit, I can't. I'm addicted to this. To her smell, her feel, the way she moves against me, all of it. I want more, and I can't have it, and that just sucks.

The song ends all too soon, and she pulls back, her eyes sleepy, hair tussled, and crazy sexy.

"I'm tired," she says during a brief break in the music.

I check my watch and see that it is well past two in the morning. "Let's get you to bed then, sleepy girl."

"I had so much fun tonight, Ryan. This has been the best," she grins, half-asleep as we walk through the hotel over toward the elevators that lead up to our rooms. Once again our rooms are next to each other, and the thought of her sleeping on the other side of the wall isn't doing me any favors.

"I did too, sweetheart."

My fingers glide through her hair as she rests her heavy head against my side. Leaning down, I press my lips to the top of her head, relieved she's so short that even with stilettos, her lips aren't more accessible. I need a distraction, and if it wasn't so late, I might actually consider going back into the club to pick someone up.

"If I tell you something, will you not speak of it again and pretend like it never happened?"

I smile at her cuteness and kiss the top of her head again before we step off the elevator onto our floor. "Promise."

She sighs heavily into me. "I miss sex." My eyes widen, and I suppress a groan, because this girl is killing me. My cock hears her words, thickening against the zipper of my pants, and I nearly groan again. "Part of me thinks I should just find someone and get it over with. You know, rip the Band-Aid off, but the other part of me has been holding onto it. Afraid to experience that with someone else." She sighs again, leaning into me a little more and our walk has all but stalled in the hallway. "What if I'm bad at it?"

I chuckle softly at the absurdity of those words.

"No, I mean it." She stops me, pulling away and looking at me earnestly. "I've only ever been with Eric. What if I'm not good at sex?"

I cup her face with my hand so she's force to look into my eyes. "You will be," I tell her honestly, because I know this beyond a shadow of a doubt. "No one who moves their body the way I saw you move yours tonight could *possibly* be bad in bed." I'm desperate to offer up my services as a test, but I keep quiet because I know she'll say no and laugh it off and then things could get weird between us. "You're an incredible woman, Katie. Beautiful, sexy, smart, funny, a bit of a wiseass. The whole package." My fingers glide down her face because I can't seem to stop them. I've never wanted anyone the way I want her. "When you do decide to have sex again, it should be with someone worthy of you, not a meaningless fuck."

"Why does it sound so hot when you say it like that?"

Now I do groan. "You're killing me here, Katie. I'm trying to be a good and honorable man, and you're telling me that what I'm saying sounds hot and that you miss sex. I'm a *guy* sweetheart; there is only so much I can take." *And I'm about at my end.*

She laughs like I knew she would, and then she leans back into me, and we start to walk again. "You are sort of a perfect guy, aren't you, Ryan Grant? I'm jealous of the woman who gets you, and I don't even know her."

I want to tell her that she could have me this very second, but I don't.

I can't.

She doesn't actually want me.

Katie is still very much stuck in the past and in love with her husband. She'd regret me before the condom even came off, and I know I couldn't handle that.

"Back at you, babe. I sort of want to take down the guy who gets you." Actually no sort of about it.

She leans her head back against the door to her room. "You're a liar, but a sweet one. So I'll let you get away with it just this once," she winks at me and I'm not exactly sure what she's talking about. "Good night, Ryan." She leans up and kisses my cheek before pulling back and going into her room, leaving me in a world of horny frustration and emotional confusion.

In all the many ways I've thought of her—imagined her—over the years, I never quite did her justice. She is so much better than any fantasy I ever conjured up, and I have a fantastic imagination. Katie is my wildest dreams and greatest hope combined into one stunningly perfect package. And I want to open it up so damn badly. But there is no way that will ever happen. There is just no way.

8

K *ate*

I WAKE to a loud pounding in my head and that sick, icky feeling in my stomach, which can only be the result of too much alcohol the night before. More pounding, and then I realize it's the door.

Crawling out of bed, I grab the robe and wrap it around myself before I open the door to a frowning Ryan. "What's up, dude? Why the early morning wake-up call?"

"Well, *dude*," he mocks, walking past me into my room. "First of all, you need to tie that damn robe because I can see you're only wearing panties under it, and it's more than I can deal with at the moment."

I shrug a shoulder, not really caring that he saw my stomach and panties. It's not like he saw my boobs. He's grumpy today.

"Second of all," he continues as I tie a knot and turn around to face him. "It's not early morning. It's after eleven and checkout is at noon."

I yawn, rubbing my face. "I thought we said we were going to stay here another night?"

"We did, but that was until I saw on the Weather Channel this morning that we're going to get hit with a hurricane tomorrow."

"Oh."

"Yeah. Oh."

"Why are you being a grumpy bear?" I flop down onto my bed, raising an eyebrow at him.

He smirks despite himself, and it's the reaction I was hoping for. "I'm not being a...grumpy bear." I love that he just said those words. "I just didn't sleep well."

"Too much ETOH will do that my friend." I lean back on my hands, my legs dangling off the edge of the bed.

"ETOH?"

"It's the acronym for ethyl alcohol, also referred to as ethanol or drinking alcohol."

His lips quirk. "You're a nerd."

"So said the computer geek. Anyway, I'm sorry you didn't sleep well last night." I sit up, leaning forward and resting my elbows on my thighs. His eyes graze down my body before he shifts and looks away. "I guess this means that Key West is out now too?" He nods. "All right. So then where to, kemosabe?"

"You're a bit of an odd duck, aren't you?"

"So said the man who used the phrase *odd duck*."

"Are you going to keep starting your sentences with, *so said the*?"

"Maybe." We're both smiling now and I think feeling a little better for it. "Give me twenty to shower and pack up. I need some greasy food, and then I'll drive wherever you direct me. You can nap in the car."

"Let's head toward New Orleans. We'll stop somewhere along the way when you don't want to drive anymore."

"That's a plan, Stan," I wink, standing up and grabbing a pair of shorts and a vintage Beastie Boys tee out of my bag along with clean panties and a bra. "Are we checked out?" I ask as I move to the bathroom.

"I'll go take care of it while you shower."

"Awesome. See you soon."

I shut the door behind me, strip down and start up the shower. Other than my stomach that feels gross, I don't feel terrible. Probably due to all the water I drank when I got back here last night. I wash quickly, dress, run a brush through my hair and teeth, and then finish packing everything up.

I'm ready in under fifteen and feeling a lot less nasty.

Ryan is hard at work on his phone, leaning against a large pillar as I approach him. "Ready, sunshine?" I ask once he tucks his phone in his pocket.

"Ready, rainbows," he smiles, but it doesn't quite reach his eyes. Something feels... off. More than just the impending hurricane. Ryan grabs my bag, and we head out to the valet, who has my car waiting.

We hit the highway quickly, and let me tell you, Florida drivers are insane. They weave in and out of lanes without signaling. Some drive dirt-ass slow, while others speed twenty over the limit. Ryan passes out quickly after we hit up a fast food joint.

Normally I don't eat that crap, but desperate times and all.

I'm lost in thought, listening to music when I start to see signs for Orlando and Disney World. The familiar burning behind my eyes begins automatically. Eric and I had talked about taking Maggie to Disney World. He wanted to do it that winter, but I wanted to put it off since she was so young. I regret that now. I wish I could have seen her face light up the way I know it would have. I wish I could have seen Eric experience that with her.

I've been driving for almost four hours. I need to get out and stretch my legs, but the thought of doing it in Orlando makes me ache. I also have to pee, and I'm stiff as hell and thirsty, and really want to curl into a ball and cry my eyes out. My fingers clasp my necklace as I take the exit for Disney World, wondering if this will prove to be cathartic or counterproductive.

Ryan starts to rouse, lifting in his seat until he's sitting up again and looking out the window. "Are we stopping?"

"I need to stretch my legs and get something to drink." My voice is so quiet that I know he won't miss it.

"I can drive after this for a bit if you want to keep going, or we could stay in Orlando? Go to a park?"

"No," I say far too quickly. "I want to keep going."

He looks over at me, but I keep my eyes trained on the road. "You okay?"

I shake my head, swallowing a few times and trying to keep my tears at bay.

"Disney World?" he guesses, and all I can do is nod. "Pull in here, Katie." He points to a Walmart, and I do as I'm told, parking the car near the front. "Let's go inside, grab some snacks, stretch our legs, and see what kind of weird shit we can find."

I look at him, but can't seem to manage a smile.

The second we're out of the car he pulls me into a hug and I have to try so much harder not to cry. I push him away, shake my head and start to walk towards the entrance.

He gets it.

I know he does as he walks next to me leaving a wide berth of space between us. The entire store is full of Disney and Universal Studios merchandise.

"I never got to read Harry Potter to her." And that does it. I break down in the middle of Walmart.

Ryan starts toward me with that sad, remorseful look on his face and I wave him off, pointing to the restroom as I run away. I crash through the bathroom and go directly into the stall.

I pee, because, well, I need to, doing my best to get control of my tears. I wonder if a day will come when I don't cry at least once. I long for it and dread it at the same time. I want to be able to move on, get my life back together, and start fresh. Yet I don't want to ever do that because I'm afraid that means I'll have forgotten them, or that my love for them has diminished. If I cry and hurt, then I know they're still a part of me and that my love is still as strong as it ever was.

I wash my hands, splash water on my face, and when I come out, Ryan has a cart that is filled with crap. A ridiculous t-shirt that says

Because I rule, Pringles, Chex mix, bottles of water, a deck of playing cards, and a checkerboard.

"Jesus, how long was I in there?"

"This store is awesome. I've never actually been inside of a Walmart before, but you can get everything here, and it's super cheap." He's excited, and it's sort of adorable. I think I meant it. I'm insanely jealous of whatever girl gets him. I know it's not me. I know he doesn't want me like that. But I still can't help that nagging jealousy at the thought.

"Lead me to the candy aisle. I need gummy candy and I need it stat."

"This way, doll," he gives me his crooked smile and then points me over toward the food.

I grab four bags of various gummies and a Diet Coke since the one I got at the fast-food place this morning wasn't real Diet Coke. Ryan thinks my little habit is nasty, and I concede that it is, but I don't drink coffee or tea, so he'll have to deal with it.

I also purchase a Hufflepuff scarf because I've always wanted one. Yes, if I had been sorted, it would have been with Hufflepuff, get over it. We leave Walmart fifty bucks broker, but it was worth it, and I feel a little better after my cry.

That's a new sensation for me too. Usually crying makes me feel worse, but today I somehow feel lighter for it.

Ryan gets in the driver's seat, and we continue heading northwest to the Florida panhandle. We don't stop for several more hours. Instead, we eat our junk food and talk and listen to music, and argue about the finer points of Harry Potter and Star Wars.

"All I'm saying is that Star Wars is the greater franchise," Ryan says, using one-handed exaggerated gestures as the other is thankfully affixed to the steering wheel.

"Greater in what respect? I mean, sure it spans a larger generation gap, but the fact that Harry Potter is both a book and a film series, I think makes it better overall."

"Okay, I'll admit that I liked the books. But the Star Wars movies are way better than the Harry Potter ones."

I shrug, conceding that point. "So would you rather be a wizard or a Jedi?"

"Damn, that's a great question." He rubs his hand along his dark bristly jaw as he thinks on this. "Jedi. Lightsabers are badass and they can do pretty much anything a wizard can do."

"Except apparate. And Jedi can't really fly."

"True. Apparation would be awesome." Ryan turns to me with the biggest grin ever, a twinkle in his vibrant green eyes, and for a moment, I get lost. And then I get butterflies that I don't quite understand.

And then I turn away because it's all making me way too jittery and uncomfortable for my liking.

I turn up the music, and we fall into a companionable silence, lost in our own reverie.

By the time we do stop, it's well after dark, and I have no idea where we are, but Ryan assures me that we're close to Tallahassee.

We manage to find a hotel that has a restaurant in it, which is a double bonus at this point. We've been driving for eight hours, and the thought of having to get back in the car to find food is not appealing.

Ryan and I eat in silence, go to bed in our separate rooms, and wake up early as hell.

Before lunchtime the next day, we're in New Orleans.

It's raining. A lot.

The hurricane that hit the Florida coast has sent a wave of moisture in this direction, so the thought of traveling around and looking for a place to stay the way we normally do does not work. We google hotels, and Ryan books us at the Ritz-Carlton, which is around the corner from Bourbon Street. We check in and as I talk to the front desk, Ryan is over by the concierge, I assume making dinner reservations.

When he returns, he has this shit-eating, triumphant grin on his too-handsome face as he pushes his black frames up the bridge of his nose.

"I sort of did something for you, and I don't want you to complain, challenge, or protest."

I raise an eyebrow because this sounds serious. "What did you do, Mr. Grant?"

He gives me his crooked smile. "Is it weird that I think it's hot that you just called me that?" I make a circular motion with my hand encouraging him to spill it. "I made you a spa reservation."

"You did *what*?" My eyebrows shoot up to my hairline.

He's grinning. "Yup. Your appointments start in an hour."

"*Appointments*? As in more than one?" I shake my head, trying to hold in my grin. "Ryan—" I start, but he quickly cuts me off.

"And it's on me." I'm shaking my head adamantly. "Like I said, no protests. I want to do this for you, so please accept it."

Jesus, this guy. I throw my arms around him, burying my head into his chest. He's the sort of man a woman falls in love with.

"I don't deserve you, Ryan. You truly amaze me. I may, in fact, love you in this moment." I pull back with a smile that he readily returns. His knuckles brush my cheek, his eyes feasting on mine before they dip to my lips. They linger there, and with each passing second, my heart beats faster. I don't want him to kiss me, I don't, but I can't make myself step away either.

Finally, he clears his throat. "Go get yourself settled in at the spa, they're waiting for you. I'll take your bag up to your room." I lean up on my tippy-toes and press my lips to his. It's quick. Nothing more than a peck really. Because a kiss on the cheek just won't do it for this.

It's not a real kiss. More like the ones I used to give Maggie. So it doesn't really count. But I feel it. Even in its brevity, I feel it. The warm softness of his lips. The scent of his skin. The feel of his touch against mine. I feel it all and it feels...well, I'm not exactly sure *how* it feels.

Confusing? Yes. Nice? Definitely.

I leave Ryan immediately after. My brain is in overdrive and I need to shut it down. The spa is beautiful, and when I get there they give me first-class treatment. Ryan ordered me the works. Massage, a body scrub thing, lunch, facial, manicure, and pedicure. I'm told by the staff that I am not allowed to ask how much everything costs. They're under strict instructions to make me feel like a princess.

Who does that?

I mean, I've known this guy for a week, and he orders me hundreds of dollars' worth of spa treatments?

I don't know how to process any of this, mainly because...I could like him. I could, and I don't want to because I *know* I'm not ready. It's just... I don't know how to make it stop. This building crush I'm developing for him. I have no idea if this pampering is out of friendship, or pity, or something else entirely, but I'm scared to ask.

Scared because I don't know what I want the answer to be.

I'll be conflicted no matter what.

I spend almost five freaking hours in the spa, and by the time I emerge, I feel and look like a new woman. I haven't been this relaxed in years, since before Maggie was born. Recharged? Yeah, I'm that too.

My room is decorated in a very New Orleans French way, full of heavy fabrics, gold and damask patterns. It's gorgeous. I wish I had someone here with me to share it. Eric wouldn't have liked this, though. He would have thought it was too ostentatious, which it sort of is, but come on.

Ryan texts me that dinner is set for eight. Perfect. I have time for a nap.

I wake at seven to shower, loving how smooth my skin is as I change into a dress—a sexy as hell, silver mini dress that I almost threw out when I was packing, but decided to keep at the last moment. I'm glad I did. I want to look how I feel. Radiant. I pair it with my silver strappy wedge sandals.

When Ryan opens the door to my knock, he pauses, taking me in from head to toe. "You're breathtaking, Katie. So absolutely gorgeous."

I smile, unable to help it, and then I launch myself into his arms. He catches me with an oomph and a laugh. I want to wrap my legs around him, but I don't dare. Instead, I hold him, and he holds me, and wow, this is just so...

"Thank you, Ryan. Today is on my list as one of the top five best days ever, and it's all thanks to you."

He steadies me, running his hand across my cheek and staring at me the way only he does. Like he sees me. Like he cares, and that's only making this growing ache in the pit of my stomach worse.

"I'd do it every day to see you smile like this."

Normally a comment like that would make me frown and feel sad, but it doesn't for some reason. For some reason, it makes me feel bubbly in a way I can't really express. He means it. And it only makes me want to smile more for him just to see the way he looks at me when I do.

"You ready, Katie?"

"I'm ready, Ryan. Dinner and drinks are on me tonight, and you can't complain, challenge, or protest," I smirk, throwing his words back at him.

He laughs, but begrudgingly agrees.

I don't really give him a choice anyway.

We walk out of the hotel into the balmy night, and even though the rain has stopped, the air is heavy and humid. I can feel my hair raising up to a frizz factor of five, so I run my fingers through it and start to try and tame it into a ponytail.

"Don't," Ryan stops me with his fingers in my hair. "I like it down like that."

I give him a look that says, *you must be joking*. "My hair is a frizzy mess in this humidity."

"No," he disagrees. "It's sexy."

"Fine," I surrender. "But promise me that when it becomes an out of control puff of hair, you'll let me put it up."

He laughs. "I promise."

We walk around the corner to Bourbon Street, and even though it's a Tuesday in September after a day of rain, the streets are packed. The majority of the one and two-story buildings are brick with a lot of wrought-iron balconies with intricate balustrades and spindles. Bright neon lights beckon you into each of the different bars, all promising real New Orleans jazz.

And there are people selling sex everywhere.

Lots and lots of sex.

Oh, and you can drink openly on the streets. I've never experienced that before.

"Despite the obvious debauchery, it's really a very pretty city. I mean, the architecture and the old world classic vibe are unique, but I don't think I could live here."

"Why not?" he asks as he opens the door for me to some restaurant I didn't even pay attention to.

"The weather," I tell him as we enter the dimly lit room that is filled with a lot of red silk and velvet. "I'm not a fan of super-hot and humid. I think the south is out for me."

He nods in agreement. "I'm the same way. We can head north after this if you'd like. See if any of those places appeal to you."

"Sure, though I'm not sure if I'm a Midwestern girl either. I love the ocean," I laugh at myself. "I'm sort of a walking contradiction, huh?"

"No, just particular with what you want. That's a good thing, especially when looking for a new place to live."

I smile at that as I slide into the plush, red velvet bench seat. Our table is set up so that Ryan has to sit next to me in the small space instead of across from me. A lot of the tables are situated this way, and I can't really figure out why.

Ryan is a big guy and he takes up a lot of space, and given the confines of our table, our thighs and arms are touching.

"Do you want me to see if they have something bigger?" he asks, noting our points of contact.

I look around the very crowded restaurant and it doesn't appear to get any better anywhere else.

"Nah," I wave him off. "It's a good thing I like you, though," I tease. An unexpected blush creeps up my face at that. *Whoa!* I clear my throat. "What made you pick Seattle? Or was it the job that drew you there?" And then I realize in the week that I've known Ryan, I have yet to ask about what he does for a living. "God, you must think I'm the biggest bitch in the world." I cover my face with my hands, leaning my head against his arm. "I'm so sorry I never asked about your work until now."

He nudges my head with the arm that I'm resting against. "I don't think you're a bitch and in truth, I don't like to talk about my work all that much, so I don't mind in the slightest."

I look up at him. "Why not?"

"Because some of what I do is... sensitive."

"Okay." I draw out the word scrunching my eyebrows.

"Seattle seemed like as good of a place as any for my company to grow, and I have a good buddy there who wants to run a particular portion of it that I'd rather not, so it all works out."

"Wait," I hold up a hand. "You own your own business? I don't understand."

He stares at me with the most serious of expressions. "Well Katie, much of the world's consumerism and wealth are driven by business and many people own their own. There are large companies and small companies—" I hit his arm, making him laugh.

"That's not what I was confused on, you dick."

He laughs even harder before leaning down to kiss the top of my head. Like it's all so normal. His touch. His kiss. "You're just adorable, aren't you? Yes, I own my own company. I have for years, and as much as I love Philly, I need a change." He raises an eyebrow. "Surely you can understand that."

"I can, and I sort of get why you went with Seattle, but you're awfully cryptic with what you do. Is it a secret?" My eyes widen with intrigue. "Illegal?"

He grins slyly. "No. It's not illegal, and it's not exactly a secret, but I don't like to publicize parts of it either."

"Then how do you get clients?"

"They come to me by referral and my reputation."

"Wow," I lean back and give him a big up and down once-over. "So you are sort of big-time then, aren't you?"

He laughs out loud and pulls me into his side. "Adorable, Katie. Simply adorable." Only I don't feel adorable in his arms. I feel something else entirely.

9

R *yan*

TONIGHT'S THE NIGHT. I realize that makes me sound like Dexter or something, but since I'm not planning on murdering anyone, I think I'm good. No, I'm talking about sex. And how I need to get some. Tonight.

It's the only way I'll survive being around Katie and not touching her or kissing her or doing any of the millions of other things that I want to do.

It certainly doesn't help that she looks like the goddess from my wildest fantasies tonight.

That silver dress is driving me mad, and the fact that I had to sit pressed up against her all through dinner? *Jesus.*

We ate all kinds of typical New Orleans fare with the exception of crawfish, since we both agreed that they creep us out. It was awesome and we talked and laughed and it felt like a fucking date. A good date.

No, a *great* date. The kind of date that you hope turns into all night, and all night turns into many more dates.

So now we're walking through the throngs of people down Bourbon Street hand in hand, pointing and laughing at various things—especially the oversexed and alcohol-ridden establishments and people. Finally, we set our sights on a jazz bar and enter the cave-like room. The walls are comprised of what looks like pressed dirt or clay with several bumps.

It's dark, as you would expect a cave to be.

The only illumination is coming from several fake candles set up throughout the room and the blue glow over the bar. It's sexy and intimate, and the jazz music is only fueling the fire.

Katie drags me up to the black shiny bar and we both order whiskeys before finding a small corner in the room where we can listen. The place is packed, so Katie is pressed up against me and my hand is on her hip—for safety purposes only, of course—because she keeps getting bumped into.

Her hips slowly sway to the beat of the drums and bass, and my chin is resting on her head. I'm enjoying the sensation of her against me.

My chin slips from her head, and I can't stop myself before my nose runs through her hair, breathing her in. That one not-so-simple motion does me in, and my hand snakes from her hip to her stomach where it splays against the thin fabric of her dress.

I know I should stop, that what I'm doing is wrong, but I can't.

I need this too much.

I need her.

Her small body leans back into mine, and my breath catches before speeding up along with my heart rate. Maybe this is different? Maybe she's into this too? My mind wanders in a million dirty directions. Would the whiskey taste sweet or smoky on her lips and tongue? Would her skin blush under my touch? Would she moan or whimper as I slip my fingers inside her panties and find her wet pussy?

But that other question pops in. The unsolicited one. What would this mean for the rest of the trip for us, if she wanted me the want her?

I know she doesn't want a relationship. I know she's not looking for anything, so what the hell am I doing?

And when did I turn into a woman with all of these fucking questions?

We sway like this for the rest of the song, and when it's over, she turns around to look at me. Her blue eyes are heated and dark in the limited lighting, her skin a little dewy from the humidity. She's gorgeous. So gorgeous she takes my breath away.

Katie continues to stare intently at me, not saying anything, just watching me, and I can't tell what she's thinking. Normally Katie wears her heart and her thoughts on her sleeve, but right now, she's holding them back, and this little stare down is getting my heart racing even faster. I don't know whether to be turned on or apprehensive.

After what feels like the longest moment of my life, she swallows hard and blinks, and just like that, the spell is broken.

At least for her it is, because she takes a sip of her whiskey and turns back around to listen to the next set of music that has just started. In this moment, I'm sort of wishing I flew on airplanes, because I need to create some distance between us. Both physically and emotionally, because I can say with one hundred percent certainty, I've never been drawn to anyone the way I am to her.

Ten agonizing minutes later, and with as little physical contact as I can stand, she turns to me and tells me she's ready for bed.

Awesome.

I walk her back to the hotel, which is really only four blocks away. When we reach her room, she stops to face me. Her hand glides up to her ever-present pendant, grasping it like it's her lifeline.

"In case I haven't told you, Ryan," she says softly, her sweet smile shining up at me. "You're really special to me. It's only been a week, but I feel connected to you somehow. Like we were meant to meet." She tilts her head. "Does that make sense?"

I nod once. "Yes. I agree." And I do.

"Thank you for being such a good friend to me," she smiles, and I'm gutted with that one stupid word. *Friend*.

"You're easy to be good to, Katie, and it works both ways. You're so special to me, too." I wrap my arms around her, but pull back just as quickly because I just can't. She gives me that sweet smile again and then goes into her room. The door clicks shut, and my face falls to my hands as I blow out a hot, tormented breath.

I turn slowly, not really *wanting* to do what I'm about to do, but knowing that I *need* to all the same.

Before Francesca, I slept around.

And I did so without explanation or regret. I made sure the woman knew the score beforehand, but that didn't change my methods. They used me just as much as I used them, so it worked, and I felt zero remorse for it.

Francesca changed that. But after her, I went back to my old ways because she made me believe that love and attachment lead to hurt.

And fuck that.

But as I make my way back outside, the only place I want to be is upstairs with Katie. I don't want any of these women, but I can't have the one I want, and since I'm forced to be around her constantly, I need this.

I need this, I tell myself again.

I'm two steps onto the main drag when I spot my target.

Or more like she spots me. I get the fuck-me eyes, and I barely have to return them before she walks up to me.

"Hi. You want to come with us to that bar over there?" The girl points to some place behind her, but I don't care enough to raise my eyes to see where. She's cute. Straight brown hair that stops an inch above her shoulders, and dark eyes. She's dressed for sex, and her friends who are standing a few paces away giggle at their brazen friend.

She doesn't ask my name or offer hers.

I don't care.

I'm in.

"Lead the way."

She smiles up at me coyly like she's about to offer me something entirely new. I doubt that, but what the hell?

I follow the nameless brunette into whatever the closest bar is without a cover charge, and she doesn't even bother bringing me up to the bar for the ruse of a shared drink. No, this girl is all business. She throws her friends a wink and then takes my hand, leading me through the crowd of people toward the back.

She tries the handle on a broom closet, and when it opens, she throws me a devilish smile over her shoulder. She's taller than Katie, probably closer to five-seven or eight. And she's not built like Katie either. She's leaner, more of a model-like build, which I don't normally find all that attractive. I like curves. She has none, but like I said, I don't really care all that much tonight.

We get into this small room, and the second the door shuts, I experience total sensory deprivation. I can't see or hear anything except her breathing and mine.

She rubs up against me, running her hands up and down my chest.

She feels wrong. Too rough and overly aggressive. Her hair brushes against my nose and she smells wrong too. Like strong floral perfume.

Her hands run down my body, landing on the button and zipper of my jeans.

"You're so sexy," she breathes out, and I can't stand her voice either. It's sharp and feels fake, put-on. "The second I saw you, I knew I wanted you."

I don't respond, because suddenly she lowers herself to her knees and puts my cock in her mouth. My eyes shut instantly, trying to block out the pounding thoughts in my head.

My mind swirls, toxic and sick. My stomach churns, turning the remnants of my dinner into a corrosive poison in my gut.

Suddenly I can't stand the feeling of her mouth on my dick.

I yank her up and off me, and she giggles. It's annoying, and I can't breathe, so I spin her around, sliding up her tiny skirt. She hasn't kissed me or even tried. A small win because I know, I fucking know, I would not be able to stand that.

This is quick and dirty and she's not complaining at all.

"Yes," she pants out.

I blink against the blinding darkness, shaking my head back and forth. *Focus.* I can't focus. I can't have Katie and I need this. This nameless, faceless woman. If I screw her then...

I put the condom on and stare down at myself. At where I know my condom covered dick is.

"Everything okay?"

"Yeah." Only it's not okay. Nothing is okay and what the fuck am I doing right now?

She moans loudly, trying to egg me on. It's the fakest sound I've ever heard. I'm not even touching her.

"Come on," she bites out when I don't move or speak. She inches her too-thin body back against me, bumping into my cock, and I grunt. But it's not out of desire.

It's out of disgust. With myself.

"I..."

"Just put it in me already. I need it hard and rough."

"Shhh," I snap. "Just give me a second." She keeps going, saying something I'm no longer listening to, and I close my eyes again, trying to block her out.

And then I do the worst thing ever.

Something I've never done in all my time of random, meaningless sex.

I picture someone else.

I see Katie. Her sweet smile looking up at me. Those light-blue eyes—the color of the sky—gazing at me. Her perfect body beneath mine. The feel of her silky skin against my hands. Her smell. Her taste. Her sounds.

I'm picturing Katie instead of this girl. I want Katie. Not this girl. Not any other girl.

"I'm sorry. I can't do this."

"What?" she shrieks. "What the fuck does that mean?"

It means I'm done.

I rip the condom off, zip myself up, find the door, and walk away without another word. Straight out of the bar and into the humid night that offers me no solace.

I wander around aimlessly for god only knows how long, before I make myself go back to the hotel. For a hot second, I'm tempted to go and have another drink at the bar, but I don't. Instead, I go right up to my room and take the longest hottest shower of my life, washing my body so many times that my skin is practically raw.

By the time I crawl into bed, I'm wrecked. It's late and I'm tired.

Worst of all, I don't know what I'm going to do.

I could pull away from Katie entirely. Become emotionally distant and save myself. But then her words from earlier tonight flit through my mind. She said I was special to her. That she felt like she was meant to meet me. I'm important to her.

And I know I can't pull back.

So is it better to spend whatever time I have with her knowing that I'm only going to get hurt in the end?

Maybe.

Maybe I should just take what I can get with her and deal with the consequences when they happen. And they will happen. Of that I have no doubt. The thought of hurting her is worse than the thought of hurting myself.

I'll ride this wave with her.

And when it's over, I'll completely wipe out.

10

K *ate*

WE END up spending two days in New Orleans, walking around the city, riding the streetcars, eating and drinking way too much and having a good freaking time.

Originally, we had wanted to drive north up toward Chicago, and then west through the Badlands and Wyoming. But we both want to do Vegas, the Grand Canyon, and SoCal, so that first plan didn't really make a lot of sense given our time constraints. If we had endless time, then sure, it would be game on.

So we did what we said we would not do.

We created an itinerary.

Our plan is to hit up Austin, then Dallas, drive through northern Texas and New Mexico until we get to the Grand Canyon. After that, it is Vegas, LA, somewhere along the coast, San Francisco and up the Pacific Coast Highway through the redwood forest all the way to Seattle.

All of that is to be done in the next fourteen to seventeen days max.

It's ambitious since we both agreed that we want the majority of our time to be spent in California.

We set off for Austin bright and damn early since it is a long-ass drive and will take us all day. But as soon as we start out we change our plans and decide to head straight for Dallas, which makes more sense than stopping in Austin.

We realized pretty quickly that we wouldn't get to enjoy the city at all, since we'd get in late and would have to set out again early. This drive is actually better anyway, as it takes us through actual towns in Louisiana, like Baton Rouge and Shreveport.

Today is October first and we have already been on the road nine days.

It's hard to believe, but it's true.

Ryan is scheduled to do a bunch of things in Seattle on the nineteenth and wants to be there for at least a full day before, so he's not so rushed. Knowing there is a very real and looming expiration date on our little adventure sucks. I never thought I'd want to travel with anyone like this, especially a man I didn't know, but now the thought of continuing on without him doesn't feel possible.

So I have a new goal for this trip.

Find a place I want to live *before* we get to Seattle.

I promised to take him all the way there, and I intend to keep my word, but I don't want to drift aimlessly after that is done. I want to know where I'm going. I want a direction and a mission, because leaving him is going to be rough.

I meant what I said to him the other night in New Orleans.

I feel like Ryan is a part of me.

I've heard that old cliché about people being thrust into your life at the right moment, and I never really believed it—until now.

Yes, I have fun with him. Yes, he's sweet and thoughtful and ridiculously hot and perfect. Yes, I have a crush to beat all crushes on him. I admit it, but that's all it is.

A crush.

Those are natural and normal when spending this much time with a member of the opposite sex, right? Right. It's not like I'm cheating or my thoughts about Ryan mean that I don't love Eric as much as I still do.

This is different.

And though Ryan and I flirt and occasionally get a little touchy-feely, we're just friends.

I'm sure it is the same way for him. I don't pretend to think he has feelings for me beyond what we have right now. That and I'm pretty sure he hooked up with someone when we were in New Orleans. I smelled some strong god-awful perfume on his shirt when I was helping to pack up his clothes, and there was an empty condom wrapper stuffed in the pocket of his pants. That's usually a pretty good indication of sex.

I didn't really expect him to be celibate just because I am.

I understand that he is a very attractive single guy and has needs and all that. I understand all of it. Even if I hate it. I'm grateful he didn't tell me about her, but I despise the twinge in my stomach I get when I think about it. I feel guilty and wrong for even remotely entertaining the idea that I'm jealous.

I have no right.

He doesn't want me, and I'm forever in love with Eric, and that is all there is to it. Even if it sucks a little.

"Tell me you're up for some killer barbeque tonight," he says as we hit the Texas border.

"I never say no to barbeque. I could rock the hell out of some ribs," I tell him, leaning back in my seat and stretching my legs up onto the dash. I drove the first four hours and now he's finishing off this leg of the journey. I flex and relax my toes repeatedly, improving the circulation in my lower extremities, because DVTs are real and I don't want one.

He laughs. "As long as we don't have to line dance or say y'all."

"Or chew tobacco," I add, scrunching my nose up in distaste. "Something tells me we can find fantabulous barbeque and delicious drinks." He looks over at me, and I bounce my eyebrows at him. "I bet you can even find some really nice fake tits here. I've heard Dallas is known for them."

He laughs again, reaching over to poke my ribs, making me squeal. I'm so freaking ticklish and he knows it. "I think I'm all set with that."

I shrug. "Never say never."

He looks at me for a moment as if trying to read my expression, and I'm doing my best to remain casual under his scrutiny. And as much as I want—and don't want—to ask about the mystery sex in New Orleans, I keep quiet.

"Not that I have any problems with fake breasts, but I have a thing for natural beauty." His eyes roam all over my face, down my body, and they definitely stop on my breasts for a leisurely look. I feel my nipples harden under his gaze as if to say, yes, look at us, aren't we delicious.

God, his eyes are practically devouring me. Okay, point proven. I need to change the subject stat before I do something crazy. Like maul him. "What's your favorite place we've visited thus far?"

"Hmmm," he tilts his head a little, the way he always does when he's giving something some genuine thought. "I'd have to say either Miami or Charleston."

"Really?" I'm a little surprised by this given the sex—yuck. "Not New Orleans?"

He shakes his head, something dark crowding his features. I take no relief in that. None at all. "Nope. Charleston is where I feel like we really got to know each other, became closer. And Miami..." he trails off.

I wait a few seconds, but when he doesn't finish his thought, I prompt him. "What about Miami?"

"I had fun dancing with you in the club and lounging by the pool," he says this so simply that I have to love that answer. I loved dancing with him too. Spending time with him is quickly becoming the thing I look forward to most. I don't even care where we are, just being with him is fun. "What about you?"

"I agree with you about Miami, but I really loved my day at the spa in New Orleans."

He looks over at me quickly with his crooked smile before turning his eyes back to the road. "I wish we had more time," he starts, gripping the wheel a little tighter. "I wish we could have gone north and done all of those places that we talked about seeing."

"Yeah," I draw out the word on a sigh, shifting so I'm on my side facing him, my legs still up on the dash. "But I'm really looking forward to the Grand Canyon and California, especially the redwood forest, though I'm bummed about missing Yosemite." He looks over at me, raising a questioning brow. "I'm a total national park slut."

He laughs out loud. "Really? And to think I could have taken advantage of that this whole time," he shakes his head like he's put out. He's not. "When did this begin?"

"When I was a kid with my dad. He was big into history, so he took me all around New England, and into Pennsylvania and New York to see landmarks and old battlegrounds. That sort of thing."

"That's pretty cool."

I nod my head against the seat. He looks over at me quickly, debating whether or not he wants to ask his next question. "How old were you when he died?"

"Sixteen. It was a fatal MI."

"MI?"

"Heart attack."

He nods. "That had to have been rough." His hand reaches over, covering mine, and that small gesture of comfort is incredible. How he knew to do that, that I needed it, I don't know.

"It was. We were close."

"What about you and your mom?" His hand continues to rest on top of mine, and I let it, though I feel like I shouldn't.

"She's tough. A bit emotionally detached. She loves me and I love her, but I wouldn't say we have any real bond."

"I get that. My mom and I are sort of the same way."

I hesitate, biting my lip because I've wanted to ask him about his dad since we set out on this trip, but I wasn't sure how he'd react.

Fuck it.

"Can I ask about your dad?"

He looks over at me quickly and then back to the road.

"He started drinking when Kyle was diagnosed with leukemia." Clearly, he knew what I was getting at without my needing to elaborate. "You saw my mother with a drink in her hand, and yeah, she has a problem, but she limits herself to no more than three a day, and she's functional. Crazy, but functional." He looks over at me with a wry grin, but there's sadness in his eyes too, and I know it must be hard to have not only one parent with a drinking problem but two. "But my dad never really learned his limit and refused to seek treatment for it. He *likes* drinking."

"I'm sorry." I don't really know what else to say. I can see it is hard for him. I can see it hurts him, so I move my hand out from under his and intertwine our fingers instead, squeezing him a little.

His gaze casts down at our laced hands and a small shudder rises up through him. That one small reaction to my touch means so much. Because I feel it too. This connection we have.

"He's more catatonic now than anything. He was never violent or mean. Just isolated, which is how I think he wanted to be."

"Have you ever tried talking to them about it?" I ask softly, not wanting to come off as judgmental or accusatory, because I'm absolutely not meaning to be.

"Yes. My dad said he had no interest in stopping, and my mother said she didn't have a problem. I can't help them if they're not willing to help themselves."

I nod my head agreeing with him. "True." My thumb runs across his hand. "Still, it must be hard." I squeeze again, and we fall into silence after that, but our hands never pull away.

We reach downtown Dallas and find a hotel that has a dope rooftop pool. When I initially thought out this trip, I did not intend to go first-class the entire way. I was thinking more middle of the road places, but that hasn't exactly happened.

I'm not *so* concerned about the money, and Ryan has insisted on paying for a lot of dinners, but still. At some point I'm going to need to check on how much I've actually spent and maybe pull Ryan back a little. I get the feeling he has a lot of money. He doesn't discuss it much, but he's hinted at it and spends it like he must.

I have plenty of money; I just don't like to spend it.

My father left me a large chunk when he died, and then when Eric died I inherited his trust fund as well as his life insurance. The thought of spending either of those makes me a little sick.

Whatever, for now I'm going to enjoy this and worry about the rest later.

11

ate

I WAKE UP EARLY, as usual, and head for the hotel gym. Ryan and I did find our barbeque, which was stellar, but decided after two full nights out in New Orleans, our livers needed a rest. We both went to bed like good little kids around eleven.

When I enter the gym, it is empty save for one other guy on a treadmill hauling ass.

We do the typical gym stranger nod to each other when I hop on a treadmill a few away from him. I pop in my earbuds, set my pace, and zone out the way I normally do.

Running is not new for me, but the way I run is.

Before Eric and Maggie died, I did it when I could and for much shorter distances. Now I run harder and longer and with a lot more regularity. Exercise seems to help. I don't know if it is the endorphins or the way my brain seems to shut off or what, but it's all good.

I'm about twenty minutes and almost three miles in when I feel like I'm being watched. Turning my head to the left, I catch the eye of the guy on the other treadmill who is smiling at me like he wants to say something. Great, I hate gym talkers. I pull out my earbud on the side facing him and raise my eyebrows expectantly.

"You've got great form," he calls out with an appreciative look, and I want to roll my eyes at that line.

"Thanks," I say instead and offer a tight smile.

"Are you in Dallas long?"

Really guy? I mean, I'm fucking running here and you want to make chitchat? Does this look like the time or the place to try and pick me up? No, it doesn't.

"Leaving today."

"That's too bad. I would love to show you around the city a little." Jesus, this guy. Suddenly I'm a little uncomfortable that we are the only two in here.

"I'm all set," I grin again and start to look away when the guy keeps going.

"What time are you leaving? I could give you a private tour this morning. Maybe take you out for breakfast." His tone does not suggest that he wants to take me out for breakfast, unless it is after he has screwed me. I swear the blonde hair makes men think I'm stupid and easy.

I hate stereotypes, especially that one, but men seem to be all over it.

My head snaps in his direction, and I'm about to go off on the guy when someone beats me to it.

"That won't be necessary." I turn the other way—nearly falling off my damn treadmill—and see Ryan walking toward us. "The only person who'll be giving my girl here *a private tour* or buying her breakfast, is me."

I smile so goddamn big. I just can't help it.

I would have happily laid into the guy and set down the law—something I have no problem doing, but it's nice that I don't have to. Men respond better to men in these types of situations for some stupid caveman-like reason.

"Isn't that up to the lady?"

Really dude? Take the damn hint.

"Then, I have to agree with my boyfriend here. He's the only one I'm interested in," I smile at the overly zealous guy, blow Ryan a kiss, pop my earbud back in and pick up the pace since it had slowed during this little interaction. The guy takes the not-too-subtle hint and leaves the gym.

I look over to Ryan, who has occupied the treadmill next to mine.

"Thank you," I say to him. "That guy just didn't know when to quit."

He shakes his head at me. "I can't leave you alone for two seconds without someone hitting on you, can I?"

I snort, rolling my eyes. "Don't be ridiculous. A guy like that would have hit on anything with a pulse and a vagina."

Ryan gives me a look that says I'm full of shit, but I let it go and so does he.

We start to run and begin to play the one-up game. Every time I increase my pace, so does he. Every time I add a little incline, he does too. And vice versa. After a few minutes of this bullshit, we're both practically sprinting uphill.

"Ryan, you're killing me," I pant out, barely able to keep this up. He is smiling smugly and I want to smack it off his way too-good-looking face. "To hell with this." I wheeze and begin to slow my pace and lower my incline. My thighs, calves, and ass are burning like crazy, not to mention my lungs.

He slows down too and after that little race, I'm done. I ran about three and a half miles and though I normally do a little over four, I cannot manage any more.

"Quitting on me already?"

I glare at him. "I was here twenty minutes before your lazy ass."

"Whatever you say, sweetheart," he winks and I roll my eyes at him.

"I'm going to shower. Come find me when you're ready."

"Yes, ma'am," he salutes me.

By the time I'm showered, changed, and packed up, I get a knock on my door. Ryan comes strolling in, freshly showered and smelling like his deodorant, shampoo, and his own unique scent. He's wearing a worn, dark-green tee that matches his eyes, black shorts, and Chucks. His hair looks like he ran his fingers through it after the shower and didn't bother doing anything else.

"What's our plan today, doll?" He flops down onto my bed, and for the briefest flicker of a second, I get the urge to flop *onto him*. What the hell? I push it back quickly, because that is not going to happen.

"I say we grab some food, maybe walk around a bit, and then hit the road to Amarillo, though I'm not in a huge rush to get there. I figure that is more of a sleeping stop."

"Agreed, now come here." He reaches out in a flash, snagging my hand and pulling me down onto the bed next to him. I squeal, squirming and laughing like crazy when he starts tickling me. "I thought you might be ticklish." He's lying. He knew I was ticklish. "I had to test my theory." He's smiling and laughing too.

"Ah. Ryan. Stop." I'm trying to push him off of me, but he is freaking relentless, and huge and strong, and I'm overpowered. "Please. Stop. I hate being tickled," I gasp through my laughter that has tears streaming down my face.

"No. You love it." He's enjoying this way too much. "Tell me you love it."

"Asshole."

He laughs harder.

Giving up on trying to pry his hands away from my ribs, I reach up and twist the hell out of his nipple. "Ouch. What the fuck?" He lets go of me in favor of his smarting nipple. "That hurt like hell." He's still smiling, so I know he's not really pissed at me.

I try sitting up, but he is half on top of me, so I can't really move. His body heat and weight feel incredible against me.

"Sorry." I'm not sorry at all. "I had to defend myself from your attack."

"Oh, sweetheart."

He places his hands on either side of my body, his face hovering over mine, and my heart rate begins to spike. His green eyes are sparkling, his face so close to mine—only inches separating us really.

"It's so on now." His eyes bounce down to my lips and my tongue juts out reflexively to moisten them. His pupils dilate instantly, and that one small reaction sets my blood on fire. He's a wall of muscle, so strong, all man. How easy would it be? Just a few inches really.

But I can't do that to him. He may skip the line, but I know he doesn't want this with me. He was just being playful, and I turned it into something else entirely. I have to stop this now.

"If you tickle me again, I'll go for your nuts," I rush out, so he doesn't start tickling me again. Or worse, I kiss him.

He freezes, evidently threatening his nuts is the key. "You wouldn't," he tilts his head, narrowing his eyes at me like I just crossed the line.

"I totally would, so don't try me, *sweetheart*," I push him back, and this time he climbs off of me without protest.

"Damn." He shakes his head as I stand up, adjusting my shirt and running my fingers through my messed up hair. "You are lucky I like you as much as I do. I don't let just anyone threaten my manhood."

I wink at him. "Lucky me then." I reach out for his hand, trying to yank him up, which is just impossible, but he stands anyway, helping me along. "Let's go feed me; I'm hungry."

We walk outside into the Texas sun and head in the direction the concierge told us to go. A block down, we spot a coffee shop and Ryan points to it, indicating that he wants to run in. The guy is as addicted to coffee as I am to Diet Coke. It's sad, really.

I turn toward the street and pull out my phone to check my email when I feel something tug on the bottom of the back of my t-shirt.

"Mommy, Mommy."

I spin around, and my eyes lock on Maggie.

My beautiful, towheaded angel is staring up at me.

Her hair is longer, almost to mid-back, but still has the spiral curls. Her eyes are the exact same color as Eric's. She's older, maybe closer to four.

I can't move.

I can't speak.

I'm staring at my little girl. She called me mommy, and I want to grab hold of her and never let go. But the rational part of my brain is cementing me firmly in place, because I know this is not her.

My Maggie is dead. And my whole body aches.

"Olivia," a woman calls out, and the little girl's head snaps to the right and then she runs off without another word, leaving me standing here without my daughter.

The pain is unreal.

One hand flies up to my pendant—the only piece of her I have left—and my other crosses over my stomach, trying to splint myself against the crushing agony that is taking over. I'm shaking, and just as my legs are about to give out on me, a large, strong body covers me, holding me up. I grab onto Ryan like my life depends on it, and I let out the sob that had been threatening.

He holds me close, my fists clenching the back of his shirt, balling up the material. "She called me mommy," I cry.

"I heard," he says softly as his hand gently caresses down my hair over and over again.

"She looked just like her, Ryan. Just. Like. Her."

"I'm so sorry, Katie." It's all he can say, but he continues to hold me in the middle of the street as I lose myself, again.

"Why Maggie? Why Eric, and why my baby?" I pull back to look up at him, his eyes so full of sorrow. "I'm so angry, Ryan. So fucking angry that my baby girl is gone and I don't know how to get past it. I don't know how to manage it or move on or even cope with it. Every time I think I can do this," I wave a hand around in the air. "Think I can start to find a way to live without her, I get sucked back into the vortex."

His eyes bore into mine and I see the helplessness in them. He wants to fix this, but he can't. There is no fix. Finally, after a moment, his eyes adjust on something behind me, and he grabs my hand and begins to pull.

"Come with me, Katie. I've got an idea."

I have no idea what it is, but right now, I'll try anything that makes this pain go away.

After Eric and Maggie died, I didn't take the easy road. I never drank or took pills, though both were offered to me by friends and doctors. But at this point, if Ryan pulls me into a bar and tries to get me shitfaced, I'll let him.

He drags me into a store with an obnoxiously loud bell over the door, but the second we step foot inside, I realize it is not a store. I'm immediately assaulted with the smell of sweat, cleaning products, and rubber. All around me men and women are hitting and kicking large and small punching bags while grunting and shouting. A few are even sparring in some sort of makeshift ring.

Ryan leaves me standing by the entrance as he walks up to the counter. He begins talking to the very muscular bald guy there. The guy's eyes flicker over to me, then back to Ryan, and before I can make sense of what is happening, Ryan pulls out his wallet and hands him a credit card. They both make their way over toward me because I haven't moved since Ryan released me.

"Katie, this is Carlos. He's going to get you set up."

I have no idea what he's talking about, but again, I don't care, so I just nod.

"Follow me, I have gloves for you."

Ryan takes my hand, clearly sensing that I need the help. Before I know it, my hands are forced into bright pink boxing gloves, and I'm standing in front of a hanging bag that looks huge and heavy.

"Now, would you like me to offer you instruction, or do you just want to have at it?"

I look up at Carlos who has very kind brown eyes, and I feel my chin quivering. "I don't know." Christ, I'm a hot mess.

His expression softens and he looks over to Ryan like he has all the answers. "Come on, Katie," Ryan cajoles. "Punch the ever-loving shit out of the bag. Give it all your anger."

I look at him—really look at him, and I finally understand what he's trying to do. He's giving me an outlet. A way to take out all of the burning aggression that is eating a hole through me.

Ryan nods toward the bag. "You've got this."

Carlos moves behind the bag to hold it for me, and I take a step forward, rolling my neck and straightening my back. Instead of pushing everything I feel down or away, I allow it to bubble up to the surface, and a loud sob escapes my lips.

Normally, I'd be embarrassed for doing the ugly cry in front of this stranger, Ryan, and anyone else who might be watching—but I'm not. I reach back with everything I've got and I punch the bag dead center. It barely moves. The thing is just as heavy as I thought it was.

But that one punch felt so fucking good.

I go at it again and again, switching my fists. It's uncoordinated and sloppy. I'm yelling and grunting and crying my eyes out.

But I'm doing it.

I'm pushing all the overwhelming anger and heartbreak out of me and into this bag, over and over again. I even try a couple of kicks, but those don't seem to make me feel as good as punching does.

I have no idea how long I go, but eventually, I collapse to the mat in an exhausted, sweaty heap. Ryan sits down next to me, his legs bent and his forearms resting on his knees as he waits me out. I'm breathing hard and heavy, but I feel lighter. Freer. My anger is nowhere to be found. I'm sure it will come back, I don't for a second think that this was the cure, but it helped.

It helped, and I think I need Ryan.

He just saved me.

I throw my arms around his neck, practically tackling him down to the rubber mat. "Thank you," I breathe into him. "Oh my god, thank you so much."

He holds me—sweaty, smelly, disgusting mess and all.

"If you ever want to train, let me know," Carlos says from above us.

"Thank you, Carlos. That was fantastic."

He smiles warmly down at me and then walks off.

"Come on, Katie. Let's go get you cleaned up and fed."

I pull back and kiss his cheek before prying myself off the floor.

"You're brilliant, Ryan," I beam at him. "That was exactly what I needed. How will I ever get by without you?"

He doesn't say anything back—it was rhetorical after all, well for the most part— he just helps me remove my gloves. Ryan may think my words were said in an off-the-cuff way, but they weren't.

I meant them wholeheartedly. I'm starting to get to the point where I'm no longer excited for the next location. Because each place we go brings us closer and closer to Seattle. And I'm suddenly very interested in prolonging my time with Ryan.

12

_____

K *ate*

AMARILLO AND ALBUQUERQUE end up being uneventful. They're a series of standard hotels and amazing Tex-Mex food and pools. No complaints, but the part of the trip that I'm really getting excited about is ahead.

The drive through Arizona is freaking hot, since most of it is desert. Nothing but flat dry earth and endless blue sky as far as the eye can see. I make us stop along the way and take a million pictures with my phone.

I'm sure Ryan thinks I'm nuts, but I don't care.

I've noticed he takes plenty of pictures himself.

Ever since my punching match with the bag in Dallas, Ryan has been...a little distant. I wouldn't say he thinks less of me or anything, but he has definitely changed, and I don't know why. I try to talk to him, ask him questions, and behave like I always have, but his answers are short and direct and he doesn't tease me or touch me the way I have grown accustomed to.

He barely even looks at me.

After the longest drive ever, through construction and traffic and desert, we pull into the hotel late at night. We're both exhausted and somehow dirty, and Ryan seems to be in a mood, so I offer to go and check us in.

"Good evening and welcome," a short man with black hair and dark skin says with a thick Spanish accent. "Do you have a reservation?"

"No, we were hoping you have two rooms available."

He looks at me like I'm insane. "I'm sorry, we only have one room left and it is a king room."

Crap. Ryan will not like that. In truth, I don't know how I feel about it either.

"Okay, give me a sec," I start to walk away and then pause. "Can you please hold the room for a minute while I talk to my friend?"

"Sure."

I doubt anyone is going to claim it since it is so late, but still.

"Hey, Ryan?" I call out and then find him pacing, staring at his phone. He looks up and does not look pleased to see me. "Sorry to interrupt," I nod toward his phone. No response, so I continue. "Um. They only have one room left and it's a king room."

He glares at me like it is my fault that we are in a pattern of not making reservations ahead of time. "Are you fucking kidding me?"

Okay, this is not the reaction I was hoping for. I shake my head. "No. Sorry." I bite my lip, suddenly feeling like shit, because I'm the one who really wanted to come to the Grand Canyon. "Do you want to drive around and look for another place?"

"No," he snaps, running a frustrated hand through his wild hair. "I'm fucking tired and sick of driving."

"So I'll just tell the guy we'll take it?" I hedge, shifting my weight.

"Whatever, Katie."

I guess I'll take that as a yes. Making my way back up to the counter, I give the guy my credit card and he gives me two room keys.

"Ryan?" Damn, why do I suddenly feel so nervous to talk to him? I hate this feeling. "I have our room." My voice is meek.

"Great. Looking forward to it."

We get up to the room, which is actually pretty nice, and he slams his suitcase down. We have clean clothes; we did our laundry in a laundromat at our last stop.

"Why don't you go shower first, *princess,* and I'll just make up my pallet on the floor." His sarcasm and disdain are killing me. I've officially had enough.

I slash my arm through the air in front of us. "What the hell is your problem?" I yell, and he looks stunned for a flash before his eyes narrow in anger. Well, fuck that. "I get it. You're tired. I'm tired. We've been on the road for two weeks together, and you're sick of me, but ease the fuck up."

"Ease the fuck up?" he yells back. "Katie, this is bullshit."

"What's bullshit?" We're both working up a good head of steam here. He paces around in a small circle in front of me.

"I've been stuck in a tiny ass car with you all day and now I have to sleep on the goddamn floor." He points down at the carpet next to the bed.

"I never said you have to sleep on the floor." I point at him. "*You* did. It's a king bed, Ryan, I'm sure we can both fit."

"Oh," he throws his hands up. "So now it's okay for me to sleep next to you?"

He's not even making sense. "What the hell?" I yell and push his chest with my palms. "Why have you been so cold to me since Dallas? Was it because I had my freak-out? You're the one who brought me to the boxing place."

He stops pacing instantly and looks at me. "No. It's not about that." He's serious, and I'm glad, because the thought of him becoming distant over that stung.

"Then what is it? We were having such a good time together." All of the fight is out of me and now I just feel small. "What did I do? You've been like a different person toward me."

He takes a harsh step forward, cutting the distance between us by half. "What do you think this is between us?" His tone is clipped, strident. His finger is flying back and forth, gesturing between us.

I'm stunned. And hurt. And I don't know what, but it's not good.

"I thought you were my friend," I say in a weak voice, wishing I had it in me to be stronger.

"*That's* what you think this is? *Friendship*?" Why does he sound so incredulous? What the hell else would it be?

I have no idea what's going on right now.

I'm totally at a loss, so I just stare up at him blinking.

When I don't respond, he runs his hand through his hair, mutters something under his breath that I cannot make out, and then walks past me.

"I'm going to shower first." The door to the bathroom slams behind him, startling me. Maybe I've pushed him too far on this trip, and he is finally getting sick of being stuck with me. He probably just thinks of me as some bat-shit crazy charity case that he has to deal with.

I walk over to the bathroom and once I hear the sound of the shower curtain opening and closing, I knock softly on the door.

"Ryan?" I call out, but my voice is soft, and I doubt he can hear me over the water of the shower so I open the door and try again. "Ryan?"

He lets out a harsh breath. "What, Katie? I'm in the shower."

"I know, and I'm not going to look, but I want to ask you something." I close the lid of the toilet seat and sit down.

"And it couldn't wait until I was done?"

God, there is just no give with him tonight. As much as I don't want to ask this next question, I have to. And no, I couldn't wait.

"Ryan? Do you want to forget the rest of the trip and have me take you directly up to Seattle? Or if you'd rather I not come along, you can always rent a car and go yourself." I'm trying to keep my voice even, desperate to hide the ache that these words cause inside of me. "I'll understand either way. I realize it has been a long time on the road with me and that I can be a lot. Whatever you want to do, I'm okay with it."

I'm not, but I have to give him the out just the same.

He's silent, the only sound in the small steamy space is the shower running. Suddenly I hear what sounds like his fist smacking against the wet tile wall and he curses under his breath.

"I'll uh... I'll let you finish your shower." I stand up and walk toward the bathroom door. "Just think about what I said and let me know what you decide you'd like to do."

I leave him in there to finish and go directly to my suitcase. Busy. I need to keep busy or I'll cry, and I'm so sick of crying.

I dig through my nice clean clothes and find a tank top, boy shorts, panties, and my toiletry bag. The shower shuts off, and a minute later, Ryan walks out with a towel wrapped around his waist.

I've seen Ryan without a shirt on several occasions. At the beach and the pool, but I never really allowed myself to look too closely. But as he stalks toward his suitcase, I take in every muscle and the way they stretch and pull with his movements.

He is unbelievable looking. So strong and sculpted.

Yet Ryan is so unassuming with the beard and glasses.

I sort of like that about him.

Averting my eyes, because what I'm doing just feels wrong, I grab my stuff and walk past him into the bathroom.

He lets me. Doesn't even try to stop me.

I hate that I feel like I lost the only real friend in my life right now. Turning on the shower, I strip down and step in, letting the warm water cascade over me.

I'm getting this feeling again. It is similar to the one I had after Maggie and Eric died. Emptiness. A feeling of void. Like I have no purpose or home. Like I'm lost.

And right now, that is exactly how I feel.

Lost.

I have no home. No job. No real friends.

"How did I get here?" I whisper aloud.

I really don't know. Leaving Boston seemed like the only solution to an unsolvable problem. Before, Eric and Maggie grounded me. Completed me and gave me a sense of home. When they died, that feeling died with them, and that emptiness only grew and grew until I had a great big chasm inside of me. So I foolishly thought that if I left, that feeling wouldn't follow me. That I'd be able to find something real to hold onto.

And maybe that is what I have done to Ryan.

Maybe I latched onto him, and everything I thought was mutual, was really just one-sided. How totally and completely unfair of me. He's just trying to get across the country because he doesn't fly, and has been indulging my whims because he doesn't want to be rude to the sad, lonely girl.

No wonder he's snapping at me.

The poor guy has finally reached his limit, and I'm selfishly making it all about me and my pathetic attempt at finding a life again.

I finish washing up, turn off the shower and dry off. Changing into my clothes, I brush my teeth and then my hair before braiding it. I usually don't shower at night because I hate sleeping with wet hair, but I don't have the energy to dry it, so a braid will have to suffice.

I walk out of the bathroom and the room is bathed in darkness. It takes me a minute or two for my eyes to adjust, but once they do, I see Ryan lying on his side facing the window pressed all the way to the edge of the large bed.

Christ, the guy can hardly stand the idea of sleeping in the same bed as me.

I get in on the other side and quietly try to adjust my position without disturbing him.

"Katie?" he asks softly.

"Yes."

"I'm sorry for being so distant the last few days. It is nothing you've done, and I apologize if I have made you feel otherwise." He doesn't move to look at me. Just talks to me with his back facing me.

"Do you want to go straight up to Seattle?"

"No." His tone is firm. "I don't. I'd like to spend these last two weeks with you, and I promise that I'll be more myself going forward."

"Do you want to talk about it?" I offer quietly, turning to face him though he is still not looking at me.

"No. I don't. It won't help, but thank you for offering."

"If you change your mind, I'm always here for you."

He sighs out, and it sounds sad, maybe a little resigned. "I know you are. You're an amazing friend, Katie. Good night."

"Good night, Ryan."

Sleep comes quickly for me despite the unrest inside of me.

My first thought when I wake up is that the air conditioner must be broken, which sucks because we're in the desert. My second thought is that Ryan is not going to be happy when he wakes up and finds me wrapped around him like a vine. I have no idea how I managed to crawl my body across this bed and latch onto him like this, but I did.

And the irony of it all? I've never been a nighttime snuggler.

Eric and I always stuck to our own respective sides of the bed and woke up the same way.

So just what the absolute fuck am I doing right now?

Despite how nice it feels to be against his warm skin, I need to move before he wakes up to find me like this. Ever so slowly, I try and slide my leg from between his thighs and my arm from underneath his, but as I do, he begins to stir. *Shit.*

"Mmm," he hums, rolling into me and burying his nose in my hair, further pinning me against him. He's still asleep, but now I have no idea how I am going to move because he is holding me like a vise. His arms are wrapped around me, plastering me against his bare chest, and my leg is tucked tightly between his.

I try pulling back again anyway.

"Katie," he whispers, rocking into me. Holy hell, he's practically hard. I know it's just morning wood, but damn.

I move back again, and this time his eyes flash open to find my face only inches from his. He startles, eyes wide, blinking rapidly for a moment before a soft smile lights up his sleepy face.

"Did I do this or did you?" he whispers, and I'm a bit relieved that he's not pissed about it.

"I did, I think." I bite my lip nervously. "Sorry."

He chuckles softly. "Are you always this clingy in bed?"

I laugh lightly and shake my head against his pillow. "No. Normally I'm not a cuddler."

He hasn't let me go. Why hasn't he let me go? Why do I not want him to?

"I don't think I've ever woken up with someone this way."

"Neither have I," I smile, and then he smiles, and then we're both smiling at each other like this is so unbelievable to both of us, and yet, we still don't pull away.

His eyes are looking into mine and mine are looking into his, and suddenly, I'm full of flutters and nervous anticipation.

His eyes are so beautiful. Such an incredible shade of green. His nose isn't too big or too small, and has the perfect amount of character like it was broken once upon a time and he never got it fixed. His lips are surrounded by the dark bristles of his beard, but they're full and look soft.

I scroll up his face, examining feature by feature until I reach his eyes.

They look different.

The green is eclipsed by dark, dilated pupils that bounce back and forth between my lips and my eyes. There is heat in them. There is a question in them as well, and I know I should draw back. I know I should, but I absolutely cannot make myself do it.

"Katie?" he asks softly. It's a question and a promise.

His head moves infinitesimally toward mine, and like the other half of a magnet, mine inches toward his. That's all the consent he needs before he closes the small distance and presses his lips to mine. He holds this position for a moment like he is giving me an out if I want to stop this.

I don't.

I really freaking don't, so I kiss him back.

13

K *ate*

A HUM ESCAPES Ryan's throat, and it is quite possibly the best sound I have ever heard. His lips press harder into mine, moving against me in a way that I feel all the way down to my toes. My hands glide up his muscular arms, savoring the feel of them as I continue up into his hair. This sets something off in him because all of a sudden our slow languid pace becomes passionate and eager for more.

He opens my mouth with his, and when our tongues meet, he groans into me.

God, I could live off of that sound.

One of his hands is on my lower back, pressing me further into him, his other beneath me, sliding down my braid until he reaches the elastic. He pulls it from my hair and then unfolds my braid little by little, running his fingers through the strands.

It is so freaking hot I can hardly stand it.

Ryan's head moves, adjusting the angle of our kiss, deepening it.

I can't seem to get enough. I'm starving, and he is the only thing that can feed this hunger. He rocks into me and a moan slips out between my lips, which makes him groan as if he enjoys my sounds just as much as I enjoy his.

"Katie," he breathes against my lips between kisses. "Oh god, Katie, I've wanted this for so long."

I can't respond, I just moan into his mouth again as my fingers rake up the planes of his muscular chest. The bristles of his beard brush against my cheek and neck as his mouth explores my sensitive skin.

I can't get enough.

I want more, more, more.

His kisses are the best sort of drug and I'm high on them.

Suddenly, his hand cups my breast under my tank top, making my head roll back and an embarrassingly loud moan fly out of my lips.

"Fuck," he hisses. "That was the sexiest thing I've ever seen."

That's my cue though, the wake up I needed, because my breasts are like the point of no return. I push off of him, creating some space between us. Ryan freezes, his hand slipping out of my shirt.

"Did I hurt you?" His voice sounds panicked.

"No," I pant out, shaking my head back and forth. "But we need to stop."

He leans up on his elbow, furrowing his brow, looking at me with confusion and maybe a little alarm. "Why? What did I do?"

I shake my head again, reaching out and running my fingers along his cheek. He leans into my touch, but never takes his eyes off of me.

"First of all, my boobs are really freaking sensitive and I have trouble stopping once they come into the game."

His eyes turn to molten fire, flying down to look at my chest through my thin tank top.

"Jesus, Katie, you can't tell me things like that and then ask me to stop," he groans, dropping his head into the crook of his arm.

"I'm sorry," I giggle out and then stop laughing when he throws me a look that says he is not amused. "But we do need to stop."

He sits up now, bringing me with him. "Why? Did I do something wrong?"

"No. You're incredible, but that's why I need to stop this before we keep going." He scrunches his eyebrows, totally confused. Probably because I'm not making a whole lot of sense. I lower my head slightly, suddenly unable to meet his eyes. "I'm not ready for sex, Ryan."

He reaches up, lifting my chin so that my attention is on him. "Yet or ever?"

I shrug. "Yet, but I don't know when I will be."

"But you're okay with me kissing you?"

He seems to be working this through, and I sort of appreciate that he didn't jump out of bed or get angry with me. But then I realize that Ryan isn't like that. He looks at an entire situation before he reacts, and right now, I absolutely love that about him.

He's so patient and...fuck, he's just perfect.

"Well, I rather like the kissing," I admit, and he grins devilishly. "But I'm not ready for more yet, and I'm really not ready for a relationship or anything like it."

"Huh." He sits back, the blanket over his waist leaving his spectacular chest exposed. Not helping, Ryan. "So, you're good with me kissing you whenever I want?" He throws me an eyebrow like he's daring me to argue with what feels like the formation of a new plan. "But, I can't touch your sensitive, absolutely gorgeous tits." I don't comment on that. "And you're not ready for sex...*yet*." I get another eyebrow, and I bite my lip to hide my smile. "Or a relationship. Did I get the gist of what you're trying to tell me?"

I nod my head, still biting my lip, suddenly feeling a little exposed and nervous.

I have no idea what I'm proposing between us, but it changes everything. How will that impact the next two weeks? I don't want a relationship, but if he's talking about kissing me whenever he wants, what the hell are we then?

Friends who kiss?

Yeah, that one always works out well.

But I don't want a relationship. I don't. I still feel married and taken, and suddenly, I feel like I'm cheating on Eric.

"Katie, stop. I see your wheels spinning and they don't need to." My eyes widen at him because I'm shocked he can read me so well. "All right, I'm going to be honest with you, since you're being so honest with me."

"Okay."

He shifts his position, reaching out for my hips and pulling me closer to his side. His fingers run through my messy wavy locks and he smiles deeply.

"I like you. A lot. I think you're incredible, and I really like kissing you. Do I want more than kissing with you? Of course, I do. Badly, in fact, but I would never do something with you that you're not ready for. So if all you're offering me right now is kissing with the eventual possibility of more, then I'm good with that," he smiles, leaning down to brush his lips against mine as if to prove his point before pulling back. "I'm great with it actually."

"And you're fine with not being in a relationship or anything like that?" I realize he's a guy and that is probably not an issue for him, but I need to make sure.

He looks pensive for a moment and then nods. "Yeah. I'm okay with that. I just want to enjoy the last two weeks of this journey with you and all that it entails."

"Wow."

I don't really know what else to say.

Not many men would willingly enter into a PG non-relationship with a woman without at least the promise of sex. Maybe he thinks that's eventually where this is headed, and it could be, but I just don't know.

I honestly don't, so I won't tell him yes or no either way.

"Now. I'd like to kiss the hell out of you for a bit longer until I can't take it anymore, and then I'd like to go for a hike through the Grand Canyon before we head to Vegas."

"I'm liking all of those things," I smile at his playful expression. He seems so much lighter today than he has the past few days.

"Good. Now get your sexy ass over here." He picks me up, settling me on his thighs, before lying back and bringing me up so that I'm straddling his stomach. "You're so small, Katie. In this situation, it's a good thing. I think if you were pressed against me a little lower, this would never work."

I laugh, leaning down to kiss him. "Agreed."

We kiss and touch safe areas, looking and smiling at each other a lot, until Ryan suddenly tosses me off him and onto the bed and announces that he needs to go take a shower immediately.

I get it. Actually, I see it as he walks by me.

"Don't look at me like that, Katie. You're killing me, and I'm trying so hard to be good," he says with a smile as he stands at the foot of the bed.

I'm biting my lip, trying to hide my smile. "Yes, you certainly are trying *hard* to be good."

He groans, dropping his head back and stalks heavily towards the bathroom. "I'm going to get you back for that."

"Promise?" I call out, and he groans again as he slams the door behind him, making me laugh.

The sound of the water running through the pipes fills the room as he starts the shower, and I get up and walk toward the window. It is a beautiful day. Bright and sunny.

After he comes out of the shower, wrapped in another freaking towel, I go into the bathroom and get changed, but I don't shower. No point since we're planning on hiking.

"Ready?" he asks when I walk out in running shorts, a sports bra, and tank top.

"Ready."

He smiles, walks to me, and kisses me like crazy until we're both breathless. "Now we're ready."

"Maybe all this kissing is a bad idea," I jest.

He takes my hand and leads me out of the room toward the lobby. "I'm going to pretend you didn't say that. Kissing is a perfect idea.

Definitely one of the better ones I've had," he winks down at me, and I can only shake my head at him.

He is too freaking cute when he's playful like this.

The Grand Canyon is everything I always thought it would be and more. Incredible and picturesque and phenomenal. Jagged cliffs, red earth, and the river cutting through the canyon.

We hike one of the many trails—which is actually pretty challenging—for a couple of hours.

By the time we are finished, we're both covered in sweat and sunscreen and dirt, but it was worth it. We both took a million pictures along the way, but at the top, with the canyon vast and glorious behind us, we take a selfie together.

Then Ryan kisses me hard, and takes more of us like that.

When he pulls away, he is smiling so big, it's infectious, and I'm smiling too, and I feel...happy.

I feel fucking happy, and then that turns to guilt, and the vicious cycle begins all over again. I do my best to push it down and just be in the moment with Ryan. Eventually, that wins out.

We load our stuff into the car for the short trip over to Vegas. Neither one of us has bought a whole lot along the way, so it's still just our suitcases and my boxes that I have left untouched. Once we hit the highway, Ryan is introspective again.

"Everything good?" I ask, turning in my seat to face him since he's driving.

"Yes, I was just thinking."

"About?" I prompt.

"You and me." This makes me a little nervous. "I'm thinking that we should share a room from now on. No more two rooms." He looks over at me quickly to try and gauge my reaction before turning back to the road.

"I don't know, Ryan. I mean, us sharing a room for the next two weeks is sort of relationship-y."

"You know that's not a word, right?"

I roll my eyes. "Yes, Professor, I'm fully aware. But it is, don't you think?"

"Not really, no. I think it's cost-effective and smart." He's giving me his crooked grin again, and it's hard to say no to him when he does that.

"One bed or two?"

"One. I liked waking up with you wrapped around me this morning."

"And this still stays within the realm of no sex and no relationship?" I ask dubiously. That just doesn't seem right.

"Sure," he shrugs like it's not the big deal I'm making it out to be.

"Okay, but then how will we handle splitting the room? You do one place I do the next?"

"Um no. That won't work for me." He looks over at me again. He's having way too much fun with this. "I'm going to pay for the hotels from here on out."

"No," I'm shaking my head emphatically. "Absolutely not."

He sighs. "Listen, Katie," he reaches out for my hand, intertwining our fingers. "I have more money than I could spend in two lifetimes, and this is something I want to do."

"I don't care if you have the money for it, Ryan. That just doesn't seem right or fair."

"Sweetheart," he's trying to hide his smile and failing. "I'll let you pay for *some* meals, if that makes you feel better."

"It really doesn't," I grumble.

"Look, I've never really been a first-class all the way guy, but that's sort of how I want to finish up this trip."

"I hope that's not for my sake, because I really don't need that."

"It's not." He squeezes my hand. "When the hell else in our lives will we go on a trip like this? Have this kind of time? Never. Let's enjoy it."

I narrow my eyes at him, still not sure how I feel about him paying for all the hotels. And then there is the whole sleeping together every night thing. Yeah, I'm going to have to think on that one a little more. But for now, I say, "All right, Ryan." He smiles brightly, so I hurry my words. "As long as you let me pay for meals and fun."

"*Some* meals and *some* fun."

"There really is just no winning with you, is there?"

He raises our joined hands up to his lips, kissing my fingers. "Don't kill my buzz, Katie. Try and enjoy the moment."

"Are you ever going to tell me more about your work?"

He glances over at me with a smirk. "My work? Sort of a random topic change, don't you think?"

"No. You talked about your money, which I assume is from your work."

He sighs, running a hand through his hair. "I don't like to talk about either."

"I'm not asking about your money, Ryan. Frankly, I could care less about what you have and what you don't. But I am curious about what you do for a living."

"I do a lot of things with computers."

"Vague and completely unhelpful," I smack his shoulder with my free hand, making him laugh.

"I create apps, do cybersecurity as well as other things. That's all I'm giving you."

"And it's not illegal?" I confirm, because last time he said it wasn't, but the way he doesn't talk about it makes it seem like it is.

"No."

"Do you want me to stop asking you about it?"

"Yes, but it's not that I don't want to share with you, because I do. It's just that I keep my work very separate."

"I can live with that." The Vegas skyline is now visible in the distance. "You ready to sin, Mr. Grant?"

"Oh, Katie, I've been ready to sin since I first laid eyes on you." I'm in so over my head with this man.

14

R *yan*

As the lights of the Vegas Strip get closer and closer, the more I fear Katie is going to be pissed at me. She is not impressed by money. I get it. I respect the hell out of it, actually, but I still want to treat her like a fucking princess.

So I did something I've never done before.

I enlisted my PA, Claire, to make dozens of reservations, and not just here in Vegas, but for the remainder of our trip.

Claire is really good at shit like that, and she got a sick thrill out of me asking her to do it. I'm still holding Katie's hand as we drive down Las Vegas Boulevard toward the Four Seasons. She's letting me, and anything she lets me do, I'm going to take advantage of.

Like kissing. I plan on kissing her constantly.

I have no idea how long I'll be able to keep up the middle-school, only-kissing thing, but I'm willing to give it my all and find out. Something tells me she won't last long with it either.

As for the no relationship crap?

Well, I'm hoping that also changes when this trip is all said and done.

I've got two more weeks to make her realize that she cannot live without me.

Two weeks before our forced time is up and she has a choice to make. Stay or go. I'm hoping for stay. I don't think I could ever get enough of her, and I've only kissed her. I haven't even begun to explore her, and doing that the way I would like could certainly take an entire lifetime at least.

But it is way more than the possibility of sex with Katie.

It's the thought of Katie herself.

I have to admit, when Katie first told me that she and Eric had been together since they were twelve, I was shocked in a total guy way. I mean, the idea of only one woman your entire life?

Fuck, that is unimaginable.

But after just kissing Katie, I get it. Eric realized at a very young age that there was no chance in hell of him finding something better than her, because it simply does not exist. I get it now. I absolutely do.

But she is still stuck on him.

I see it in her eyes, and I see it in the way she holds onto that pendant like it is her reason for living. I have to wonder if it's guilt that is driving it.

I know she loved him. I'm sure she still does and that a part of her always will, but it's more than that that is keeping her from living again. More than just losing Maggie too. It's like she won't allow herself to be happy because they're dead and she's not.

I'm no expert on survivor's guilt, but I'd say she's got it in spades.

She is trying, though. I'll give her that.

Maybe she just needs more time to work through all of her shit. The boxing certainly helped, and it's something I plan to do with her again.

Katie is oddly quiet as we drive, her eyes glued to the giant hotels and the masses wandering the excessively bright streets. The sun is shining high in the cloudless sky, adding to the Vegas desert mystique.

"What have you done, Ryan Grant?" she whispers, more to herself than to me as we pull into the Four Seasons.

Yeah, she's gonna be mad, especially when she sees our room. Too late now. The valet opens our door, and the second we're out of the car, our bags are being removed by the bellhop.

"Mr. Grant. Welcome to Four Seasons Hotel, Las Vegas. My name is Sarah and I am your personal concierge during your stay." A woman in a sharp black suit comes over to me and shakes my hand firmly. "Your suite is ready for you, sir, and I've made the arrangements you've requested."

"Thank you." I take Katie's hand and pull her along into the building to the private elevator for the upper floors. I can feel her staring at me, but she's remained silent while Sarah leads the way.

Sarah swipes the key for our room and then hands it to me. "The penthouse, sir," she says, opening the door for us to walk in first.

It's perfect.

There are sweeping views of the Strip, and the mountains in the distance from every window. There is a large living room, dining room, multiple bathrooms, and a huge bedroom with a walk-in closet. A bottle of champagne is chilling on ice—which I did not order, but certainly won't complain about—as well as everything I purchased for Katie. I palm Sarah some money and she graciously takes the hint and leaves us alone.

And then I wait for it.

Katie is walking slowly through the space, touching everything she comes across. The fabrics and wood of the furnishings, the drapes, even the glass of the windows that showcase the Strip.

But she's eerily silent, and I'm terrified of the explosion to come.

Finally, she walks over to the bedroom, and like a good little boy who is hoping for more kisses, I follow her in. Her bright blue eyes take in the entire room, and then she walks into the closet.

There is a black garment bag hanging inside along with a pair of shoes and a purse.

She doesn't touch them, just stares, blinking a lot, and I know I'm in trouble now.

"I don't know whether to yell at you or kiss you."

"If I get a choice, I opt for kissing," I say, lingering in the door of the closet, my hands up on the wood frame above my head.

"Why did you do all this?" She turns to face me, her hand waving to the stuff I bought and then over to the large suite.

"Because I wanted to," I say simply. I really don't have much more of an explanation that I am willing to give her. "I want to take you out for dinner tonight, and then after that, I want to go dancing with you again. The dress and the shoes are for that. If you don't like them, we can go to any of the shops and pick something else out."

"It's fucking Valentino, Ryan!" Now she's yelling. "You bought me a black sequin mini dress, and it is Valentino. The shoes are Louboutin. The purse is Prada." I won't even mention the earrings I got her. I think it might be too much at this moment. "I'm sure I'll fucking like them, Ryan. What the hell on earth were you thinking? All of this has to cost ten thousand dollars, at least." Thirteen, but I won't go there either. "Then there's the massive penthouse at the motherfucking Four Seasons we are staying in for the next two nights and whatever other '*arrangements*' you have made," she puts air quotes around the word the concierge used.

"Do you want to leave?"

I'm smiling. I shouldn't be smiling, but I can't help it.

She is too damn adorable when she's angry, and since I've never really seen her like this, I'm enjoying the show far too much for my own safety.

She sighs, taking a deep breath and then walks over to me slowly, her hands reaching up to touch my chest. Eyes boring into mine. "I would have been happy in a regular room in a regular hotel. I would have been happy sleeping with you in my car."

"I know," I smile even bigger because she means it. "Please don't be angry with me. I really want this to be special. Memorable."

She shakes her head like I don't get it. "Everything with you is memorable."

Damn. She always says the most perfect things. I lean down and kiss her, because I absolutely have to.

"Are you okay with this? I can return the dress and shoes and bag."

"I'm okay with this." Her fingers glide through my beard and I've never felt a sensation like it before. "Have you always had a beard?" she asks, and I love how she just changed the topic like that.

"No. I grew it after Francesca because she hated beards," I grin. "Do you not like it?"

"I do like it. I just can't figure out what your face would look like without it."

I laugh, leaning down to kiss her again. "Do you want me to shave it so you can see?"

She bites her lip and tilts her head, like she is giving this some thought. "No," she shakes her head. "Not now. Maybe someday." I like the way she says that, but don't comment. "So what's the plan for today, since you seem to be full of them suddenly?"

"We could open the champagne that's chilling, and drink it in bed while we kiss a lot." She's smiling her sweet smile at me.

"You don't want to go get lunch on the Strip and walk around?"

"If I get a choice, I'm always going to go for the kissing, Katie. You should have figured that out by now."

"You are sort of a glutton for punishment, aren't you?"

"A masochist to the core," I grin. "But you do know that there are other things we can do that aren't *technically* considered sex."

She smiles seductively with widened eyes. "Oh, and what would those be?"

Damn, she's playing with me now. "I'm just saying that there are other places I can kiss if we're sticking to this kissing-only rule."

"I see. Like my neck?"

"That's definitely one place, but not the one I was thinking of."

"Hmm." She places both hands on my shoulders, pulling me down to her so that she can bring her mouth to my ear. "As much as I think I would enjoy you kissing *other places*," her tongue and teeth graze along the shell of my ear, making me shudder. "For now, I think we should stay above the clavicle."

"You really are trying to kill me," I say with certainty. All I can think about right now is ripping her clothes off and doing a hundred dirty things to her.

"Maybe," she smiles sweetly, "but not until we feed me. After that, I'm all for killing you for a while."

I have never seen such a small woman eat as much as she does. She's constantly packing in the food, and I think it is amazingly sexy. Francesca never ate anything more than a sprig of lettuce once a day. It was boring as hell to go out to eat with her, and the other women before and after her? Well, let's just say we skipped over meal time in favor of other ventures.

Katie is eating the hell out of a burger right now, and enjoying every bite. We did end up going out—much to my dismay—and after this, she wants to go walk around the Strip.

I can't really say no to her.

Tomorrow I figure we'll hit up the pool or the spa, but today we can go exploring.

"I can't get over how they hand out flyers for hookers." She really can't. That's probably the third time she has said that. "We should totally get you one."

I practically choke on my fry. "Um. I'm not really a prostitute kind of guy."

"No. I guess if you wanted to get laid, you could just go out and meet someone." Shit. I wonder if she knows about New Orleans. She wipes her mouth with her napkin and then looks up at me through her dark lashes. "I would understand, you know."

"Understand what, sweetheart?" She can't be suggesting what I think she is.

"If you wanted to go out and meet someone who could give you what you want."

I reach over and take her hand. "I don't want another woman, Katie," I tell her hoping to convey my sincerity. "I want *you*. Even if it *is* just the killer kisses."

She smiles softly, nodding her head, seemingly liking my answer.
"I'm kind of crushing on you, Ryan Grant. Maybe even a lot."

I lean forward and kiss her sweet lips, wondering how in the hell
I'm ever going to be able to let her go when these two weeks are up.

We end up spending hours walking up and down the Strip seeing
the crazy bullshit that accompanies it. Rollercoasters, giant candy
stores, novelty and touristy shops.

Everything is in freaking neon.

By the time we get back to our room, it's almost five, and dinner is
—as usual—at eight.

"Nap?" I ask, since she looks exhausted.

"Lead the way."

I do, and when we reach our bed, I turn to her. "Do you trust me?"

She nods, and I know she means it, but at the same time, she
looks a little apprehensive. I reach down and lift her t-shirt over her
head, revealing her fucking amazing tits encased in a white lace bra.

Holy mother of hell.

"Ryan—"

I shake my head. "I'm not going to take advantage. I just want to
sleep next to you like this." It's true. She can see that in my eyes. So I
reach down and undo her shorts, slipping them down her legs before
an involuntary groan forces its way out of my throat.

"Ryan—"

She tries again, but I stop her. "I promise to be good; it's just the
matching white lace bra and panties."

She smiles in a way that tells me she knows *exactly* what she is
doing to me.

I take off my own shirt and shorts, not caring if she sees the tent
in my boxer briefs.

I *want* her to see it. I *want* her to know the effect she has on me.
She sinks her teeth into her full bottom lip when she notices, and
then her eyes scroll up my chest to my eyes.

"Nap time?" she whispers, and I nod, taking her hand and leading
her to the bed. When I pull her down next to me and wrap my arms

around her warm soft body, she giggles. "Do you know that I have never slept in as many clothes as I do when I'm next to you?"

"What do you mean?"

She rolls over so that we are face to face on the pillow. "Normally, I only sleep in my panties."

My eyes snap shut, and I lower my forehead to hers. "Are you trying to torture me?"

"Maybe a little," she admits, and a laugh huffs out of me.

"Well, it worked." I look down at myself, raising an eyebrow.

"I thought you said we were napping before we have to get ready for dinner?"

"We are, sweetheart. We are." I fold her into my chest, wrapping my arms around her and burying my nose into her hair.

Fucking heaven.

She sighs deeply, allowing her body to sink into mine. Her soft perfect chest pressed up against mine.

"In case I haven't told you," she raises her head so our eyes meet. "I'm having the best time."

"Me too, love, me too." I realize too late which endearment I used, but she doesn't comment, just sighs contentedly, closing her eyes.

I, on the other hand, do not go to sleep yet.

Instead, I snap a picture of her in my arms with my phone. Once that is done, I allow myself to surrender to her pull and close my eyes, never wanting to wake up from this perfect dream.

15

R *yan*

I'M ASLEEP MAYBE a half an hour when my phone rings on the nightstand behind my head. Reluctantly, I pry myself away from a beautiful and comatose Katie and slink into the living room. I swipe my finger across the screen to answer the call.

"What's going on, Luke?"

"Ah, finally. The man himself," Luke's enigmatic voice fills the phone.

"Cut the shit, man. I just sent you the code the other night. Don't tell me you've gone through it already?" I ask, sitting myself down in one of the large chairs that faces the windows and the view.

"Oh, but I have my friend, I have, and it looks really fucking good." I smile at that. I knew it was right on, but having Luke confirm it just makes it better. "How on earth did you come up with this? It's going to be killer and get a lot of hype, which is not really your thing, man. I'm surprised you want to do this."

I run a hand through my hair because he's right, I don't like hype or publicity. I like to remain under the radar, but I want to do this, so it is what it is.

"I'll manage it, and we have Claire to field a lot of the extra bullshit."

"True." He's silent for a minute. "Where are you anyway?"

I hesitate, but only for a brief moment. Luke knows pretty much everything there is to know about me. He's one of the very few people I trust.

"Vegas."

He laughs out loud and hard. "Shut up, really?"

"Yup." I look out at the evening sun as it sets over the mountains.

"What the hell are you doing there? Is this all part of your *road trip*?"

The way he says road trip sounds a bit condescending. Like he thinks I'm being childish for doing it in the first place. That doesn't surprise me, though. Luke has lived in his own small bubble since college. Since the FBI came knocking on his door. That was enough of a scare for anyone, so I get it.

"I am, but I'll be there for the meetings that you graciously set up on the eighteenth." I look over at the dark bedroom, wondering what things will be like for me by then—looking forward to it and dreading it at the same time.

"You'll thank me after the meeting. It's a big-time name, and if we can penetrate their system, which the dude tells me is impenetrable, then we're looking at big things." He's excited. I know he is.

Luke's a scrapper and he needs this. I don't. I've made all that I'll ever need and this new software that I created is only going to add to that. I do it for the fun of it now. For the challenge. So I say, "Sounds great, man. I told you about Tommy's new app bullshit, right?"

"No," he draws out the word because he knows as well as I do what dealing with Tommy entails.

"He's got something new I promised to take a look at. He's giving us twenty and a favor."

"For real?" he blows out a breath into the phone. "Damn." He's silent a moment like he's thinking this over. "I guess we can't really say no to twenty, and certainly not to another favor."

"My thoughts exactly."

I hear movement to my right, and as I look over I see Katie hovering by the bedroom door wearing what looks like only my t-shirt. Fuck, that's all kinds of hot.

"I gotta go, Luke. I'll call you." I hang up without waiting for a response and set my phone down on the small table next to the chair I'm sitting in, unable to remove my eyes from the vision that is now walking toward me. "Did I wake you?"

She shakes her head, her messy blonde waves only adding to the bedroom thing she's got going on. "No, I didn't want to sleep too long," she says with a coy smile. "We have a big night ahead of us, after all."

Katie pauses in front of me. My shirt is enormous on her and stops just above her knees. My hands reach out, grabbing her waist and pulling her so that she's straddling my lap with her bare thighs on either side of mine.

"Do we? What sort of big night?" I lean forward to kiss her sweet mouth.

"Well, I was thinking about whoring myself out." She tilts her head, her arms stretched out wide. "You know, to pay for the room and the clothes. And after that is done, I was thinking about maybe going to dinner and a club."

"Hmm." I run my fingers up and down her silky thighs, stopping just under the hem of her shirt. "Are you offering your services to me, or some stranger? Because I have to tell you, I'm willing to pay way more than the other guy," I smile, kissing her lips again just because.

"I can't whore myself out to *you*," she makes a tsking sound. "Having you pay me in cash as well as clothes and hotel rooms? That just doesn't make any sense." Her fingers come up, raking through the back of my hair.

I fucking love that.

She makes a good point, though.

"I suppose that's true." My hands slide up a little higher, wondering how far she'll let me go. "How about this? You whore yourself out to me, I *don't* pay you in cash, but you graciously accept the clothes and hotel rooms because it makes me happy to share them with you?"

"Hmm," she purses her lips to the side like she's thinking about this, and then leans forward so her mouth is hovering alongside my ear. "You drive a hard bargain, Mr. Grant, but I think I'm in."

God, this girl does it for me. I'm smiling like an idiot.

"Excellent." I lean in to run my nose along her neck, savoring her scent. "Can I shower with you, or am I pushing my luck here?"

I'm kidding, and she knows it. Well, half-kidding anyway.

"Yeah, sorry. No," she shakes her head, flattening her lips and widening her eyes like she's genuinely sorry. She's not, but I'll let it go for now.

I kiss her hard, running one hand up and down her thigh and the other hand through her hair. All too soon she pulls back, her pink lips swollen from my efforts. Damn that just makes me want to kiss her more.

"I need to go shower and get ready," she brushes her lips against mine again like she doesn't want to stop either.

"I like you in my shirt."

She smiles, biting her lip to try and hide it. "Me too."

"Can I watch you take it off? Or better yet, you let *me* take it off for you?"

She gives me a look that says I'm pushing it. "Not this time."

I get another kiss before Katie climbs off my lap and walks to the bedroom, but just before she disappears inside it, she pulls the shirt over her head and tosses it to the floor, treating me to her unbelievable backside.

"You're evil," I call out, because she really freaking is. I mean, come on. All I hear is her laughter before she shuts the bathroom door. Damn her, she's got me smiling again.

And nursing yet another case of blue balls.

When she walks out of the bathroom an hour later, she's a vision.

Her hair is piled up on top of her head in some sort of a messy updo. Her makeup is minimal as always, but her lips are red and her eyes are lined with some black shit that really makes them stand out. The dress is probably one of the best decisions Claire has ever made, and I may even have to give her a raise for the shoes, because I have never seen a woman look more beautiful and sexy as Katie does right now.

The black sequin dress goes to her mid-thigh and has a nice deep V-neckline that shows off just the right amount of cleavage without her tits being fully on display. I haven't seen the back yet, but I know there isn't much of one. The black sparkly heels give her a good five inches, and if she can walk in them, the extra height will make dancing with her that much better.

"You are a goddess, Katie." It's really all I can manage because my tongue may, in fact, be dragging against the floor. "Seriously. So crazy sexy, beautiful."

She blushes, and I think it's one of the few times I have ever seen it on her. Normally she is incredibly self-possessed.

"You look pretty hot yourself there, Mr. Grant." Her eyes wander all over me. "I think I may just keep you."

God, I hope so, I want to say, but don't.

I'm wearing a dark-gray button-down with the sleeves rolled up because I hate the feeling of cuffs around my wrists, black Armani pants—another thing from Claire, one I did not request, but hey—and some sort of black shoe. I even brushed my hair, but I left my glasses on tonight because the smoke from the casino bothers my eyes if I wear contacts.

We step outside and Sarah is waiting on us. She hands me the VIP passes to the club I requested and helps Katie into the limo. The second the door shuts behind us, Katie gives me that look again. The one that says I've gone a bit overboard with the wooing. I don't see the big deal here. I mean, it's not like we were driving around the city tonight, so why not go out in style.

The restaurant is on the fifty-fourth floor and the views are incredible. Everything in here is white, from the floors to the walls to the furnishings, and there are small glass bubbles dripping from the ceiling.

I've never been a fancy restaurant kind of guy, give me a burger and a beer, and I'm a happy man. But Claire and Sarah went top of the line, and I'm far from disappointed. We're halfway through our salad when Katie asks me something I'm surprised hasn't come up sooner.

"Why don't you fly?"

It's not a question I love answering, but she's entitled to one all the same. "I was in a plane crash about a year and a half ago."

Katie gasps and covers her mouth with her hand.

"It was a private plane, which I don't normally use, but I was in a bind and needed to get back to Philly for a meeting. There were no commercial flights available, so I chartered a small jet, and we crashed into a field in Nebraska."

Tears are pooling in her eyes, and I hate that reaction, so I reach my hand out for hers. The second she slips hers into mine, I realize that I need the comfort just as much as she does.

"Were you hurt?"

I nod. "The pilot was killed on impact, and I walked away with a broken arm, some broken ribs, a concussion, and a lot of cuts and bruises."

"Jesus." She shakes her head, wiping away a stray tear and looking out the window. She's silent for a minute, seemingly lost in her thoughts when she says, "You can't die, Ryan."

"What?" I ask, taken aback.

She turns to me, and the look in her eyes causes my breath to stall. It's a mixture of pure fear, anger, and resolve. "You can't die," she demands. "I need you to promise me." I don't say anything because that is not a promise any of us can make—something I became even more painfully aware of as a result of that crash. "My heart couldn't take it," she continues. "I can't lose anyone else that I care about. I realize that it's an impossible request, but I still need you to say the words."

Fuck. I didn't even think about what that story would do to her. "I'm not going anywhere, sweetheart."

She's not mollified, but she doesn't press it further either.

A moment of tense silence follows before she sighs out, her stiff posture relaxing. "I can see why you don't fly anymore. I guess I'm glad for that part; otherwise, I wouldn't have met you."

"Me too." I mean that with all my heart. I don't exactly believe that everything happens for a reason, but I feel like all that we have been through has led us to each other. I'll never be happy or grateful for the loss Katie endured—who would?—but it brought her to me and for that alone, I am both of those things.

The waiter comes back and we order. I manage to lighten the mood by giving Katie shit for ordering chicken instead of something expensive, and our dramatic moment is forgotten—at least for now.

After dinner, we take the limo to the club, and thanks to the passes, we not only get to bypass the psychotic line, but we end up in some roped off bar and dance area surrounded by the glitterati—Katie's term, not mine.

She and I each do a shot of some green thing that is passed around in a test tube, but we both decide we need something real, so I leave her at the edge of the dance floor and head for the bar. The music is insanely loud. The only thing I can hear is the heavy bass. It's dark in here too, but there are a million lights of every different color swirling and gliding past me.

Actually, it reminds me of the club in Miami almost to a T.

The bartender smiles and asks me what I'd like by shouting. I order the tequila shot Katie requested, as well as my whiskey. But when I'm done ordering, I notice he's not paying any attention to me. His eyes are fixed on something—or should I say someone—past my left shoulder.

"Are you here with that hot blonde in the black dress?"

"Yes." He looks very interested in whatever he sees, so I turn and notice some asshole who looks like Captain America—minus the spandex—talking to her.

"Dude, you should go get your girl." My eyes snap back to the bartender and he nods his head in Katie's direction. "That's Jamie Cole." That name means dick all to me. "He comes in here a lot and *never* leaves alone. Always with the hottest woman and he could care less if she's attached or not." Another head nod in their direction. "It looks as though he's set his sights on yours."

I turn back, and no doubt about it, he's trying to work her. Hard.

The full lean-in, brushing his fingers across her cheek, tucking a loose hair behind her ear and smiling at her with fuck-me eyes. She's not uncomfortable or distressed—though she is leaning away from him—so I let her handle it and turn back to the bartender with an easy shrug.

His eyes widen slightly like he can't believe that I'm not storming over there after her. "You're either dumb as fuck or confident as hell, and you don't look dumb to me." The bartender shakes his head in disbelief.

I get it. Most guys would be all over that. But I know for a *fact* that Katie won't go home with that guy.

If it had been Francesca, I'd have been over there in a flash.

Franny would have wanted me to think that she was going home with him. She was just that kind of woman—always making me work for it, and mind games were her specialty. Katie is *nothing* like Franny, and I trust her. It is really that simple.

"He steals women all the time, man. That's all I'm saying," he holds his hands up in surrender and then goes about pouring our drinks.

Small hands glide up my back, and as I turn, I'm treated to Katie's soft smile and twinkling eyes. "You left me to the lions," Katie shouts in my ear, and I smile down at her.

I had no doubts with this one.

"I knew you could handle your own." I brush my lips against hers.

She rolls her eyes dramatically. "What a douchebag."

I can't help but grin at my girl.

Our drinks are placed in front of us, and I hand the shocked bartender two twenties. Apparently, Katie is a rare creature around here.

After drinking our drinks, we head to the dance floor and don't leave each other's arms for the rest of the night. It's heaven, and I just pray it never ends, knowing I'm officially on the clock to convince her to be mine.

16

 ate

I WAKE in a similar fashion as the day before, wrapped in Ryan's arms. It's only been twenty-four hours of this, but already I'm used to it. And that has me troubled.

I know I should pull back.

I tell myself that constantly.

I'm blurring lines and pushing boundaries further, and I cannot stop myself. Every time I try to take a step back, Ryan does something wonderful—which is often—or he gives me a look that I find irresistible.

Or he does nothing, and I'm still hooked.

I'm falling for him.

I know I am, and I haven't a clue as to how to stop it.

"Don't go," he rasps out in his sleepy voice, pulling me closer into his body before I can escape. "I like you just where you are."

I do too, Ryan.

I give up the fight against my conscience and roll over in his arms to face him, kissing up his neck and through his scruffy beard. I like the beard. And I *love* the way it feels on my skin.

"You keep doing that, I'll have trouble holding back."

I sort of don't care right now. I mean, I do, but I really don't.

It's a conundrum if ever there was one.

I think conflicted should be my new middle name, instead of Anne. His mouth finds my mouth, my jaw, my neck, my ears, and before either of us knows what's happening, we're going beyond my kissing rule. Not much, but enough because his hands are groping the hell out of my ass—my bare ass, since I'm in my thong and bra—and I can tell he's struggling with his restraint.

His cell phone rings from the bedside table and Ryan groans out in frustration. "Fuck." He rolls over and grabs it, about to silence it when he checks the caller ID. "Fuck," he says again with a bit more annoyance because I can tell he has to take it. I'm relieved. He throws me an apologetic look before swiping his finger across the screen to answer it. "Yeah?" he snaps and then listens. He huffs out a loud angry breath. "I'm on it. Give me a few hours." He hangs up and rolls back to me. "I'm sorry, Katie, but I have some work that needs to get done."

I smile at him, running my fingers through his hair. He loves that. So do I.

"Don't be. I'm fine. Go work." I kiss his jaw before hopping out of bed and heading for the bathroom. I debate going to the gym, but I'm fried from getting home late last night, and frankly, my mind is a mess.

I need to walk, not run, if that makes any sense.

By the time I make it out of the bathroom, Ryan is on the phone and computer at the table in the dining area. I wave bye and blow him a kiss, and he covers the mouthpiece of the phone, asking whomever it is to hold.

"Where are you going, baby?"

Baby? Yup, I'm a total mess.

I manage a smile somehow. "I thought I'd go walk around the hotel. You do your thing," I blow him another kiss and head for the door before he can stop me. I need to get out of here.

"I shouldn't be more than a couple of hours," he calls out, and I throw up a hand so he knows I heard him.

I walk through the lobby but get bored quickly, so I decide to check out the casino. I've never been much of a gambler. In fact, I've only done it a couple of times and both times were at a casino in Connecticut. I only played the slots, so I guess that's where I'm headed.

"Excuse me?" a soft, male voice questions, and I look around. "Would you mind helping me out?"

I turn and see an older man, probably in his late-seventies, standing by a long table that I think is a craps table. He's got bright blue eyes, similar to mine, light, almost-white hair, and a kind smile. "Me?"

He nods with a wide grin, so I take a step closer to him.

"I was hoping you could help me play some craps here," he gestures toward the long oval table in front of him.

His clothes are reminiscent of Steve McQueen from *The Magnificent Seven*—very cool cowboy, with a faded pink denim button-down, tan pants, and matching cowboy hat.

"My wife is off getting her hair done, and I have no one to play with." He looks down before meeting my eyes. "Would you mind being an old man's good luck charm?"

I can't help but laugh. "I don't even know how to play."

He smiles, waving me off. "That doesn't matter. I do, and I'd like to teach ya if you're interested." His voice is thick with country and I find it oddly comforting.

I shrug. "Sure. Why not?" I sidle up next to him and pull out four hundred dollars from my wallet, handing it to the dealer to change out. It's a fifty-dollar minimum, which is a little—or a lot—rich for my blood, but I'll give it a go.

The guy, whose name I learn is Mo, gives me the rundown on

how to play, so we both place a fifty-dollar chip on the pass line, and then he hands me the dice.

"Me?" I ask, feeling a little nervous.

"Yes, you," he nods firmly. "You're my good luck charm today, remember?"

"No pressure then," I half-laugh.

"Just toss the dice down in that direction," he points to the far end of the table. "And don't worry about anything else."

I roll the dice around in my hand a few times, and then do as Mo instructed. The dice hit the green felt wall and then bounce back in opposite directions on the table.

"Seven," the dealer calls out, and Mo is beaming at me.

"Is that good?" He may have given me an overview, but there are a million rules to this game, and I've already forgotten most of them.

"That's good, cookie. We just won."

My eyes widen as the lady places more chips in front of the ones I had already put down. Mo stacks his winnings on top of his initial bet, so I do the same. The dealer slides the dice to me and we go again.

"Eleven. Winner."

Holy crap. That's twice. More chips and once again, Mo stacks his winnings. We both have a rather large pile building here. "What's your name, cookie?"

"Kate."

He looks at me with a smile, but there's familiar sadness in his eyes. "How old are you, Kate?"

"Twenty-seven." I'm searching his face, trying to figure out why he looks like a mirror.

"You look just like my daughter did." And there it is. That one word. *Did*. Mo and I have a shared pain.

"How old was she?" I don't even need to clarify my question. He knows what I'm asking him.

"Seventeen. Prom night. Drunk driver." His words are somber, but the soft smile on his lips gives the impression that it's always there when he thinks about his daughter. "Yours?" So he's observant as well.

I swallow hard then blink twice. "Almost three. Drunk driver."

He shakes his head, the smile slipping from his thin lips. "A baby."

I toss the dice in my hand, needing the distraction.

"Eight."

Mo and I fall into silence for a moment, letting the game lead us. I put money behind the pass line—the same as him—and more money on six. I don't even want to think about how much I have in play on this table right now.

"What was your daughter's name?" I ask, while the dealer does her thing with the new people joining the table on the other end.

"Chloe. She was my angel. Now she's up in heaven." He looks up at the ceiling and smiles again. "Yours?"

"Maggie," I swallow again, suddenly needing to ask a very personal question to a total stranger. "How did you...?" I can't even finish my words.

"Get through it?"

God, this guy just knows me. I nod.

"Well, cookie," he touches the brim of his cowboy hat, sliding his finger back and forth across it. "It was the hardest thing I've ever done. I still struggle with it, and I know I always will." The dealer slides me the dice again and I reach forward to retrieve them. "But it took me finally accepting that there are things in this world I cannot change. Death being one of them. And that I was beyond blessed to have had her at all." He doesn't rush me. No one does. Mo just continues to talk while I hold onto the dice for a moment, rolling them in my hand. "Now when I think about Chloe, I focus on the happiness her brief life brought me. Not the sorrow of her loss."

I nod, understanding but not fully on the same page. When I think about Maggie and Eric, I still feel the heartbreak of their loss. It's true, though, I am missing out on remembering the joy of their lives.

I throw the dice down the table.

"Six," the dealer declares, and the people down on the other end of the table cheer, as does Mo.

"We won again, cookie," Mo looks at me with his sparkling blue eyes and easy smile. "I think you *are* my good luck charm after all." His expression turns serious. "And maybe I can be yours, too."

"I think you are, Mo," I smile, pick up my chips that I just won and toss the dice again. This pattern continues—us winning—for the next twenty minutes. I have no idea how much money Mo and I won, but the two guys at the other end of the table have been hollering and cheering and singing my praises. All four of us are laughing and smiling, because this is just fun.

Winning always is.

Eventually, I crap out, which is fine. It's scary to think how far this could go and how easily my head would swell with it. But after I do crap out, I place a hundred-dollar chip on snake eyes.

"That's a sucker's bet, cookie," Mo warns me.

I nod my head in acknowledgment. Thirty-one to one odds *is* a sucker's bet. But Maggie was two when she died, and for some reason, I want to bet on that. The guy down at the far end picks up the dice and tosses them, and as they fly across the table I shut my eyes, picturing Maggie's sweet smiling face.

Maggie was always smiling.

That girl had no shortage of happiness.

When the shouting erupts, I don't notice right away that it is for me until someone shakes me. "Holy shit, you just won over three thousand dollars," one of the guys who was playing on the other end of the table, says. He's smiling with wide, excited, brown eyes.

"You did it, cookie!" Mo pulls me in for a hug, which would be strange if we hadn't just shared way more than most strangers do in under thirty minutes. "Remember, the key is to find your happiness in the life you shared with her." I don't reply, I just hug him back and then release him. "You take care of yourself now. Find your peace with what's done and live your life. That's all any of us can do in this short go-around that we get."

"Thanks, Mo. You're something very special."

He smiles, pats my cheek like my grandmother used to, and leaves to go find his wife.

Someone hands me my chips and I silently walk away, far too stunned to react the way they want me to. I have no idea how much money in chips I've stuffed into my bag, but I think it's a lot. My phone buzzes in my back pocket as I wander past some dinging slots, but I'm not ready to answer it. I want more of this moment of suspended time.

It's almost like I'm floating, watching myself from the outside.

Maybe it's the constant noise—the buzzing and ringing, and humming and talking, and laughing—all around me. Maybe it's the artificial lights combined with lack of daylight. Who knows? But I'm reveling in it right now, surprised by how oddly good it feels.

A roulette wheel is spinning, and there are maybe six people standing around the felt, reaching and placing chips and markers all over the numbers. I've never played roulette either, but the concept is simple. Way easier to get than craps.

I take two one-hundred-dollar chips out of my bag and place them both on the number nineteen, drawing the curious gazes of a few fellow gamblers.

Eric was born on March nineteenth and Maggie on July nineteenth.

One hundred for each of them.

Seems a bizarre thing to gamble money on them, but for some reason, it feels like the right thing to do.

It's as if I can sense their auras. Like Maggie thinks I'm being silly, and Eric's laughing and shaking his head because I'm wasting money, but would never tell me not to, regardless. The dealer calls out: "No more bets!" and the small white ball clickety-clacks against the multi-colored wooden wheel, landing finally on red nineteen.

People are screaming and grabbing me, and a large man walks over with a fake smile, congratulating me.

I'm too stunned to speak.

Then I'm being pulled into a large, familiar chest.

"Katie? What's going on?"

It's Ryan. *Thank god he is here.*

I don't know why that's the reaction I have to him holding me, but it is. He steps back, tilting my face up to his.

"Why are you crying?" Concern is etched on his handsome face. I didn't realize I was, so I have no answer for that.

"Sir? Is everything okay? Should I call for some help?" That's the guy who congratulated me, and I think it's time I start talking before they have me committed.

"Yes," I wipe my face with my hands and smile. "I'm fine. Just surprised I won is all."

The guy nods at me like this reaction happens all the time, then hands me my chips, which is evidently several thousands of dollars.

"What the hell did I miss while I was working?" Ryan's flabbergasted. I don't blame him. This is a lot of money, and he hasn't even seen what I'm hiding in my bag.

I look up at his bewildered face, reaching up to touch his prickly, soft, nearly-black beard.

"So I was walking around the casino when I met a man named Mo. He taught me how to play craps. His daughter died at seventeen in a drunk-driving accident on prom night. I rolled the dice and won insane money," I'm rambling a mile a minute, but can't seem to stop the verbal diarrhea. "Then Mo left, and I was walking around like some mindless zombie for I don't know how long. I saw the roulette table and I decided to play nineteen," I point to the table we're still next to. Amazingly, Ryan is standing here listening to me, and not running off screaming from my crazy. "Because it's the date of Eric and Maggie's birthdays," I blow out a breath. "And I won, Ryan. I won everything, and Mo told me to remember the happiness of their lives and not the sorrow of their deaths, and I'm just so tired of being sad. I want to think of them and be happy that I had them in my life, because they both made *me* so incredibly happy. Does that make sense?"

He brushes his knuckles along my jaw and nods with a half-smile that says I may be onto something.

God I hope so.

My head falls into his chest and his arms wrap around me, holding me to him like I'm precious. He kisses the top of my head.

"We should go cash in your chips. Get them out of your bag and then feed you. Do you want me to take care of that?" I nod into him. I love how he knows exactly what I need. "Come with me, sweetheart."

And I do.

I might just follow Ryan Grant anywhere.

17

K *ate*

THE MILD OCTOBER air outside the casino is like a balm on my overheated skin and muddled brain. Ryan holds my hand, swinging it a little between us as we walk down the Strip. I imagine we make quite the odd couple.

He's so tall and I'm so short in comparison.

"What are you in the mood to eat?" He's as casual as ever, acting as though I didn't just have some sort of minor psychotic event back there.

Why does he have to be so wonderful? I mean, I'm not looking for judgment or anything, but he makes me seem so...normal, when I feel anything but.

I think on this for a moment. "I want a Vegas-style buffet." He turns to look at me. "You know, the kind with everything from caviar to egg rolls to breakfast. I'm talking a full boat, self-indulgent, glutinous dining experience."

He's giving me that crooked smile that I like so much, and his green, bespectacled eyes are laughing at me. "You got it," he winks, and I can't help but beam at him. Is it wrong that I want to climb him like a tree in the middle of the sidewalk? Probably.

Ryan doesn't miss a beat, just keeps walking, so I follow. Sure enough, a few minutes later, we're headed into Caesars. The buffet is as promised. An all-encompassing dining experience. We eat a million different kinds of food and talk about nothing of importance, and it is beyond perfect.

So perfect, in fact, that when we leave to head back to our hotel, I want to die.

"I need to throw up everywhere," I groan, holding my severely bloated belly. "Thank god I'm wearing yoga pants," I look up at him. "That's all I'm saying."

Ryan laughs out, but I know he's feeling this hurt too. "I don't think I've ever eaten so much in my life."

"Ditto," I groan again, rubbing my food baby.

"Do you want to cab it back to the hotel?"

"No, I need to burn off the eight thousand calories I just consumed."

"Right," he deadpans. "That should only take us twenty years. What are you going to do with the money you won?"

I shrug. "I don't suppose you'd take it to even the expense score?"

He shakes his head with a smirk. "No way, I was promised sexual favors for that."

I snap my fingers in an aw-shucks way. "Ah, that's right. Damn. Then I guess I'll save it, or donate it, or both. I really don't know."

We make it back to our room, and I swear we both waddle our way into the bedroom, where I proceed to flop down onto the bed. He climbs in beside me, pulling me up so I'm sitting next to him, leaning against the headboard and his arm.

"Don't you think it's weird that we met once upon a time as kids, only to meet again as adults and go on this insane trip together?"

"I guess so," he shrugs a shoulder. "You haven't changed much since you were six, you know." He looks down at me with his crooked smile.

"How can you remember me so well? It was ages ago."

"You did make quite the impression—" I can hear the smile in his voice, "—especially knocking that huge chocolate cake onto the floor."

I bolt upright, staring at him with wide eyes, and startling him a bit. "That was you?" I ask, bewildered. There's just no way.

"What do you mean?" he looks confused.

"I remember dropping that cake."

He smiles, pleased. "You ran off crying. I followed you, since you went into my room." I get an eyebrow for that. "For some reason you went in there to pout. You were more upset about not getting to eat the cake than you were about your mother yelling at you," he chuckles lightly at that.

Sitting back on my haunches, I inch towards him on the bed until my knees are touching his thigh. With my hand covering my mouth, I speak through my fingers. "You sat me on your lap." I cannot *believe* that was him. "And ran your hands down my hair while I cried before you kissed my cheek and said—"

"Don't worry, Katie," he interrupts, repeating what he said to me that day. "When we're old and married, I'll buy you cake whenever you want."

I nod, so totally mystified. "Yes. How was that you?"

He laughs. "What's the big deal? You're looking at me like I'm a ghost, or a figment of your imagination or something."

"Dude," I reach out and smack his shoulder. "Because you basically are." I can't get over this. I crawl onto his lap so I'm straddling his thighs, his hands automatically come up to grasp my hips. "Your hair was lighter," I run my fingers through his dark strands. "And when we left your house, I cried a lot. I told my mother that I had met a prince and since I couldn't remember your name, I called you Peter."

He laughs lightly, smiling a lot. He likes this story. "Peter?"

"Yup. You reminded me of Peter Parker for some reason, but I was

heavy into princesses at the time, so I thought you were my prin
held onto that, onto *you*, for a very long time."

"Really?" He's having trouble believing me.

"Promise. But as time went by, you became more of an imaginary
friend than a memory or a real person, but you always saved me." I
lean forward to kiss his lips softly, before pulling back and resting my
head against his hard chest. His hand runs down my hair, much the
way it had that day twenty-one years ago.

"I begged my mother every day to have you come and visit us, or
to have us go see you." The sound of his speaking vibrates through
his chest into my ear. His heart beat a steady staccato. "I was ten, and
you were only six, but I couldn't get you out of my head," he lets out a
shaky breath, my head rising and falling with the effort. "I saw you
again when I was twenty-two, and you were eighteen."

I sit up in his lap, staring him in the eyes. "What?" I scrunch my
eyebrows in confusion. "When?"

He smiles, but his eyes are hesitant, nervous even. "It was my last
semester at school and I was returning to Boston from a weekend at
home. My mother had given me a package of some kind to deliver to
your mother, so I went to your house to drop it off." My mouth pops
open. "I rang the bell, and no one was home, so I left the box on the
front step, when a car pulled into the driveway. A girl with dark hair
was driving, and when you stepped out of the car, our eyes met, and
you smiled at me." He runs his hand across my cheek and through
my hair tenderly. "The second I saw you, my breath caught in my
chest." A small smile curls the corners of his lips and his eyes sparkle,
full of memories. "I couldn't even speak. It was like I had been
stunned. I knew who you were instantly, and I figured you wouldn't
recognize me, but just as I was about to call out to you, a guy—who I
assume was Eric—got out of the car and diverted your attention away
from me. He put his arm around your waist and pulled you in for a
quick kiss, and any nerve I had died right there."

I don't know what to say to that, so I just sit here and stare at him
in quiet disbelief.

"I was almost done with school and I knew I'd be leaving Boston.

You were only eighteen, not even graduated from high school yet, and you clearly had a boyfriend. So I left without speaking to you, even though I really wanted to." He leans forward to kiss my lips, pulling back to rest his forehead against mine for only a moment. "You stayed with me after that day, *again*," he emphasizes. "One way or another, Katie, you've been on my mind since I was ten years old. That's why when my mother told me you were leaving Boston, driving across the country, and were willing to take me, I called you. I debated it, believe me, I did. I knew what you'd been through. That you'd lost Eric and Maggie," he grimaces a little as he says their names, like he's afraid of hurting me.

It does hurt. It always will, but I need to start being okay with that hurt instead of always running from it.

"But I also knew that if I didn't at least contact you and see what your situation was, I'd always regret it." He leans forward, dropping his forehead to mine again. "And Katie? I'm so fucking happy I made that call. Whatever happens—or doesn't happen for that matter—I'll never regret these weeks with you."

"I'm scared," I whisper before I can stop the words.

"I know, baby. Me too."

"I don't know what to do, Ryan. I really don't."

He cups my cheek, holding me in place so I have to meet his eyes. "We don't have to decide anything now. We can just continue on and see where we end up. I don't want to pressure you, Katie. I don't. I'm in this no matter the outcome, but I'm sure I don't have to tell you what I'm hoping for," he sighs out. "But I'll take what I can get with you. Even if it's just friendship. I'm okay with that. I just want you around."

I have no answers. I'm all unknowns and paradoxes.

So I kiss him. I run my fingers through his beard and I kiss him hard. Telling him with my lips what I can't with my words.

"Katie," he whispers against me reverently. I love it when he does that. He groans, running his hands through my hair and down my back to the top of my bottom, where he freezes.

I'm tired of all these rules.

I'm tired of a lot lately, but I know in my soul that I'll never find another man like Ryan. If I'm going to sleep with anyone else again, I can't think of anyone I'd rather do that with than him. Reaching up, I pull my shirt over my head, making him gasp.

"Katie?" This time it's a question.

My fingers find his hair again. "I want you to touch me, Ryan."

His eyes turn into twin pools of heat and he swallows hard. "Are you sure?"

I take his hands away from the back of my hips and place them on my lace-covered breasts, eliciting a moan from both of us. "Jesus, Katie."

His mouth finds mine again and he gets to work with his hands on my chest. I reach behind my back and unclasp my bra, letting the straps fall from my shoulders before taking it off and tossing it aside.

Then Ryan loses it.

I'm on my back on the bed before I can even process how I got there. His mouth and hands find me. My lips, my neck, my chest, my nipples. The pads of his thumbs roll across my nipples as he squeezes my breasts. I moan. So loud. My head falls back and my eyes shut. I'm so close already. His mouth takes over, nipping and sucking and even biting lightly.

"So perfect," he hums against me, the sound reverberating through me, settling every single place I need it to. It's the most incredible thing. *This* is the most incredible thing.

It's been more than two years since I've been touched by a man, and Ryan certainly knows what he is doing. I can't stop the buildup, and he's only on my boobs. I come. I come so hard I see stars behind my eyes as my back arches, pushing my breasts further into Ryan's greedy mouth. I cry out loud and long, and when I'm done, I realize Ryan is watching me. I blush something fierce.

"Don't be like that," he kisses me. "You're so fucking beautiful, Katie. I could watch you all day, every day, and never grow tired of it."

I smile up at him. "Come here." I reach for him, and he kisses me happily. Grabbing the hem of his shirt, I pull it up and over his head, running my hands all over his chest and back. And god, his muscles.

They're just...absolutely perfect. All I know is that I want more of him. He helps me out of my yoga pants, and I help him out of his jeans.

His warm, slightly calloused hand glides down the smooth expanse of my stomach until he finds my pussy. My eyes cinch shut and a shaky breath passes my lips.

"Open your eyes, Katie. Look at me so I know this is okay."

I do open my eyes and this is so much more than okay. It's new and it's scary and I'm nervous as hell, but I trust Ryan. I trust him and I want this. His eyes are locked on mine as his fingers swipe against me, rubbing my clit before they sink inside of me.

My eyes are closing again when he says, "Open. Watch me touch you, Katie."

Oh God.

"It feels too good," I pant, and I can practically feel his smile even though my eyes are still closed. His mouth finds mine, kissing me with ardor as his fingers slide in and out of me, rubbing my clit with firm, deliberate circles. I'm hovering on the brink. Already. How? I have no idea. But I'm not ready for another. I want to explore him. I push him onto his back. He chuckles at my enthusiasm, lying back and watching as I move against him.

It doesn't last long. There is only so much control we both have.

We're all mouths and hands, exploring and touching, kissing and tasting and licking each other like we have an endless amount of time. Neither of us are rushing the moment, wanting it to last forever.

"Talk to me, Katie. If you want me to stop, I will." He's on me, skin to skin in the most delicious of ways. We're both already sweaty and smiling, but I'm not done with him yet. I need more. I can't seem to get enough.

"No stopping, Ryan. I want you too much."

His eyes lock on mine. "I've wanted you for so long. So fucking long, Katie." He kisses my lips, my cheek, the tip of my nose. My eyes close, and he kisses them too. "Look at me, sweetheart." My eyes flutter open. "I want to look into your eyes when I'm inside you." I moan just at his words alone, but when he slides inside of me, I'm a goner. My fingers grip onto his strong arms and my back arches. "So fucking beautiful," he rasps. "You feel so good, Katie. Fucking unbelievable. So perfect."

I nod my head, my voice caught in my throat.

We find our rhythm quickly, like we've been doing this forever, and it is perfect. Everything about it. The way he moves inside me. The way we move together. So different, and yet, so amazingly incredible. He rolls me so I'm on top, looking down on his gorgeous flushed face. His heavy-lidded eyes are burning into mine, the intensity like nothing I've ever felt before. My head rolls back, and I lose myself completely, riding him until we're both moaning and panting. I come on him, and he follows a half-second behind, roaring out his release, before I collapse down onto his sweat-slicked chest with an exhausted, sated smile.

"You do realize we're ordering room service and never leaving this hotel room, right?" he asks, still breathing heavily, his fingers gliding up and down the skin of my back.

"Oh good. More food," I deadpan because I'm never eating again. I look up, resting my chin on his chest, him peering down at me. "I think I still have another six thousand calories to burn off. You up for the challenge, Mr. Grant?"

He smiles that crooked smile and then flips me onto my back, grinding himself into me. "What does that tell you?" Christ, he's already hard.

"Hmm," I purse my lips to the side, pretending to think about it. "I really couldn't say. I think a closer inspection is warranted."

He laughs and kisses my lips. "A closer inspection, eh?"

"Absolutely," I nod emphatically. "How else am I supposed to formulate an educated opinion? I mean, I think this type of inspection could require hours of field research."

"Good," he smiles wide. "I plan on testing you and your limits for several more hours."

Awesome. I'm so in.

By the time we're done with his testing and my research, we're a heaping pile of smiles and sweat. You'd think showering together would help that, but it really doesn't, and we end up testing more limits.

I feel like I should be freaking out about now. Like crying in a corner, wanting to die, freaking out.

But I'm not.

I feel good. Happy. Satisfied.

And I'm not sure how to feel about that. Ironic? Yeah, I get that. It's weird, really. It's been hours and multiple times, but I want more.

And it's not necessarily the sex, though that is fan-fucking-tastic.

It's Ryan. It's the way he holds me, and touches me, and looks at me and talks to me.

It's the whole goddamn Ryan Grant package that I want to buy into.

"What now?" I whisper into the darkness we've been snuggled up in for the last half an hour. We did get out of bed and managed to have a sex-free shower. We even put on clothing, ate some food, and watched mindless television.

But all of that turned into naked bedroom time. Again.

"You tell me. I want you. It's really that simple for me."

Shit. I want him too, and I also want Eric. Yes, I get that I can't *have* Eric anymore, but I feel like as long as I still want him, I shouldn't be with anyone else. Isn't that how it's supposed to be?

"I want you, Ryan. Like mad." He smiles, but he can feel the but coming, so he holds back. "But I'm still not ready for something more than what we've got going."

"Do I still get to have sex with you, and kiss you whenever I want?"

I smile. "You bet your sweet ass you do."

"Then I'll survive. But just."

18

ate

I WAKE up the next morning much the way I do any other, but this
time, Ryan is up before me. He has been on the phone since four in
the morning doing work, and when I got up at six, he was ready for a
break. We both went to the gym in the hotel and ran our butts off.
Ryan then lifted all kinds of insane weights while I did some yoga. I
used to do a mommy and baby yoga class with Maggie, which was
really the most absurd thing on the planet, but she loved it.

Maggie loved everything. She was always smiling and talking and
playing and making my world a better place.

I miss her.

I don't know how not to, and I think I'll feel like this forever.

I miss Eric too.

As I breathe and stretch, I think about the fact that he's no longer
the last man I kissed, or had sex with. I knew this moment would
come, but it's not the sort of situation one can ever really prepare for.

Eric was an amazing lover. Generous, sweet, and fun. But Ryan is a different animal all together. He's more carnal. More aggressive. More devouring. Neither is better than the other, just different.

A difference I'm so grateful for.

Eric used to think my wild sexual fantasies were amusing and something to play with, but not fully explore. I get the feeling Ryan would not only embrace them in a second, but push them to the next level. Again, neither is better, just different.

Eric could kiss the hell out of me. In fact, every time he'd press his lips to mine, I felt a comfort I haven't been able to duplicate since he died. A love unchallenged and unparalleled.

Ryan kisses like a fiend. Like a hungry man desperate for the food my lips give him.

Both hot. Again, both different.

The main issue is that I still feel like I'm married to Eric. Like my being with Ryan is somehow betraying him. I know it's not. I. Know. It's. Not. Which is why I'm doing it. But that doesn't change my mentality. How can I be with one man when I'm mentally still with another?

I can't.

Do I feel like the world's biggest bitch? Absolutely.

Can I stop this new train that I've found myself on? No, probably not.

I'm addicted to Ryan. I want him constantly. And not just the sex, though that's certainly part of it.

I want *Ryan*.

His brain. His sense of humor. His touch and smile. His every-thing. I don't know how to *stop* wanting him.

"Off to LA today?" I ask, my ass in the air as I do a downward-facing dog.

"Yes, though if you keep that position up, our getting there may take a bit longer than planned."

"As tragic as that would be," I look up to find him staring at my ass in the air. "I could be okay with that."

He laughs, walking over to me and smacking my ass. Hard. "You're insatiable, Katie. Not that I'm complaining or anything. I'm more than happy to keep up this pace, but it seems to me that if we do, we won't have time for anything other than me being buried inside of you."

One thing I learned about Ryan last night? He's really good with the dirty talk. *Really* freaking good. Bringing myself upright, I stretch my arms up over my head.

"You're right. We should shower and get going."

He wraps his arms around my waist and begins to walk me to the exit of the gym, his nose inhaling the skin of my neck.

"Katie?"

"Hmm?"

"Should we talk about last night?"

I tense, and I know he feels it because he pulls away from my neck to a standing position, though his arms are still around me.

"Probably." I know we should. I know how he feels about me. What he wants.

Me? I have no fucking clue what I want. What I can handle. Why do we have to put a label on things? Why can't this just be what it is? Fun. Sex.

Because it is so much more than that, I remind myself.

I hate how selfish I'm being. I *know* I'm being selfish. But how do you stop something that just feels so...right?

"Are you okay with everything?" Could he be any more considerate?

"What are you asking me, Ryan?" I angle my head up to see him. "Are you asking if I'm okay with all the sex we've been having, or something else?"

"I'm asking about the sex. About this," he squeezes me with his arms that are around my waist. "Other than what we talked about yesterday, you've been very quiet about where your head is with all of this." I know he doesn't want to ask about it. I can hear it in his voice and see it in his eyes.

He's uneasy. So am I.

Leaning back into his chest, we step onto the elevator and make our way back up to our room.

"I like being with you, Ryan. You put me at ease. Relax my mind and somehow seem to understand me. I have fun with you. I think you're an incredible man. Smart and funny and charmingly sweet." I spin around, reaching my hands up and wrapping them around his neck. "I can't get enough of you."

He smiles big, bending down to kiss my lips and when I push him back a little, his smile falls.

"But?" he asks cautiously, sensing it coming.

"But I'm a mental mess, and the last thing I'd ever want to do is hurt you. I care about you way too much for that." He looks up at the ceiling of the elevator and lets out a sigh. The doors open and we step out into the hallway. We're silent for a moment as we walk toward our room. The heaviness between us is tangible. "Ryan?" He doesn't look at me. "I know how selfish I'm being. I'm trying to just live in the moment, and it's not fair to you. Maybe we should—"

"No," he snaps out, interrupting me. "I don't want to stop."

"I don't know what I'm doing here, Ryan. I'm going moment to moment, and that's just fucked up and wrong."

"Katie." He spins me around, stopping me in the middle of the hallway, his hands on my shoulders. "If you can live in the moment, so can I. I told you I'd take anything I could get with you, and I meant it."

"How is that fair to you? Is that even what you want?"

"Yes. Being with you in whatever way I can have you is what I want. I'm a big boy, Katie. I can handle myself, so stop worrying about it. I want fun and sex and you. Beyond that?" he shrugs like it doesn't matter. "I'm not asking for a relationship; you're the one who keeps going on about that. I'm just asking if you're okay with what we've got going on right now."

Oh. Well, now I feel stupid for assuming he was looking for more.

"Yes. I'm okay with it," I smile slimly. "More than okay with it."

"Good," he shrugs again. "Let's go shower and hit the road. It's getting late." With that he brushes past me toward our room.

Shit. What just happened?

I follow after him, and by the time I reach the bedroom, I hear the shower running. Apparently, he wasted no time. Stripping out of my sweaty clothes, I tentatively walk into the bathroom.

"Ryan?" I call out, but he doesn't respond. Either he doesn't hear me or he's ignoring me.

He's standing, unmoving under the stream of the shower, his head lowered to tiled floor.

"Ryan?" I try again, and this time he raises his head, turning to look at me. "Can I come in?" I ask, uncertain.

He shrugs.

I'm going to take that as a yes.

His face is completely blank. Impassive. Pouring some body wash into my hands, I rub the soap into his warm, wet chest, creating lather and filling the steamed glass enclosure with the scent of jasmine. He doesn't say anything, his eyes trained on my hands as they work soap all over his body.

"I'd wash your hair, but I don't think I could reach." That gets a half-smile, but nothing more. "Here, sit." I point to the bench on the far wall, walking him over there when he doesn't move right away. Now that his body is clean, I go to work on his hair.

His head falls back into my hands and his eyes flutter shut. Very few things feel better than having someone else wash your hair for you. My nails scrape along his scalp as I work the shampoo through his thick, inky strands. When I'm done, I adjust the showerhead so that it reaches us and wash out the soap. Leaning down, I place a chaste kiss at the corner of his mouth before I set to work on myself.

"Let me," he whispers and runs his hands through my hair, lathering it up with shampoo, washing it out, and then repeating the process with the conditioner. His strong hands run down my wet body, spreading soap as he goes. "Katie," he says in that way of his, before his mouth connects with mine. Ryan lifts me up into his arms, walking me until my back is pressed against the tile wall. My fingers run through his sodden hair, our eyes locked as he enters me. "Katie," he says again, though this time it's more of an expletive.

We've never done it like this—without a condom. Skin to skin. The sensation is overwhelming. My fingers are digging into his arms and shoulders, my eyes rolling back into my head.

"Look at me, Katie," he demands. "I want to see your pretty blue eyes as I fuck you." Jesus, his words aren't helping with the whole opening my eyes thing. Then he pounds me into the shower wall. Over and over again. I moan long and loud, clinging to him and saying his name over and over again. "Yes, Katie. Just like that. So beautiful when you come for me."

He pulls out of me after I come down from my heavenly high and finishes with a heavy grunt all over my belly. Washing ourselves off, we get out of the shower, and he wraps me in a towel. Whatever heaviness he was carrying seems to have lifted and his eyes are light, playful even.

"I realize this is an odd question at this point, but are you on the pill or anything?"

I shake my head, looking down at the floor and pulling my towel tighter around my body.

"No," I whisper, unable to meet his eyes as guilt, and maybe even a little shame, takes over. So much for living in the moment and working on not feeling sad. Eric and I were trying to get pregnant when the accident happened, and I never felt the need to go back on anything after that.

This rollercoaster feels like it is never-ending. Just as I'm up, I go flying back down.

"It's okay, baby." He brushes my chin with his fingers, drawing my eyes up to his. "We'll use condoms. I was just asking."

"I know." I nod my head.

He leans down to kiss my lips. "Come on, sweetheart. Checkout is in one hour." Ryan leaves me standing there in the bathroom, and I wonder if he's hit his limit with my mood swings.

I have, so I can only imagine the frustration he must feel from them.

We've entered into new territory, and though I certainly don't regret sleeping with Ryan, I don't know how to navigate this either.

I've only ever been with one man before, and that was the man I fell in love with, married, and had a child with.

I don't know how to do casual.

I don't know how to do just sex with no strings.

I don't even know if that's what I want. Ryan has also become a hotbed of mixed messages. Worst of all, I'm terrified that our friendship is over.

Walking back out into the bedroom, Ryan is already dressed and running his fingers through his hair instead of using a brush. I don't say anything as I walk over and grab what I want to wear out of my suitcase and begin to get dressed.

It's not awkward between us, but it's not comfortable either.

This is how he was the two days before the Grand Canyon.

Distant. Introspective.

I don't know how to breach this divide. Is it better this way? Maybe I'm not as ready for sex and another man as I thought I was. I mean, I knew I wasn't ready for a relationship, but maybe I'm not ready for this either.

What have I done?

One thing is for sure, I need to make friends with Ryan again. I don't think I can handle the alternative.

19

R*yan*

KATIE and I don't talk much on the three-hour drive into Los Angeles. She's been typing away on her phone, doing god only knows what. I fucked up. I get that. She has told me time and time again that she doesn't want a relationship. That she isn't ready for something more than fun.

And I told her I was good with that.

No wait, I told her that's what I want too.

So when she sticks to her word, I fail at mine because I'm going into hibernation, self-preservation mode again. I decided when this all began with her that I'd live in the moment and enjoy whatever time we had together.

Then we had sex, and everything I thought I had managed to control fell apart.

I'm totally and completely ruined, and I have no idea what the fuck I'm going to do about it.

Claire booked us in an amazing hotel right in Beverly Hills. Katie's eyes finally leave her phone in favor of the view, but as we pull into the hotel, she starts to shake her head ever so slightly.

"What? You don't approve?" My tone is clipped. Even I can hear it.

Her head snaps over to mine with wide eyes. "Oh. No, it's great." She doesn't mean it. I know she thinks it's beautiful here, but all of this luxury just isn't her.

"Do you want to stay somewhere else?" My voice softens.

"No, this is fabulous." She reaches over for my hand now that we're parked in the valet area. "Thank you for seeing to all of this." She leans in to kiss me and then looks at me with a shy smile. "Do we have plans for tonight?" Her teeth sink into her lip, her eyes apprehensive.

We do have plans for tonight, but it's just dinner, and judging by the look in her eyes, I'm happily canceling it. "Nothing important. What did you have in mind?"

"I sort of got us Dodgers tickets."

I smile, because how fucking cute is she? "Sort of?"

"Well, yes, I got us tickets. It's the last game of the regular season."

She's trying to make me happy, knowing how much I love baseball. Trying to lesson this bullshit tension I've created between us.

"That sounds great. I can't wait." I lean in and kiss her lips, her nose, her cheeks. "Thank you for doing that for me."

She beams, squeezing my hand before stepping out of the car. I check us into our overly posh suite, but we don't have a lot of downtime before we have to head back out to the game. The hotel arranges a car service for us, since driving in LA sucks and neither one of us wants to deal with it.

We arrive at the stadium, procure our tickets and make it to our seats—right behind home plate—as they're singing the national anthem. The park is crowded, and as I sit down, I get the buzz that you only get from watching professional sports live.

This was the perfect idea, and I'm so glad that she did this.

Another night of being dressed up and going to an expensive

dinner seems over the top. And that's certainly not who Katie is. She's down-to-earth and easy-going.

How stupid am I for thinking that if I wine and dine her full of lavish things and big price tags, that she'll be more inclined to stay with me? So fucking arrogant. The way to Katie's heart is not through money. Francesca really jaded the hell out of me.

Katie doesn't drink beer, but when the beer guy comes by, she throws her hand in the air and orders one up. Then hands it to me. She does the same thing when the hotdog vendor approaches, though this time, she gets one for herself too.

It's the perfect night. The air is mild and just the right temperature. The crowd is into the game, despite the fact that the Dodgers are not headed to the post-season, and Katie is even heckling the umpire over a bad strike call.

I want to freeze-frame this moment and hold onto it.

Katie is able to stay in the moment. To live in it. At least that seems to be the way she's been doing things for the last few days.

Me? I'm trying. Trying like hell actually, but it's hard.

"Can you believe that call? That was so obviously a ball." She's full of ire, her eyes on the field.

"You're adorable when you're angry," I lean over and kiss her cheek.

She smiles. "You're adorable all the time," she nudges me with her elbow. "Now shut up with the compliments and watch the damn game." Fuck I love this woman.

And apparently I'm admitting that to myself now. Great. That should help with the in-the-moment thing.

"Yes, ma'am," I kiss her again, and then I relax into it. I drink beer; she drinks water. We eat hotdogs and ice cream and have one of the best nights of my life—even if it's not the Phillies playing.

The Dodgers lose, but it was still a good close game, and as we sit in the back of the car, stuck in never-ending traffic, Katie takes my hand, resting her head on my shoulder.

"I was seven the first time I went to see a game in Fenway Park," she starts, her voice distant, lost in the memory. "I thought it was the coolest place ever. My dad and I didn't have great seats, we were high up in the bleachers, but it didn't matter. It was the whole spectacle of it, you know?" She tilts her head up to look at me and I nod, grinning down on her. "It was just...fun. Hotdogs and Cracker Jacks, and people yelling all around us. Tonight reminded me of that, so thank you for canceling whatever incredible thing you had planned for us so we could go."

"Katie, in case you've missed it, I'll do anything for you."

She smiles, snuggling into me, silent for a few moments before she speaks again. "Eric hated sports," she laughs lightly like this amuses her. "We were the odd couple like that, because I love them. On Sundays in the fall, when I wasn't working, he'd take Maggie out for the day and I'd sit around watching football," she snorts. "He wouldn't even get into the Super Bowl when the Patriots were playing." She angles her head up to me again with an incredulous look. "What kind of guy doesn't like the Super Bowl?" It's a rhetorical question, so I don't answer. "He and I were so well-matched with some things, and so at odds with others."

It's the first time I've ever heard her say something about Eric that didn't include him being flawless. It's hardly disparaging, but it's certainly different for her.

She sighs, tightening her grasp on my hand.

"He was not the best driver, either," she says after another quiet beat.

And this comment surprises me completely. I know he died in a car accident, but I was under the impression that it wasn't his fault. Maybe I was wrong.

"He always got speeding tickets. Had a lead foot that would not be thwarted. I constantly worried whenever he drove Maggie around. I used to tease him that he'd die in a car accident." She's laughing, but it's the saddest laugh I've ever heard, and my heart breaks for her. "It was a drunk driver. Did you know that?"

I shake my head, relieved somehow that Eric didn't cause the accident. I don't know why really, but I am.

"The driver walked away with only a two-inch laceration to his forehead. He was in the ED at the same time that they were working on Maggie."

Jesus, I can't even imagine. I find myself pulling her closer into me, holding her tighter.

"I can't forgive him, Ryan," she whispers like this admission somehow makes her a bad person. "It was his third DUI that he got *caught* for. He had a penchant for going to the bar and getting himself good and drunk before driving home. He left the bar that evening earlier than normal, and slammed into the side of Eric's car, going over sixty in a thirty-five zone, after running the red light. His blood alcohol was three times the legal limit."

My eyes slam shut and my breath stalls in my chest. My insides are on fire, anger being the most prominent emotion swirling inside of me. My parents are alcoholics, but they've never hurt anyone— other than themselves—or driven drunk as far as I know.

Would I be able to forgive them if they did?

"He emailed me this morning. The driver." She looks up at me, her eyes glassy with unshed tears. "He served four months in jail and was forced to go to rehab for a month. He also lost his license for an additional six months. That's it. He killed a husband, a father, and a child, and that's all he got. He's out free, and they're gone forever."

I pull her onto my lap. She's sitting sideways, her head resting on my chest.

"In the email, he asked for my forgiveness. It's the first time I've heard from him, including after it happened. I never even got an apology. Nothing. And now he sends this via email and asks for me to absolve him of his sins. I don't even know how he got my email address."

I don't know what to say to her. I wish I were one of those people who always knew the right thing to say. Who could spew out sage words of wisdom, and anecdotes, and bullshit that would turn her world into sunshine and fairies. But I'm not one of those people, so I just wrap my arms around her and hold her as close as I can so she knows she's not alone.

"I always thought I was a forgiving person, and truth be told, I haven't given the fucking prick much thought over the years. But now he's invaded my world once again, and I can't forgive him, Ryan. I can't."

She pulls back to look at me with such heartbreaking grief in her expression.

"Does that make me a bad person?"

"Katie, my sweetheart, the mere fact you're even worried about that shows you're not. I'm not sure many people could ever truly forgive someone who not only did that to their family, but showed such little remorse in doing it."

She sighs heavily into my chest, my fingers gliding down the back of her silky waves. I know we're getting closer and closer to our hotel, but I don't want to let her go until I know she's not berating herself over this.

That she's not letting it consume her.

"I don't hate him, Ryan, though a huge part of me wants to. But I still want to find him and beat the shit out of him for all the life he wasted. For the future he took away from Maggie, Eric, and me."

"That doesn't make you a bad person either, you know? It makes you human."

"Yeah, maybe. But I feel like I should be further along with the stages by now. I keep bouncing back and forth between anger and depression. Bargaining I feel like I hit and passed, but acceptance is like a million miles off."

I can't offer much, but I can tell her the truth that I've been holding back for fear of her reaction. "Katie, if I were Eric, I would want you to find that acceptance. A guy who spent his whole life loving you the way he did, doesn't want you to be like that. He'd want you to be happy and live your life to its fullest."

She's silent for another minute as we pull up to the hotel. "I know he would, Ryan. I know that. But knowing something and being able to do it are sometimes two very different things."

She climbs off my lap and hops out of the car, but instead of walking away like I expect her to, she waits for me, reaching out her hand for me to take. Our fingers intertwine and she grins up at me.

By the time we're thirty seconds into our room, she's naked and so am I. I'm devouring her, unable to get close enough. To taste enough. To kiss enough.

"More," she whispers, and I can only oblige, because I want the same exact thing.

She's so incredible. From her amazingly soft, yet firm, large breasts, to her slender waist and curvy hips. Don't even get me started on her other deliciously marvelous parts, because I swear I could write a fucking sonnet about them.

Katie is my dream girl. My goddess, and I am worshipping at her altar.

Hours later—and I do mean hours—we're both lying in bed, facing each other with only a sheet covering our bare skin. We're smiling and talking and laughing. I'm in heaven because nothing has ever been this good. *Ever.*

"Tell me about the first girl you kissed," she asks with her devilish smile.

We've been playing this game for a while now, and so far, I've told her about the time I broke my wrist skateboarding, and the time Kyle punched me in the face and broke my nose for taking his Xbox. She's told me some stuff too, but nothing too revealing. I fully intend to change that.

"The first girl I kissed was Jessica Higgins. I was eleven and she was thirteen. It was behind the big tree in my backyard on a dare. *Her* dare."

"Really?" she raises an eyebrow, like I'm a master seducer. "A player even at eleven."

I laugh lightly, leaning forward to kiss her lips. I do that every time she says something adorable, which is often.

"Was it good?"

I shrug a shoulder. "Sure. For a first kiss that had no tongue and lasted all of three seconds."

She laughs, biting her lip to try and hide her smile. That may, in fact, be my favorite of her smiles. "Your turn. Was Eric your first kiss?"

I've mentioned Eric a few times, and so has she, but it has been in a happy context.

That's what I want for her. To talk about Eric with a smile attached to her face and through happy memories.

"Yes, but he almost wasn't. Eric and I had gone out for our first ice cream date and then on another to the movies, but all we had done was hold hands. So we went to a birthday party at my friend Sam's house, and of course, the boys wanted to play spin the bottle." She's smiling big, her eyes are sparkling and a little distant, loving the hell out of this story. "So Sam spun the bottle and it landed on me. It was a half-assed attempt at a spin and everyone knew it. He had wanted it to land on me and as he got closer to me with his big, shit-eating grin, Eric blew up."

"What do you mean?"

She laughs, resting her head on her tucked hands. "He started yelling before Sam got close enough to kiss me. Claimed that Sam cheated—which he had—and that he should have had to spin the bottle for real and see where it landed," she laughs again. "Sam wasn't having that at all, and the two of them got into it. My friend Chrissy—who liked Sam—was agreeing with Eric that Sam should re-spin, and so it went. Finally, Eric got really angry and decided to leave. I got up and left with him, and on our walk home he apologized. Told me that the reason he was so upset was because *he* wanted to be my first kiss. So I stopped him in the middle of the street and kissed him."

"Wow. That's a really good story."

"Yeah. It is," she sighs heavily. "Thank you for letting me share it with you."

"Katie, baby, I don't mind you telling me about him. Eric and Maggie were the biggest part of your life, though I technically did meet you first." I raise an eyebrow, but am smiling so she knows I'm kidding.

"Is that so? Well then," she pushes me onto my back and climbs on top, chest to chest, her face inches from mine. "I guess it's a good thing I'm in bed with you. I'd hate to ever be with a man I haven't known my entire life."

"Sarcasm will get you nowhere." My fingers slide up the sides of her body, across her silky skin.

"Really?" She rolls her hips against me. "It feels to me like I'm getting somewhere." Her hand glides down my stomach to grip me.

"Fuck," I hiss out, my head tipping back onto the pillow. "Jesus, Katie, what are you doing to me?"

"I should think that is fairly obvious, Mr. Grant." God, I love it when she calls me that. "But since I assume you were being rhetorical; I'd like to show you just what I want to do to you."

She kisses me chastely before lowering herself down my body and settling between my legs. She takes me in her mouth, licking and sucking me, cupping my balls, and generally giving me the best head of my life. Katie's mouth is like fucking magic. *Katie* is fucking magic. She puts her whole heart and soul into everything she does, and sex is no different. I can honestly say I've never been with another woman like her and I hope to never be again.

She's it for me; she just doesn't know it yet.

20

K *ate*

WE SPEND the entire next day doing the typical tourist bullshit all over LA. It's a cool city, but the smog and the traffic and congestion make it not for me. I couldn't see myself living here. I'm all for a city, but something smaller and more intimate is what I have in mind. Something less dirty and polluted too.

We end up at some trendy Hollywood hot spot for dinner that Ryan says his assistant Claire—who I found out made all of our reservations—says is a good place for spotting celebs.

Not my thing.

I figure they're people who are just trying to go out and eat a meal like everyone else, but whatever.

Ryan is all over me. His distant mood forgotten once again. I swear his mood swings can be worse than a teenager's.

The restaurant is all low lighting with elegantly appointed tables, topped with white linens and fuchsia roses. Every woman here is gorgeous, tall, very thin, and showing more skin than I think I've ever seen—and I'm a nurse. The men aren't so bad either, and while my eyes haven't stopped scanning the room of beautiful people, Ryan hasn't taken his off of me.

Swoon.

Ryan is wearing his dark-gray pants, a black button-down, and the new gray fedora we bought today. Holy hell, can this man rock a hat. His dark hair is sticking out from the bottom, and his whole look says dark, sexy, and mysterious, especially with the beard and glasses. He's definitely getting checked out by the local fanfare here, and I can't say I blame them.

His hands are gliding up and down my bare legs. Apparently he's got a thing for my legs, because he bought me yet another dress, despite my protests, and it's very short. So short I have to cross my legs the second I sit down or everyone in this restaurant is going to get a show.

Our food comes, and tonight I ordered lamb since both Ryan and our waitress talked me out of the chicken.

"We have two options for tonight after dinner."

"Oh lord," I roll my eyes dramatically, earning me a pinch in the ribs. "Ah." I slap his hand away, making him chuckle and kiss the side of my head. "What are our two options, Master?"

"Is it wrong that I love that you just called me Master? I think I might have to implement that into our bedroom activities tonight."

I snort. "Bedroom activities? What are you, seventy? You can say sex or fucking, or even lovemaking if you want to be totally cheesy about it."

"Fine." He leans in right up to my ear, his hot breath sending shivers down my skin. "I'm going to tie you up and make you call me Master, while I spank your ass red before I fuck you into tomorrow. How's that?"

I flush. It only took like two seconds too. "That sounds like something we could try, *Master*," I wink at him, and he presses his lips to mine with a fierce kiss that leaves me breathless.

"Now, as I was saying, slave girl," he raises an eyebrow at me and I can't help but laugh. Ryan leans forward, placing his elbow on the table and propping his head up with his hand. "We have two options for after dinner. One, we could go to the beach and walk around, or we could go to a club that Claire got us passes for."

"Hmm. Well, I don't know how safe the beach is at night here. I don't really feel like getting mugged or having to run for my life in a mini dress and five-inch heels."

"Good point. The club then?"

I reach for my wine glass and take a sip, mulling it over. "Nah. I'm not really feeling clubby tonight. What if we just went to a bar or something?"

"Sure. I'm up for that. Besides, we have a long drive tomorrow."

I nod. "True. Where are we stopping anyway? We never did decide."

"No." He leans in to kiss my head before taking my hand and kissing my fingers. Did I mention how he can't keep his hands off me? "We haven't. What are you thinking? Do you want to go up the Pacific Coast Highway toward Big Sur and Carmel, and see how far we get before we want to stop?"

I shrug. "Sure. That sounds like a plan. But we should probably leave on the earlier side then. That's more than a six-hour drive, right?"

"Yeah, I think so."

Our food arrives and we eat, chatting about the various places we'd like to stop along the way. We decide to spend two nights in San Francisco because neither of us has ever been, and two nights in Redwood National Park because I want to hike and explore and even camp—gulp. Then it's a long haul up to Portland, and after that, Seattle—another gulp. Both of us turn inward after that realization.

Yes, we knew this trip was eventually going to end.

But the question lingers in the air, unspoken between us.

Then what?

I don't know. I really freaking don't. Part of me wants to ask Ryan if he wants me to stay. But a slightly larger part tells me that is a bad idea. Not because of him, but because I'm not ready. I don't want to just grab onto someone and not formulate any sort of life for myself. I want to stand on my own two feet for a while. Find my bearings and see where and how I end up.

That was always my plan.

Then Ryan came along, and now I find myself rethinking things I shouldn't.

Do I want him? Without a doubt. Am I in love with him? I'm not going there. I like him. A lot even, but that's as far as I'm allowing my brain to go. The thought of loving another man feels...well, it just feels wrong. I know it's not. I know it would be a good thing, a healthy thing, but that idea kills me.

How can I love another man when I still love Eric?

And isn't that betraying his memory just a little bit?

I always thought of Eric as the love of my life, so what would that mean for the next guy? Will they always be in second place? That's not exactly fair, and I don't want Ryan to ever be second. He deserves to be first all the way, and I don't know if I can give him that—at least not right now.

Here's the kicker though, last night before I fell asleep in his arms, I imagined what our life together could look like. Would our children be dark or blonde? Blue- or green-eyed? Tall or short? Would he want boys or girls? Does he even envision a wife and family?

It's hard to go from having a family to not, but the idea of never having any more children is a bit more than I can handle.

Having Maggie was the best thing I ever did. She was the light of my life. The love of my life. My entire world. I miss her desperately. Every day I wonder what she'd be like if she were still alive. What new and exciting things would come into her world.

I want that again. Not this minute, but eventually.

And I can see myself doing that with Ryan.

Probably because he's the first guy I've been with since Eric. Yeah, that must be it. I'm sure I'd be doing the same thing with any guy I was...whatever the hell it is I'm doing with Ryan.

We leave the restaurant hand in hand, after I finally convinced him to let me pay. *That* was an argument. Stubborn man.

We end up walking two blocks down and then find a small but nice-looking bar. I order another glass of red wine. If we're waking up early tomorrow and driving a million miles, the last thing I want to be is hungover. Ryan is feeling me on this because he orders a beer instead of his usual whiskey.

We get back to the hotel early, and true to his word, Ryan does tie me up and spank my ass. It's a first for me, and I have to admit, I am totally into it. It's not something I want to do every day, or even go beyond his hand, but it's hot and fun.

He passes out quickly after our nightly workout, and just as I'm about to fall asleep, I feel it. The crazy sense that everything is the way it's supposed to be.

But instead of filling me with comfort, it makes me uneasy.

Our alarm goes off at eight, and after hitting up the gym, we shower, pack up our stuff and get on the road. The Pacific Coast Highway is everything you read about. Gorgeous, unparalleled views of the Pacific Ocean, and windy, scary-as-hell roads along cliffs with nothing between you and the edge but an occasional guardrail. I let Ryan drive for that part because I'm far too distracted and nervous to do it myself.

We have all the windows down and are blasting music and having the best time when we stop for lunch in Santa Barbara. We grab sandwiches and take them to the beach for a picnic, sinking down into the sun-warmed sand. It's only in the low seventies with a good breeze on us, but I'm comfortable in my jeans and t-shirt.

We sit in silence, just watching the Pacific crash onto the shore and a few surfers having at it in the waves. It's beautiful here. Palm trees and sunshine. Could I live in this type of world? Maybe? Being able to go to the beach every day certainly wouldn't be a bad thing.

"I know we're not really talking about the end of this trip," Ryan's voice snaps me out of my reverie. "But if I haven't mentioned it, I'm having the time of my life."

I turn to him and smile brightly. "Me too. It's been the best."

"You like it out here? Don't you?" he asks, trying to sound light but not really managing it. His eyes are fixed out on the ocean.

"I do, actually. I think I may add it to my short list, but I don't know if I'm really a California girl," I laugh. "Despite having the hair for it."

"Well, we still have a few more places to visit. Maybe you'll find something further north that you like better."

Yeah, like Seattle, I don't say. "True," I offer instead. But I think we both know what we're not saying.

Taking a small stroll along the beach and then through the town of Santa Barbara, we get back on the road. After almost another five hours of driving, we're both fried. We're somewhere near Big Sur. It's almost seven in the evening and the sun has just set over the Pacific, which we had stopped to watch.

Beautiful doesn't even begin to describe it.

Sunrises are still my favorite, but damn…there is just something to be said about watching the sun set over the ocean. We find a local grocery store and get a few things before getting back into the car and parking on a secluded bluff by the ocean.

"Are we going to look for a hotel or something?" I ask through a yawn.

A shrug. We've been on the road way too long today. "I don't think I can drive anymore, Katie. I'm tempted to sleep right here."

"I would normally say yes to that, but you're a tall dude and I'm afraid it won't be very comfortable for you."

"What if we move our suitcases to the front seats and lay the back seats flat?"

"You're serious?" I look over at him with scrunched up eyebrows.

"Yeah," he says through a chuckle. "I can barely move. Are you okay with that?" I look around us, but it's getting pretty dark outside and there isn't much to see. "No one is around," he adds like that will sell me on this idea.

"What if someone comes, though?"

"We'll lock the doors. Besides, the only person who would ever come up here would be a cop."

"It's going to get really cold."

He takes my hand, kissing my knuckles. "We have that blanket you bought outside of Dallas, and I'll hold you all night." He makes a pretty good argument. "Come on, Katie, where's your sense of adventure?"

I laugh. "Fine. You got me. I'll help you move the bags to the front."

We turn on the flashlight apps on our phones and get to work. With the seats folded flat, the back is actually rather spacious, at least for someone my size.

"I've been meaning to ask you, what's in those boxes?" Ryan nods his head to the two small boxes I have that are tucked in the well behind the front seats.

"Things I couldn't part with. Photo albums, Maggie's stuffed bunny, her hospital blanket, Eric's Boston College hat, his wedding band. Stuff like that."

Ryan's eyes are wide and he blinks at me a few times. I crawl into the wide open back and cover myself with the blanket, because now that the sun has set, it is getting rather chilly. Ryan follows, wrapping his arms around me and spooning me from behind.

"Can I see some of the pictures, or is that too painful?"

I look into his eyes in the extremely dim lighting; all I can make out are shadows. I haven't looked at pictures of them in a long, long time. Not since right after the crash, and then it just got to be too hard.

But now?

I swallow hard and say, "I'd like that."

Leaning forward over the edge of the seat, I flip open the top of the box that I know holds my rather large photo album. Most people only have digital photos, but I like the real thing, so I was always having pictures printed out and set into this book.

Crawling back over toward Ryan with the very heavy book, I set it down, angling my body so that it's in front of me on the bed we've created. Ryan is still behind me, but since he's so much bigger than I am, he won't have any trouble seeing. I flip on my flashlight again and set it in such a way so that the pages are illuminated.

The first picture is of Eric and me.

We were fourteen, smiling with mouths full of braces and his arm around my shoulder. I don't know why we didn't have any pictures of us before that, but this is where our photo story begins. Ryan is silent as I flip the pages, through high school graduation, college, and even our vacation to Cape Cod.

The next page is of our wedding.

These are pictures people took of us, not our professional ones. I always liked these better for some reason. They seemed more real. More like us.

"You were a beautiful bride, Katie," Ryan whispers, his voice full of emotion. I have no idea what's going through his mind. He's been very quiet, but I'm actually okay with that.

I don't think words are needed right now.

More pictures of Eric and I dancing, laughing, kissing, and cutting the cake. Then into our honeymoon.

"Where is this?" he asks, brushing his fingers over a picture of a waterfall.

"Hawaii. We went for ten days on our honeymoon."

He nods his head against mine, but that's it. Then I flip the page, and I gasp. I can't help it.

It's one of my favorite pictures.

It's me with bright red cheeks, laughing as Eric is squatting in front of me, pointing animatedly at my then flat belly with the world's biggest smile lighting up his face. It was the day we found out we were pregnant with Maggie, and I swear I had never seen him as happy as he was in that moment.

I feel the tears running down my cheeks before I can even try and stop them. No point, I realize, since I'm sure more are to come. But I also realize it feels good to cry through this. To see these moments in time and remember the pure joy we both felt.

We were so happy, and for the first time, I'm not so sad about that.

I'm frozen on this picture, so Ryan turns the page for me, and I'm hit with an image of my rather large belly with Eric's hands cupping it tenderly, lips pressed to the swell, his eyes closed.

"That's an incredible picture," Ryan whispers, and all I can do is nod. I miss him. I miss him so much. He wasn't just my husband, but he was also my best friend, and sometimes I miss that the most.

Then comes Maggie, and that first picture of her on my chest in the hospital wrenches a sob from me.

"Katie, we can stop if you want. I don't want to make this hard for you."

I shake my head, but can't formulate words. I'll lose it if I try and speak. More images of Maggie. As a newborn, an infant, a toddler. Smiling, getting her first teeth, and taking her first steps. Hugging and kissing.

There are lots of those.

Family pictures.

I can't look anymore and end up burying my head into Ryan's chest and letting go. Poor guy doesn't deserve this, but he holds me tight, running his hand down my hair and kissing my head.

"She was so beautiful, Katie. A perfect blend of both of you. You were so very blessed." The tears come harder at that, but I can't help but agree.

I'm so tired of this grief, but I can't seem to stop it either.

It's so completely consuming that I feel it in my mind, body, and soul. It's everywhere, suffocating the life from me, and I would do almost anything to get it to stop.

"How do I make this pain stop?" I'm gripping Ryan's t-shirt with one hand, pulling it toward me like it has the answers I need. My other hand is clasped tightly around my pendant.

"I don't know, sweetheart, but I would give anything in the world to make it go away. But think of this, love, if you had never known them, never had them in your life, never loved them as much as you do, you wouldn't be hurting this way."

My head snaps up to look at him, the illumination of the flashlight set across his face.

"Don't you think all of these amazing memories, all that love you had with them, was worth it?"

I swallow, blinking away my tears.

"Would you give up everything you had to never hurt from their loss again?"

"No," I say without any hesitation.

"Right. You wouldn't." His hand cups my jaw, his eyes burning into mine with profound meaning. "So instead of focusing on the hurt that will always be there, focus on the love. Focus on the amazing memories this book is filled with. The memories your heart is bursting with. Feel the comfort and wonder and fucking bliss you felt in these moments," he kisses me deeply before brushing his lips across my cheeks, taking my tears away with his mouth. "Focus on the future, Katie. On all that you could have again if you let yourself."

I know what he's saying, what he's offering, and maybe even asking.

I see it in his eyes.

God, the way he's looking at me.

I really want to take that promise and never look back.

I reach up, grab his face, and pull it down to mine. I kiss him with everything I've got—a world of hurt and anger, and passion and love.

We moan in unison, our mouths dancing together in a way that is as familiar as it is new. I'm pulling at his clothes frantically, trying to rip them from his body, which is easier said than done in the small confines of this car.

The second he's about to slide inside me, something unspoken shifts between us, and our frenzied pace slows to something much more intimate. Our eyes lock, mere inches from each other, our breath mingling.

His fingers intertwine with mine as he stretches them above my head and we become one. This is so different than anything we've done before. Every other time was sex—mutual pleasure, and sometimes pure, carnal fucking.

This is making love.

Something I haven't experienced in years. Something I know is entirely new for Ryan. It's intense and fiery, and so goddamn good. So heavenly perfect that I never want this connection to end.

His eyes sear into mine, before he buries his face in my neck and whispers something I cannot hear. When we both come, we do so together and then hold each other in silence, letting what just passed swim between us and instinctively I know. There is no going back now.

21

R *yan*

OUR ROOM at the Ritz-Carlton San Francisco is awesome. It's huge, boasting a living room, dining room, large master bedroom with a gigantic bathroom, and views of the bay all the way out to Alcatraz. I shoot Claire a text telling her that I will be giving her a raise, and I get an emoji of a smiley face showing lots of teeth.

I also got an email from Luke stating that the software I wrote last spring is ready to go live.

It's that holy shit moment.

The one where you realize that your life will never be the same again. It's a weird dichotomy of emotions, because, on the one hand, I'm balls to the wall excited. On the other, I'm terrified. I've spent all my adult life living under the radar and this will thrust me into the limelight.

Thrust my company there too.

Katie is in the shower, so I call Luke while I have a moment.

"Motherfucker," he answers on the third ring, and I roll my eyes, sitting on the couch. "We're going to make Cisco security look like a pansy-ass joke. Your lawyer says we're good to go, and I've already sent out feelers. Guess who the first fucking call was from?"

"Who?" I have a guess already, but I know he's in the moment, so no sense in ruining his story.

"The goddamn FBI, bro. And I am *so* tempted to tell them where to shove their shit after everything that went down at Caltech."

True story: Luke went to Caltech, and I went to MIT. Both schools have underground hacking rings that compete. Luke and I were in the finals, and our mission was to hack into a global banking company. Stupid? You bet. But hackers sort of live under the umbrella of *no guts no glory*, so that's where we found ourselves. Luke got nailed by the FBI the same night he broke through the bank's firewall, and I didn't. No idea how they didn't see me—because I was in— but they didn't. Luke had every opportunity to turn me in. He knew who I was, where I went to school, and even what my handle was. The guy never said a word, which was stupid really since he was a poor kid from Oklahoma attending Caltech on loans and whatever he earned doing side jobs. I had already sold a few apps and had more money than I needed. So I procured him a kickass legal team that got him off with six months parole and community service. We've been tight ever since.

"Can we handle this new software going live, plus the clients you're trying to bring in, plus Tommy's app, *plus* our other shit?" I run a tense hand through my hair, feeling the overwhelming anxiety creep up my spine.

"We need to hire some people, Ryan. Like yesterday. If you don't want us to go big-time, then why did you give me this software to look at?" He has a point. "You've worked really hard to get here, man, and no one deserves it more than you. Between the accident, Francesca, the shit with your cousin trying to nab your money and turn you into the FBI, you've been through enough. I get that you're private, but you can stay low-key and still do this if that's what you really want."

"Fine," I sigh out, resigned. "Do what you think is best. I trust you with this." And I do. He's the only one I would.

"Right on. Where the hell are you *now*?"

I laugh. "San Fran."

"Same woman?"

Does he have to know everything? "Yes."

He laughs. "Awesome. Can't wait to meet her. Later." He hangs up, and I toss my phone down on the couch next to me.

If he gets to meet her.

I made love to Katie last night. I've never done anything remotely close to that before, but hell, that's exactly what I did. I even told her that I loved her, though I don't think she heard me since I mumbled it into her neck and she didn't react in any way.

I don't know what to do.

I know she's going to leave me when we get to Seattle.

I can feel it like the calm before the storm, and I have no idea how to stop it. I'll try, though. I'll try like hell because I can't imagine my life going forward without her in it. The idea of life without her feels colorless and dull, much the way it was before she entered it. I was simply coasting through. Working constantly and fucking faceless women as needed to release the tension.

I can't go back to that.

I need Katie.

But I'm trying to prepare myself for the inevitable all the same.

She walks through the double French doors into the living room. Her wet hair is braided over one shoulder, dampening the material of her white, long-sleeved shirt. Her jeans are tight and strategically ripped in various places, and she's got her black Chucks on.

She's so unbelievably beautiful it's almost too much.

"That shower is killer. I could move in and never want to leave," she says as she walks over to me, reaching out to run her fingers into my hair. "You ready to go exploring, or do you need more time?"

"Waiting on you, love," I stand up, looking down on her, daring her to challenge me with the moniker I've been freely giving her. She won't, of course, too afraid of the answer.

"Then let's shake our asses."

I laugh, leaning down to kiss her before taking her hand and leading her out the door of our suite. It's a sunny day, but only in the mid-sixties. Chilly, considering what we've been used to, but nice to walk around in.

We're only here the rest of today and tomorrow, so our plan is to explore near our hotel today and do Golden Gate Park tomorrow. We also have reservations for dinner, and I know Katie wants to hit up a particular bar tonight, so I think we'll do that after.

Walking hand in hand through Chinatown, Katie is the most animated I've seen her yet. She's talking constantly and pointing at a million different things.

She likes it here.

I can tell.

And for every positive thing she points out about the city, I find myself saying something negative. I realize it's a dick move, but I can't seem to help myself.

I just made some comment about the exorbitant cost of living when she stops me in the middle of the sidewalk, looking up at me with an expression I cannot read. Then without warning, she jumps up into my arms as I reflexively reach out to catch her. I'm laughing as I adjust her ridiculously light weight in my hands so that I'm holding her up by her ass—yup, I'm a pig like that.

Her arms are wrapped around my neck, and she's looking at me with a contemplative expression. "You don't want me to move here."

It's not a question, but I feel the need to respond anyway. "No."

"You want me to move to Seattle," she tilts her head, trying to read my face. Her platinum blonde hair glowing in the sun.

Again it's not a question, but I answer her without hesitation. "Yes."

She doesn't smile, and I can't seem to read what she's thinking, which is not the norm for her. After a beat of staring into each other's eyes, she leans into my ear and whispers, "What if I don't like Seattle?"

"You will," I tell her simply.

She pulls back to look at me and a wry smile is pulling at the corner of her mouth. Leaning in, she kisses me hard before wiggling herself free and standing on the sidewalk again.

"It *is* rather expensive to live here," is all she says, taking my hand and pulling me on. There's not much more I can say on the subject after that.

We spent hours roaming around, which was incredible. After our mini moment in the street, I stopped making disparaging comments and just enjoyed how cool the city is. It's really something else.

Streetcars and old Victorian-style houses and buildings, the ridiculous hills. I think my favorite was Chinatown. Katie's too.

We took a long nap and ate dinner in our previously appointed restaurant—again, thanks, Claire—before heading over to the bar Katie had heard about.

It is in a converted warehouse, so it's essentially a large open space with sky-high ceilings and exposed piping. Very trendy, with a heavy bass beat in the background as well as black mood lighting and candles. The bar takes up an entire wall with more shelves of alcohol than I've ever seen.

Katie spots a tiny place to sit off to the right, and goes to snag it while I get us a couple of drinks.

I finally manage to get the attention of the bartender and order Katie's apple martini and my whiskey when I feel hands sliding up my back. I spin around with a smile on my lips expecting it to be Katie, but it's not.

It's Francesca.

My smile dies instantly.

"Ryan Grant," she purrs, her dark eyes eating me up from top to bottom and then back again. "Fancy seeing you here. You look amazing. I like the beard." *Liar*, is the main thought that filters through my mind before, *what the fuck*?

She looks good too, but I'm not about to say that to her.

Her dark, stick-straight hair is down her back, and she's wearing the smallest of dresses that show off her curvy figure. As always she has on more makeup than I like, but that too looks good on her.

No doubt that Francesca is a beautiful woman, but she pales in comparison to Katie. It's not even a contest.

"Hello, Francesca. Nice to see you." It's not. That was a lie, but I couldn't think of anything else to say.

"What are you doing in San Fran? I know you didn't fly here," she muses as if my newfound fear of flying is comical. She was not the most attentive or nurturing after the accident, and that alone should have tipped me off to the type of person that she is.

"I'm traveling with someone. What about you?" And why is the bartender taking forever to make our drinks?

"I'm here for business, of course," she says as if I should already know. Then she leans into me, running her hand up my chest. "I've missed you."

I take her hand and pull it away from me, trying to extricate myself from her venomous clutches.

Francesca takes a step back, and as she does, her eyes widen before her expression turns superior and calculating. A small hand curls around my bicep, and I look down into Katie's sweet, smiling face.

She looks stunning in an ice-blue dress that brings out the color of her eyes, and dips low enough to give me the greatest view of her perfect cleavage. The only makeup Katie has on is eyelash shit, something that makes her cheeks glow, and lip gloss.

And she blows Francesca out of the water.

"That seat that I found for us was already taken," she says, either oblivious to Francesca's presence or ignoring it entirely. "It was too small for you, anyway. I would have had to sit on your lap in my tiny dress." I can feel Francesca stiffen, that's how close she is to us, before Katie's eyes turn in her direction. "Oh sorry," Katie grins at her. "I didn't mean to interrupt."

Francesca's dark eyes narrow as she scrutinizes Katie and then she reaches out a perfectly manicured hand. "It's not a problem. I'm Francesca. Ryan's ex-girlfriend," she purrs like it's a badge of honor. Does she not get the *ex* part?

"I'm Kate," Katie smiles, shaking her hand, before tilting her head to the side like she's thinking long and hard about this. It's an act. I know it is, but it's also driving Francesca wild that Katie didn't instantly admit to recognizing her name. "Francesca?" she muses. "Oh right." She looks up to me. "You mentioned her once, I think."

Francesca is fuming, and since she majored in bitch, I'm a little worried as to where this is headed.

"Well, I'm sure you haven't known Ryan all that long, since I've never heard of you."

I laugh, running my hand around Katie's tiny waist, pulling her into my side and kissing the corner of her mouth. "I've technically known Katie since I was ten and she was six, but we didn't reunite until recently. Anyway, it was nice seeing you again, Francesca." I turn my back to her and face Katie full on. "Don't worry about the seat," I shrug. "It's fine. Though the thought of you sitting on my lap all night in that dress does sound good," I smile, kissing her irresistible lips again. Her damn gloss tastes like raspberries. "The bartender is backed up, but our drink order is in the queue."

Katie waves me off. "Great. I'm in no rush. This bar is fun."

"Ryan?" Francesca places her hand on my arm, turning me toward her. "I need to talk to you. Surely your little *friend* here under-stands." Her eyes glare in on Katie before turning back to me with what is meant to look like an adoringly seductive grin.

"Not interested."

"Ryan, you can't be serious about this flavor of the moment." She looks at Katie. "No offense honey, but before me he was a fuck 'em and leave 'em sort of guy."

"Stop it, Francesca," I warn.

"No, it's fine," Katie says to me with her sweet smile. "You two should talk. I'll just run to the ladies' room."

"Katie—"

"Ryan, just let her go. Clearly, she wants to," Francesca says, step-ping into me.

I step back, toward Katie, who crooks her finger, drawing my head down to her height. "Talk to her, Ryan," Katie says in my ear. "It's not a problem, and if you decide you want her back, well, I get it. She's beautiful, and clearly still interested."

She kisses my cheek, and before I can say anything in response, she's gone. Now I'm fucking furious because Francesca just made my Katie feel like she's less than she is, and I can't stand that.

I turn on Francesca, ready to unleash holy hell on her. "What the fuck, Franny? How dare you speak to her like that?" My hands are fisted at my sides. The people standing around us all turn to look, but I don't care.

They can look all they want.

She waves me off like it was nothing, placing her hands on her hips. "Oh please," she steps into me again. "I've missed you, Ryan. So much." Her brown eyes, that I once thought were the be-all, end-all, shine up at me. "We were so good together."

"Good together?" I scoff. "Franny, you cheated on me." I don't really want to focus on that right now. It's hardly the point, and it doesn't matter. I shake my head slightly. "Whatever. I'm happy with Katie. Please, Franny, just go."

"You can't be serious about her, Ryan." Her mouth forms into a frustrated frown. "You barely know her." She's stomping her foot at me like a child who was denied a new toy.

"I *am* serious about her. I'm fucking in love with her," I point in the direction that Katie just went. "Katie is *all* I could ever want. So. Go."

"You can't be in love with her," she yells at me, pointing a finger into my chest. "She's using you for your money." She leans back, crossing her arms like she's just made the point of the century. "Or can't you tell what she's really after?"

I laugh out, humorlessly, crossing my arms the way she has. "Sort of the pot calling the kettle black, don't you think?" She looks confused. So dumb. What did I ever see in this girl? "Do you know where she and I slept last night? In the back of her damn Prius. She never complained once, because she thought it was cool and romantic." Franny rolls her eyes like that's beneath her, muttering something that sounds like *whatever*, but it's hard to hear in this stupid bar. "Katie could give two shits about money. In fact, she hates it when I spend any on her, which I love doing by the way." Yes, I'm being petulant, sue me. Francesca scoffs, turning her head to the side, her eyes rolling again. "She likes to run and hike and watch the sunrise, and she's goddamn perfect. I want *her*," I point again toward the bathroom. "Not you."

"She'll never love you the way I do," she sneers. "You think you love her, but she doesn't know you like I do."

"Oh. You mean she won't cheat on me with my friend? Or try to suck my money dry while complaining that what she has isn't enough and that she needs more?" I calm down.

Why am I entertaining this? Francesca is old news and I'm so done with her.

"But really, I should thank you. Without you being a cheating, money-grubbing, narcissist, I probably never would have gotten together with her." Does it make me a dick if I'm being completely honest with her? Probably, yeah.

Francesca tosses her silky mane over her shoulder and stalks off. I'm not usually one for confrontation like that, but I have to admit, it felt really good to do that. The irony of all of this? I'm not even angry with Francesca. I could care less about her and my blowing up like that was misplaced.

I'm angry with myself, and maybe with Katie a little too.

Finally, the bartender places my whiskey and Katie's martini down, and before he can walk off, I'm tossing my drink back and ordering two shots. Katie's hand glides along my arm as she slides in next to me, her back leaning against the bar as she turns to face me. Her drink in hand, she takes a long pull then licks her lips.

She always does that after she tastes something she likes.

It's sexy and adorable. Just like her.

"Yummy. That's good," Katie twists, placing her drink on the bar behind her before turning back and scanning the large open bar behind me. "Where's my new BFF?"

I reach my arms around her, placing my hands on the bar on either side of her, essentially caging her in. Katie and I have been dancing around this thing between us, and that little confrontation with Francesca made me want to clear the air...well, for the most part, anyway.

I know Katie doesn't feel the same way about me as I feel about her, but I don't want any more confusion.

This may be a stupid move that backfires on me, but we'll see.

"Katie?" I say quietly, but loud enough so she can hear me over the constant hum of voices and the heavy drum and bass beat. I'm a few inches from her face, and her eyes are widened in surprise and anticipation. No doubt as a result of my expression. "Francesca is a non-issue. She's gone and will never be a part of my life again." The spark of pleasure in her eyes drives me forward. "But you need to understand something once and for all."

Her teeth sink into her lip as the tension between us builds.

"I want you, Katie. Only you," my tone softens, and I reach up to cup her cheek, her head leaning into my touch. "I'm crazy about you."

"You are?" she breathes, but it's reluctant, as if she wants to hear the answer to the question, but is terrified of it all the same.

I nod. "Yes, but I know you already know that." She swallows hard, blinking up at me a few times. Her long dark lashes fanning her cheeks. "I'm not telling you this to pressure you into anything. I'm not asking you for anything. I know you're not ready for that. I'm just making sure you know, so there's no confusion going forward."

She swallows again and nods at me, her eyes glistening.

She's so damn gorgeous. Leaning in, my lips press against hers, and she instantly returns my kiss with the same level of intensity. When we pull back, she grabs my shirt, pulling me so we're against each other, chest to chest.

"I'm crazy about you too, Ryan," she says, looking up at me, our eyes locked. "I am. That's not what's holding me back. I can't...," she looks down quickly before meeting my eyes once more. "I'm not ready, and I'm sorry about that. I wish I were different. I wish things were different because I'd keep you forever. Part of me even wants that. I'm just...," she huffs out a heavy breath. "I'm just a mess."

"No, sweetheart, you're so unbelievably amazing." I wrap my arms around her, kissing her again. When we pull back, I can see the conflicted agony in her gorgeous blue eyes. "Let's not talk about this anymore. You know how I feel and where I stand, and I know the same about you. Now we can put it aside and try to have some fun tonight." I brush my lips against her jaw.

"I'm good with that," she smiles brightly, turning around for her drink only to notice the two shots I ordered are waiting for us. "Shots?" she throws me a raised brow.

"Yup," I raise a brow of my own. "You with me on this?"

"Hells to the fuck yeah," she laughs, bumping her hip into me. The serious mood from moments ago is gone, and we're back to being playful.

To being us. Even if being us hurts like a motherfucker.

22

I WAKE up the next morning sans clothing, with an alcohol-muddled brain and a mouth that feels like I swallowed sand. This is what two martinis and two shots gets me.

Ugh.

Rolling over onto my side, my hand slides to the spot next to me where Ryan usually sleeps, only to find it empty. Slowly I sit up, testing the waters to see just how roughed up I am. My head feels heavy, but not awful, and my stomach seems intact. In fact, I'm needing to get my hands on something greasy, stat.

"Ryan?" I call out, pulling the sheets up to my chest.

No answer.

Crawling out of bed, I throw on a pair of yoga pants and his t-shirt since it's on the floor and I like wearing his clothes. I think he likes it too. Walking through the doors into the living room, I find him sitting at the dining table, typing a mile a minute on his laptop while his cell phone is wedged between his shoulder and ear.

"No, Luke. I can't do that." He's listening, and I feel weird about standing here when he doesn't know I can hear him. "Because I can't," his tone is firm, but not mean. "I'm not going to be in Seattle until the middle of next week, and after tomorrow I'm going to be in the middle of nowhere, so I have no idea what cell service I'll have." I start to walk toward him, but he is too engrossed in what he's doing to notice. "You can handle it, Luke. I've known you to be very capable when it comes to wielding a computer's wiles." His eyes flash up to me and he smiles appreciatively, taking in what I'm wearing. "I gotta run. My distraction just got out of bed and I'd like to put her back in it."

I blush like a bastard, because I have no idea who this Luke is.

He laughs at something the guy says and then hangs up the phone.

"Morning, gorgeous." He places his phone down, clicks another button or two on the keyboard, and then closes his laptop. "I like you in my shirt, but those pants have to go."

"But if they do then I'll be naked underneath." I hold my hand up to my open mouth, widening my eyes in mock horror.

"True," he nods solemnly. "But I'm afraid I'm still going to need you to remove them."

Maintaining eye contact with him, I shimmy out of the offending pants, letting them rest on the floor next to me as I step out of them. "Now what, Master?"

His eyes heat instantly.

He likes it when I call him that, which I find just the tiniest bit amusing.

"Come here and sit on my lap, straddling me." He scoots his chair back, patting his thighs like I'm a puppy who needs to heel. I do as I'm instructed like a good little girl, and his hands slide up my naked thighs until they reach my ass where he adjusts my position to how he wants me. "Perfect," he breathes in my ear. "Now your shirt, love. I want to look at this beautiful body before I have my way with it."

Damn. The dirty talk gets me every time.

I remove his shirt from my body and then lean back in his arms so that my back is against the solid wood of the table. His eyes roam over me greedily, every freaking inch, and instead of feeling exposed or self-conscious, my blood heats like nothing else.

"What about you?" I ask, tilting my head. "You're wearing all of your clothes." He is. He's wearing running shorts and a worn gray tee.

"We'll get to me soon, but for now, I'm going to focus on you."

He lifts me off his lap in an effortless motion and sets my bare bottom down on the edge of the cool table. *Now* I feel exposed, especially when he spreads my legs wide open before dipping his head in between them.

Holy mother of Moses.

My back arches as my hands fly down to his thick hair. His mouth devours me, eating me out like I'm the best thing he's ever tasted. Like he can't get enough. He doesn't stop until I've cried out his name a full two times. After we're both completely sated, we shower and get ready to go out.

"Can we go eat now?" I moan, running a brush through my hair. "I'm so hungry; I'm wasting away over here."

He chuckles at me. "Yes, I can see that clearly. If we don't feed you soon, I'm afraid your health may suffer."

"Don't be a dick, Mr. Grant," I smack his arm. "You gave me lots of alcohol last night. With that comes the need for lots of greasy food."

"All right, all right. Let's go feed the hungry beast." He throws his arm around me as we walk out of our suite. "Do you want to eat in the hotel or go and find a place near the park?"

"Um," I look up at him blinking. "So I checked and Off the Grid is open on the far side of the park today."

"And what is Off the Grid?" he asks, scrunching his eyebrows.

"Food trucks," my eyes widen with excitement, and he laughs at me.

"You want to eat from a food tuck?"

"You bet your sweet sculpted ass I do," I tease, pinching his butt and making him laugh.

"Whatever my girl wants, my girl gets," he jests, kissing the top of my head.

But his words make my stomach flip, and I can't tell if it's in a good way or a bad way. I like his words. I like him calling me his girl. But at the same time, I can't stand it. Eric called me that when we were in high school, and now I'm feeling the sting of guilt.

Ryan knows where I stand.

I'm not ready.

I didn't hold back at all last night when I told him that, but still.

I choose not to say anything to him about it. I don't want to hurt him with the reminder, and at this point, it's like beating a dead horse —I've always hated that idiom. His arm is slung over my shoulder and my fingers are laced through the hand draped against my chest as we take in the beautiful city around us.

I could live here. I like San Francisco. A lot. But I'm not going to say anything about that to Ryan either.

After we scarf down some amazing Korean barbeque à la food truck, we set off into the park. I'm dying to see the waterfalls and botanical gardens. Ryan is interested in the Japanese tea gardens. I think tea is a vile substance, but what the hell? The architecture will be killer.

"So you're really up for camping in the freaking redwood forest for the next two nights?" he asks as we get closer to Strawberry Hill. Have I mentioned that I'm in love with this park?

"I know it sounds crazy, but how else will we be able to explore it?"

His head nuzzles into my hair. "I'm okay with it, sweetheart, but it's going to be balls cold, especially at night, and there won't be showers or probably even a lot of bathrooms."

I laugh, nudging his ribs. "You afraid of me being smelly, or that I can't handle roughing it?" I'm actually a little—or maybe a lot— nervous about this camping thing. I've never done it before, and I'm not known for being all that outdoorsy.

"Smelly I can handle, I may even like it, but it's not as if we can swim in the streams or anything."

"All right. I get it. How about we do one night of camping, and another night in a hotel?"

"I just want you to be happy, love. I don't know how happy you'll be freezing your ass off with no shower or toilet paper."

"Point taken. What if we got a sleeping bag and camped out in my car again? That was fun in a weird, hysterical crying, sort of way," I look up at him with a bashful smile.

Talk about a night of ups and downs.

"Maybe. Let me look into some stuff and we'll go from there. Agreed?"

I nod emphatically. "Agreed."

"Help!" someone cries out as we get closer to the falls. "Oh my god. Help us!"

I look at Ryan, and before I can think too much into it, I'm running at a full-out sprint toward the sound of the voice. More cries for help guide my way, and as I reach the wooden bridge that overlooks the falls, a man is hunched against the railing, holding his chest.

Fuck. It's an MI.

"Hi," I touch the shoulder of a tall, thin woman with spindly graying hair, and wildly terrified brown eyes. Her head snaps around to me, and the second she sees me, relief flashes through her. "My name is Kate and I'm an acute care nurse. What's going on?"

I walk over to the large-bellied, middle-aged, balding man who is sweating profusely despite the cool temperatures. He's panting, grabbing his chest, and as I get closer, I see his coloring isn't right.

Shit. This is bad.

"I don't know," the woman says frantically. "We were just standing here, and then Gerald started grabbing his chest saying that it hurt. A lot of pressure, he kept saying."

"Gerald, I'm Kate," I touch his shoulder, trying to pry him away from the railing so I can move him over to the bench that's not too far off. "Can you walk at all?"

"I don't know. It hurts. A lot of pressure." He's rubbing his sternum and can barely hold his weight up.

I look to the woman. "Did you call 911?" I'm trying to stay calm, but this is dire. If I don't get help for this guy, he's going to go down. Soon.

"I don't have my phone with me," she starts sobbing.

Ryan finally catches up to me, looking around anxiously. "What's going on, Katie?"

"Ryan," I'm so fucking glad he's here right now. "Call 911. Tell them we've got a probable MI. A male complaining of chest pain, shortness of breath, and diaphoresis." He's looking at me like I just spoke in Chinese. "Just call 911, Ryan. We need them here, stat," I bark at him. He gets where I'm going and pulls out his phone. "How long have you been having pain, Gerald?"

"I don't know," he manages, but it's getting harder for him to talk, and his breathing is even more labored. "Five minutes, maybe? I wasn't feeling all that good this morning." I sling his arm around me and walk us to the bench, using Herculean strength to get him there since he weighs a ton and isn't able to help much. Setting him down, I lean him back so I can evaluate him better and give his body a rest.

"Are you on any medications?"

The woman who I assume is his wife is next to me now, hovering over him.

"Yes. He's on Atenolol, baby aspirin, and Lipitor."

Awesome. "Do you happen to have any of those medications on you?" I ask, putting my fingers to his wrist to try and get a pulse rate. I'd fucking kill for my stethoscope right now.

"I have his aspirin," the lady says, and I can't help the mild relief that flashes through me.

"Perfect." His pulse is thready. Not good. We're in trouble here. Big time. "Take out four of them and give them to Gerald to chew."

"He already took his dose this morning and he's only supposed to take one," she tells me like I'm trying to kill her husband instead of helping him.

"I understand that...," I trail off since I don't know her name.

"Sharon."

"Sharon," I echo, "but I'm trying to save your husband's life right now. Aspirin is first-line treatment when you're concerned about a heart attack, which is exactly what I believe Gerald is having." Both of them look at me, but there's no sense in candy-coating it. "Give him the four pills now, please," I look over at her with a grin that says I'm in charge, but is also calm and reassuring. I've mastered it during my tenure in the ED and ICU. "I know what I'm doing. This is my job."

She nods, fishing through her bag to find the bottle.

"Ambulance is eight minutes out," Ryan announces, joining us by the bench. That's not stellar, but not much I can do about it. "The operator is on the phone and she'd like to speak to you."

He shoves the phone into my hand and steps back, not knowing what else to do.

"Hi. This is Kate," I say as I bring the phone up to my ear.

"I'm Sophia, the 911 operator. This call is being recorded on an open line. Can you tell me more about the situation? I have dispatch listening in as well." This chick is all business. I freaking love 911 operators. It may be the hardest job in the world, but they do it damn well, and I have nothing but the utmost respect for them.

"Yes. I've got a man in his mid-fifties, I'm guessing," I get a thumbs-up for that, "complaining of chest pain times seven minutes. He's diaphoretic and short of breath. Describes a lot of chest pressure. His wife informs me he's taking Atenolol, Lipitor, and baby aspirin. She had the aspirin on her, and I've instructed him to take an additional four of those. He's bradycardic with a pulse of forty-six and it's thready."

"Okay, Kate. I've noted the patient's condition and dispatch has been notified as well. Can you tell us anything else about the situation that would be helpful for the responding team?"

"No," I turn away from them and take a few steps and speak quietly. "But they need to hurry up because this guy is going to go down soon. I can just feel it."

"I hear you," Sophia says in a deeply soothing cadence. "They're four minutes out. Just do what you can. I realize that since you are a nurse, you're at least familiar with basic lifesaving."

"I'm an ED and ICU nurse. I'm ACLS certified. I'm on it, but let's hope we don't get there." I turn around and walk to Gerald, who's looking like he's seen better days. "I'm going to hand you back to Ryan so I can attend to Gerald. Thank you, Sophia. You're aces."

I hand the phone back and sit next to Gerald, trying to check his pulse again. "I feel like I'm going to be sick," he rasps out, still clutching his chest tightly.

"I know, Gerald." I squeeze his other hand. "I've got you. Just keep taking slow deep breaths. Help will be here soon." And just as the words leave my mouth, I hear sirens getting closer.

Thank Christ.

Ryan looks like a fish out of water and is constantly running his hands through his hair with the phone pressed to his ear as he paces an apprehensive circle. Sharon is trying desperately to hold herself together, but is losing this battle quickly as tears are starting to stream over onto her cheeks.

"Sharon, I hear the paramedics coming," I look her dead in the eyes. "You need to hang on and stay strong."

She nods, understanding the gravity of my words. We're all scared, no doubt about that, but pacing and falling apart will only make this situation worse.

Suddenly in a whirlwind, paramedics, police, and maybe even the fire department descend upon us.

They're shooting questions a million miles a minute, and everyone, including poor Gerald, looks to me for the answers. I relay everything I know about the situation and the paramedics get Gerald hooked up to oxygen and set up an IV of fluids while checking his vital signs—which are not stellar.

They strap him to the gurney in no time, and before I can even process what's happening, they're running off with him. Sharon follows, calling a thank you over her shoulder. Once everyone is gone and the scene is calm again, I drop onto the bench in an exhausted heap and then burst out laughing.

"What?" Ryan looks at me, startled by my reaction.

I shake my head. "Whew," I run a hand across my forehead wiping away fake sweat. "That shit was intense. I really thought poor

Gerald was going to crash any second and that I was going to have to perform CPR on him in front of his wife."

I'm still laughing, which is just a weird reaction for me to have.

Must be the adrenaline aftereffects or something.

I've done this hundreds of times. I've been in dozens of codes, held hands while people died in front of me, but that was always in a work setting. Always surrounded by other healthcare professionals and in the hospital.

I had nothing with me to help him, other than myself, and that's a terrifying thing.

"Damn, that was a crazy rush."

Ryan laughs now too, coming to sit down next to me. "You were incredible. I was scared shitless. I didn't know what the fuck to do."

"You were perfect," I take his hand. "You called for help and didn't panic on me."

"Do you think he'll make it?"

I shrug. "I honestly don't know. The fact that he was still conscious when they got to him is a good sign, but if I had to guess, I'd say he was having a rather large MI."

We're silent for a few moments before Ryan asks, "What do you want to do now?"

I look up at him and smile. "It's a beautiful day, Mr. Grant. We should go and enjoy it while we can. Life is too goddamn short and unpredictable not to." And I want as much time with you as I can get before this trip is over. Clock's ticking.

23

R *yan*

"HOLY BOOGERS, IT'S COLD," Katie says, huddling into herself as we hike down one of the bigger trails in the redwood forest. We left San Francisco at seven this morning, and the drive up here took almost six hours.

We did stop at a camping outlet store near here, which was a good thing because Katie's right, it's cold. Northern California is having an unseasonable cold snap.

Lucky us.

It's in the low forties and there is no sun in the thick forest to warm us.

"Katie, baby, as much as I applaud your rugged spirit and all that crap, there is no freaking way I'm camping tonight. Not in the car or on the ground."

"Totally freaking agree," she nods emphatically. "But you have to admit that despite the cold, it's so pretty here. I love hiking. I think I'd like to live in a place where I can go for hikes."

Looking down, I nudge her with my elbow. "You realize Washington State has plenty of places to hike?"

"I see where you're going with this, Mr. Grant," she arches an eyebrow at me.

"Actually, I was thinking."

"Oh?"

"Since the weather is less than wonderful here, what if we head up to Portland tomorrow and get to Seattle a day early?"

Katie stops dead in her tracks, looking up at me. "Why?" She's trying to keep her expression neutral, but I can see the hurt in her eyes. She thinks I'm trying to end this.

Why can't she see that I need her to stay?

That I just plain need *her*?

"Because we haven't really factored any Seattle time into our plans. I mean, I'm moving there, and hoping you'll consider doing the same," I raise two eyebrows up at her, seeing if she'll balk at that. "What if we get there a day early and spend it going around the city?"

She blinks up at me. Once. Twice. "Okay," she eventually says in a slow, even tone. "We could do that."

I sigh, because I have been avoiding this shit, and it's just absurd at this point. After that near-death escapade with Gerald yesterday, I'm sort of in a carpe diem way of life.

"Katie? What are your plans for when we get to Seattle?"

She's silent for another twelve steps. I know because I can't help but count them out.

"I don't know, Ryan," she tilts her head up at me. She's so short when she's wearing her sneakers, it requires some effort to actually look down at her while maintaining our pace. "I uh...I haven't really let myself get that far," she laughs out uncomfortably. "I mean, I know it's coming up really soon. Sooner now than before, but I was sort of doing my *living in the moment* thing."

"Okay. But if you *had* to think about it? Do you think you'd consider staying on, or do you plan to leave shortly after getting there?" I need to know. I need to prepare myself for the reality that I'm almost positive is coming.

She's leaving me.

"I might," she half-whispers. "I have no doubt I'll love Seattle, Ryan, and it is possible that I will choose it as my new home. You'd certainly be a very strong reason for that." She reaches out a small hand, grasping my jacket and pulling me to a stop to face her. "I care about you. So much. I hope you know that."

She looks down at the worn dirt and gravel-covered path.

"I've told you I'm not ready for a relationship. That hasn't changed despite my feelings for you. I uh...," she looks up at me again. "I need more time. To think, ya know?"

I nod. I do know. I have known, which is why I tried to separate myself from her in the first place. Create some distance once I realized the true nature of my feelings for her—realized just how completely obsessed with her I was.

But then we kissed, and everything I tried to stop, could no longer be.

I love her.

I want to tell her that, but it's not right.

Not the right time. It would just confuse her more. I don't want her to stay with me out of manipulation or a sense of obligation, or anything like that.

I want her to stay with me because she wants me. Wants a life with me. A future with me.

She doesn't, and I have to learn to live with that.

Despite how it fucking destroys me.

"Okay. I was just curious," it's all I can manage, so I start walking again, and I hear her shoes crunching against the earth, indicating that she's doing the same.

We're silent for a while, just walking and looking around at the natural beauty surrounding us, but it's gotten progressively darker the farther in we go. I'm about to suggest we turn back when she stops, her hand out, palm up to the sky. "Was that rain I just felt?"

Just when I'm about to tell her I don't feel anything, I do. *Shit.*

"Yup. It's rain. We should head back before it comes down on us." And then the sky opens up and it begins to pour.

"Shit. Run." I grab her hand and we run like hell.

We're a few miles in and it's coming down hard, so when I spot a fallen tree trunk that's hovering several feet off the ground, wedged against another tree, I lead us there.

"We'll have to wait it out. Let's hope it's just a passing shower."

"Seriously," Katie laughs, ringing out some of the excess water from her hair and then throwing it up on top of her head into a bun. "Dude, it's freezing now. What the hell?" She shivers and I throw my arms around her, keeping her against me, because I'm cold too. And wet. Being cold and wet sucks. "So Ryan, now that we're stuck in the forest in the middle of a rainstorm, we should get to know each other better."

I laugh at the playful tone in her voice. Katie really does just roll with the punches, doesn't she? "Sounds like a plan." I kiss the damp, rain-scented top of her head. "What do you want to know?"

"I want to know about your work, but if you still don't want to tell me, that's cool too."

Shit. Why does it always come back to that? "What specifically do you want to know?" I'm trying not to get annoyed, and I get her wanting to know since I've been way too cagey about it, but still.

"I know you do cybersecurity. That you own your own business. That you do favors for your friends. But I also know there's more you're not telling me."

"Look, Katie, I've had trouble in the past with people I thought I could trust. I'm sorry for being so secretive about it, I'm just...cautious."

"You don't have to tell me. I get that you don't know me all that well, so I can understand you not trusting me with something like that."

She's not saying this in a harsh or mean way. Or even a scheming, fake-hurt way. She's being totally genuine, which makes me feel awful.

Do I trust Katie? Yes. I do.

But I also trusted Tristan, and look where that got me. Fuck it. *Katie is not Tristan.* Katie may in fact be the purest, most honest person I've ever met.

"I started out as a computer programmer in college. I'm *very* good at writing code and creating software and...that led to hacking into things." She's silent, just letting me speak with her head still pressed against my chest. "You know I created some apps in college, and that's true. I also did other things that weren't so...legal. That all stopped when a fellow competitor got busted by the Feds and I didn't."

She pulls in a rush of air, but doesn't comment or react beyond that.

"After that, I used my skills to help *prevent* cybercrime," I emphasize. "And yes, friends ask me to check out their stuff to make sure it's good, and as it should be," I sigh because here comes the rough part. "I've created a piece of software that is going to change cybersecurity. It's—thus far—an impenetrable system that will protect servers and systems from cyberattacks and malware. It's going live in the next few weeks, and that's going to give me and my company a lot of press."

"And that's a bad thing?" She can tell by my voice that it is. At least, it feels like it could be. I squeeze her tightly against me, needing her warmth and comfort, her smell and essence.

Just fucking needing Katie.

"Shortly after college, I told my cousin Tristan about some of my misadventures in school, and how I got some of my money," I breathe out hard, the air fogging in front of me. Damn, it's cold. "Katie, you need to know, I never stole from anyone. I wasn't going around taking what didn't belong to me. But I did some things I'm not entirely proud of and...I profited from them." I rush through the last part, feeling as ashamed as always when I think about it. "I'm a different man now. You understand that, right?"

She nods her head against my chest. "Yes. I believe you."

The sincerity in her voice causes my eyes to slam shut, before opening them just as quickly. I'm so crazy for this woman.

"My cousin tried to blackmail me. Said he'd go to the Feds and turn me in if I didn't pay him several millions of dollars."

Her head snaps up to look at me, eyes full of pain and sympathy and maybe a little overprotective indignation for me. Jesus, that feels so good to see.

"He was in with the wrong people, which I didn't know about at the time. Needed the money to pay them off. Anyway, he ended up getting arrested before any of this could happen, and then he tried to tell the Feds about me, though they didn't seem to care much. There was no proof of anything against me, and all my money *appeared* to be explained by the software and apps I had created." I stroke her cold moist cheek, her chin resting against my chest. "That's why I don't like press or attention. That's why I don't like notoriety or to talk about what I do. I'm trusting you with this because I don't think you'll go behind my back, and I doubt you're after my money." I try for a smile, but I'm sure she can see how bitter it is.

She snorts. "I could care less about your money, Ryan. Believe it or not, I have plenty of my own. Some of it I have no intention of spending. *Ever*," she punctuates with widened eyes. "As for going behind your back, I could never ever do that. You're a good man," her fingers glide across my bristly cheek as her eyes sear into mine, "and I understand that you may have done some things that were not on the level, but we've all done things that we regret. I'm not judging you, and I'm certainly not going to betray the trust you've just imparted in me."

I love you.

I want to say those words to her so badly my chest and throat are burning with the restraint to hold them in.

So I do the only thing I can do.

I kiss her and let it tell her for me. Her words mean everything to me. I've never met anyone quite like Katie, and I'm going to have to fight like hell to keep her.

"What do you mean you never intend to spend some of your money?" I ask when I'm done kissing her.

She shrugs a shoulder against my chest. The rain is still pounding all around us, but the large tree trunk is keeping us reasonably dry. Definitely not warm, but we'll take what we can get right now.

"My dad left me money when he died. My mother already had more than enough for herself, and he left me a large chunk. I've spent that on occasion throughout the years, but I've saved most of it. I also have money from the sale of my house, which I've also used as needed, which again, isn't often."

She sighs heavily, puffing the plume of white exhaust at me.

"Eric had a trust fund that he had set aside and was going to leave to our children. When he and Maggie died, it was passed onto me. I will never spend that money." Her tone is so unyielding that there is no room for argument. "I've offered it to his parents, but they declined. They've got more than they'll ever be able to spend, and Eric's older sister has a trust of her own and didn't want it either. So I'm stuck with it," she sighs out. I can tell she despises that money. Loathes everything it represents. "I could donate it, and eventually I probably will, but I can't decide where, so it just sits accruing interest."

"Why don't you want to keep it? Use it?"

She turns her head, looking out into the rain, staring out into the thick forest without really seeing it. "Because I hate the idea of profiting from his death. That money makes me sick."

"I can understand that."

"Do you need to find a place to live in Seattle?" she asks, changing the subject after a quiet moment.

"No. My assistant, Claire, found me a furnished house to rent in the city."

"That's cool. Do you know what it looks like?"

I shrug. "It's a house. Bungalow-style or something. Updated, but not overly modern. I like more comfortably nice than modern or stuffy nice, if that makes sense?"

"It does. What made you go for a house instead of an apartment or condo?"

"I didn't want to buy yet. That would definitely require me being there to see the places, and I like houses. I'm not big into strangers living above or below me."

She laughs. "No, I imagine you wouldn't be. And yet, you've

managed well with me for the last however many days, haven't you?"

She's teasing me now, but that doesn't make her wrong.

I've never been one to live with other people. Even in college, I always had my own space. But living with Katie is easy. She's not demanding or needy, and I *like* spending all my time with her.

"It will certainly be an adjustment if you make me give that up." I'm trying for light and failing miserably.

"If?" she asks, looking up at me again. "You don't want me to live with you? Right?"

How the fuck do I answer that loaded question when she asks it like that? "What if I said I did?"

She blinks up at me before breaking eye contact. "I don't think I can do that, Ryan."

"I know, Katie. I'm not really asking anyway."

"So you have a house." She keeps going like that small *living together* moment didn't happen. "What about a car?"

"It's being shipped along with the rest of my stuff."

"Ah," she says like it all makes sense. "I was wondering why you only had one suitcase with you."

"I have more stuff than what I brought with me. My car, boxes of crap, more clothes, that sort of thing."

"Why didn't you drive your car out yourself?"

I'm shocked it's taken her this long to ask. "For one, my car is a bit on the older side and I was worried it wouldn't love the trip. Two, you offered to drive me, and there was no way I was going to pass that up." I pinch her side through her puffy jacke,t making her giggle and squirm. "The rain looks like it's letting up. Do you want to risk it?"

"If you can deliver me to a place that is warm, dry and possibly offers access to a large bathtub, you'll be my personal hero."

"Who the hell can turn down that challenge? We might have to run a bit, though."

"Then it's a good thing my ass is in excellent shape."

"Yes, it is, so move that hot ass before I decide to spank it again."

Katie throws me a wicked grin. "We can play that game later."

She winks and then starts to run. We were further in than I

thought, and it takes us close to a half an hour of running in the wet, freezing cold to get back to the car. By the time we do, we're both exhausted and drenched.

"Whose brilliant idea was it to go to the freaking forest?"

"Yours."

"Oh, right." We turn on the car, blasting the heat and head back toward the highway and the coast. "Do you know where we're going?"

"No," I laugh out. I pick up my phone, unlock it, and call Claire, who picks up on the second ring. Bless her. "Claire, we're outside the fucking redwood forest, and I need a hotel that is warm, dry and has a large bathtub." I throw Katie a wink, and she laughs under her breath.

"On it like a bonnet," Claire says. "But you do realize you're in the middle of fucking nowhere, and it may be difficult for me to find the type of accommodations you're used to, right?"

"Whatever you can find for us would be great. We're stuck in the car and internet access sucks around here."

"You got it, boss."

"I hate it when you call me that."

She laughs in that raspy tone of hers. "I know. That's *why* I do it. I'll shoot you a text in a moment. Later, skater."

She hangs up on me, and I can't help but smile.

Claire was born decades too late, but she's adorable in a twenty-two-year-old little sister sort of way. Two minutes later she texts me an address, which I punch into the car's GPS and we head off. We arrive at a bed and breakfast that is situated on a cliff overlooking the ocean. It's really just a small house, but I don't care and neither does Katie.

The innkeeper—I guess is what they are called—seems like a friendly enough guy, and leads us up to a large room with a king-size bed, a fireplace that is already lit with a roaring fire, a terrace over-looking the ocean, and a large en suite bathroom. He tells us break-fast is at eight, and then he leaves us alone.

Katie stands in front of the fire, enjoying the heat. "I'm going to take a bath," Katie wags her eyebrows suggestively. "Wanna come join me for a swim?"

I laugh, but it quickly gets stuck in my throat when she starts to shimmy out of her wet jeans. I swear, watching Katie strip naked will never get old.

"Lead the way, doll."

She starts the bath, making sure it is up to temperature and dumping some smelly, flowery shit into the water to make bubbles. I light the candles that are strategically placed throughout the space.

She smiles up at me softly and then slips into the water, closing her eyes briefly as her cold skin makes contact with the warm water. It's a claw-foot tub, and not a large one at that, so even as I climb in behind her, it's awkward and uncomfortable.

"You don't have to stay," she laughs out as I try again to change my position, sloshing sudsy water everywhere. "But if we ever do this again, I'm demanding a gigantic tub."

"Noted," I laugh, getting out and wrapping a white fluffy towel around my waist, but I don't want to leave her, so I pull the small stool that was sitting in the corner over, and perch myself on it next to the tub. "Can I wash your hair?"

She shakes her head.

"It will be a pain in the ass in this little tub," she gestures to the limited space around her small wet body. *Fuck.* "We'll shower together after?"

"I'm good with that," I say, leaning in to kiss her soft, full lips. "What's our plan for tomorrow?" Resting on the edge of the tub against the cool cast iron, I continue. "Portland is like a seven-hour drive. I'm not against it, just curious what you want to do."

She leans back, her wet hair resting on the tub as she cups handfuls of bubbles, placing them over her exposed skin. I'm completely mesmerized by the motion.

"I'm liking the idea of a day in Seattle." It's something I did not expect her to say, but can't help feeling good about.

"Then Portland tomorrow it is. We'll have to wake up, eat breakfast, and go."

She frowns. "It's the last of our long trips." I nod but don't say anything else. She knows where my mind is. "I'm sorry," she whispers, looking down at the disintegrating bubbles. "I shouldn't have let this happen."

"What?" I'm both alarmed and pissed, because just what the fuck?

Her blue eyes are watery when they find mine.

"I've got a shit ton of baggage. We've been talking around and over this again and again. I feel like I'm playing with you, and I hate that. Fucking *hate* it, Ryan." Her glistening eyes bounce back and forth between mine. "I'm still a mess, and I knew that going in, and yet...I couldn't resist you. I've never felt like this before," she continues. "So conflicted. So unsure of what to do." A tear spills out over her eyes and down her cheek, but neither of us moves to wipe it away. "I don't want to hurt you," she says on a sob.

"I know, Katie. I know. I got into this with my eyes wide open. You've hardly made your feelings for me, or about us, a secret. If I get hurt, it's on me."

She shakes her head, her expression pained. "That doesn't make me feel better."

"What would?"

She bites her lip, sinking lower into the tub. "That's just it. I don't know. It's like I can't stay away from you, though I know I should because I'm no good for you."

"Don't I get to decide who's good for me?"

I'm starting to get exasperated again. It's not like she lied to me. Not even once. She's been crystal clear on everything. And sure, maybe I should have heeded her warnings before this became all that it is, but too fucking late.

"Any time with you is better than no time at all." I mean that.

"That's how I feel too." She bites into her full soft lip.

"So, no plans then. We'll see where we go and how we end up."

"I'd like to go to Seattle and look around. See if it fits."

Fuck, I can't stop the smile. "I'd like that too."

"Okay then," she offers up a weak smile. "It's settled, but I have an idea for tomorrow that you may or may not like. We'll see, but I'd like you to promise me that you'll keep an open mind about it."

I narrow my eyes at her, and she just blinks up at me innocently through her ridiculously long lashes. She's fooling no one, and she knows it. "I'll do my best to keep an open mind."

Katie smiles triumphantly. "That's all I can ask for. Now, help me out of this tub so we can shower together and go have sex in front of the fire."

"Such a demanding little sprite, aren't you?"

"And you wouldn't have me any other way," she winks as I pull her up from the tub. Water splashes all around, dripping down her body. Damn, that's one hell of a sight.

"No. No, I wouldn't." *I'd keep you as you are forever if you'd let me.* Now to get her to agree to it.

24

K *ate*

"WHAT THE FUCK?" Ryan practically yells as we step out of the car early the next morning. We're on the long strip of land they call a private airport around here.

I know I'm really pushing my luck here, but I don't want him to be controlled by his fear. Ryan means the world to me, and I need to do this for him before I leave. *If I leave.*

"What the fuck, Katie?" he asks again, and I step in front of him, which does not block his view of the private jet since I'm so short and he's so tall. But I need his attention for a moment all the same.

"Ryan. Look at me." He does, but it takes a moment for him to pull his eyes away from the small plane. "I'd like us to fly up to Seattle today. It's a short flight. A little more than an hour, but I think you need to conquer this."

I can see the dread radiating off of him. He's terrified, and though I feel bad about that, I think it's something he can do. He's so strong.

"I can't, Katie." It's a whisper. "Please don't make me." It's a plea.

"Baby?" I call up, and his head snaps down at the endearment because I've never called him anything other than Ryan. "I won't make you do anything." My eyes burn into his so he knows my words are one hundred percent sincere. "I would *never* force this on you. But you're living across the country from your family. What happened to you was a freak thing. An awful thing, but rare all the same. All I'm asking is that you try. Maybe just step on board with me and see how that goes. Can you do that?"

He stands there, frozen, for the longest time. His eyes bounce back and forth between mine and the plane.

"I'll be with you the whole time."

He takes in a heavy breath and releases it slowly. "I'll step on board, but no promises, Katie. I don't think I can do this."

I smile up at him. "That's all I'm asking." I reach out and take his hand, interlacing our fingers. His hand is clammy as hell, but I won't release him.

As we approach, his grip on my hand tightens, pulling back a little, but I urge him on and he reluctantly follows.

We walk up the short staircase that leads into the main cabin of the small plane. It's nicer than I thought it would be, and the pilot is standing outside the cockpit waiting. I've never been on a private plane, and in truth, I'm a little excited by it, but I quickly curb my enthusiasm.

"Hello," the pilot who looks like he's in his mid-forties says with a smile and deep, sparkling chestnut eyes. "I'm Steve, the pilot of this vessel. It's nice to meet you both." He reaches out his hand to shake both of ours.

"I'm Kate and this is Ryan. Thank you for letting us sit on board for a bit. We're still not sure if we'll be flying today," I inform him.

He smiles wider. "Not a problem. Take all the time you need. I'm available for questions if you have any."

"Thank you," I say, and try to take a shell-shocked and silent Ryan further into the plane.

Steve goes into the cockpit, giving us our privacy.

The cabin looks like it can seat about eight people. There are two leather seats that are side by side, directly facing another pair of matching chairs, with a long, narrow, wood table between them. On the other side, a small couch is pressed against the window, and further back behind the chairs is a forward-facing love seat with another narrow table in front of it.

That's it.

All the seats are cream-colored leather, and look comfy and plush. The wood accents and tables are all dark mahogany stain.

"Katie," he says my name in a panicked tone, staring at the seats like they're going to jump up and attack him at any moment.

"Come sit on the love seat with me," I say gently.

I can feel his raised body temperature even though I'm about a foot away from him, and his hand is trembling in mine. He follows me to the back of the plane where the love seat is.

"Look. There's a minibar." I point across the aisle at a small bar stocked with a mini fridge, a small ice maker, sink, glasses, and a few bottles of alcohol. "I know it's early, but do you want something to help you relax?"

"No." He shakes his head and sits down rigidly, his eyes are the only thing moving as he takes in his surroundings. I walk around him and sit down right up against his side. "Why are you doing this to me?"

Damn, his words cut me.

"Because you're too strong to live in fear. Your family is far away from you now, Ryan, and there may come a time when you *have* to fly to them. I don't want your life to be restricted by this."

"I don't think I can do it."

I climb onto his lap, staring into his bright-green eyes that are stocked full of fear.

"I think you can, Ryan, and I'll be here next to you the entire way. If it becomes too much, Steve said he could land somewhere along the way. But if you can't, I *completely* understand, and I will support you no matter what."

"What about your car?"

"I've made arrangements for it to meet us up in Seattle if we do this."

"What about Portland? You wanted to go to Portland."

I smile, running my fingers through the black bristles of his beard.

"I can go to Portland whenever I want. You're more important than Portland, Ryan." I brush my lips against his. "Do you think this is something we can do together, or do you want to leave?"

He stares at me, looking deeply into my eyes for the longest of moments. I let him. He needs this time and I won't be the one to interrupt it. Finally, he takes a long unsteady breath.

"I'll try, Katie, but I don't know how well I'm going to do." He's shaking his head back and forth. "I haven't been on a plane since the accident, and that was by far and away the worst moment of my life. Not just the sheer terror I felt when the plane was going down and then crashed, but waking up with broken bones and incredible pain, and seeing the dead pilot, not knowing where I was, or if I could even get help...," he trails off.

I get it. Fear is a nasty fucking bug that can take over and control everything.

I cup his face in my hands. "I will be right next to you the whole time. We'll do this together."

He gives me the tightest, smallest nod I've ever seen, but I'm going to take that as a yes.

"Steve?" I call out. "We're a go."

"Sounds good," he yells back. "I'm going to start the engine and notify the car service of your plans."

"Thank you."

I smile up at Ryan and then we hear the rumble and loud keening sound of the engines starting.

"I'm going to move so that I can buckle up next to you." His hands become rigid on my thighs, holding me in place on his lap. His eyes snap shut, clenching tightly. "Or I can just sit like this the entire flight." Another nod. "I'm really proud of you, Ryan." I lean in to kiss him.

I really freaking am. He's so goddamn brave.

"Save your praise. I'm not sure I can do this." He shakes his head again, and when his eyes open, they're wild. "This is crazy." His voice is manic. "What the hell am I doing? You're lucky I love you as much as I do; otherwise I'd never do this. I couldn't stand flying before the crash, and right now, I'm about two seconds away from embarrassing the hell out of myself and crying like a little bitch."

I smile. Fucking hell, he just said he loves me.

Shit, that shouldn't make me as happy as it does.

"You said you love me." I'm grinning like an idiot, but I'm also trying to distract him since the plane is officially moving now, albeit slowly.

His eyebrows knit together, and he blinks at me a couple of times, then he realizes what he said, and his expression softens. "I did," he confirms. "I do." His hands tighten on my hips as he looks at me so adoringly, my breath hitches. "I love you, Katie. So much."

The plane rumbles and I can feel the motion of us moving, but Steve had told me on the phone that he would just go and not say a whole lot unless it was needed, and right now, I think Ryan is adequately distracted.

"I know I wasn't supposed to say that, and I've been holding it back for a while now, but apparently it just slipped out, so..."

I interrupt his rant by pressing my lips to his.

Softly at first, and as I feel the plane start to pick up momentum, I deepen it, running my fingers through his hair and driving my body closer to his. His hands slide back to my ass and he squeezes.

I should be freaking out about the "L" word, but I'm not, which feels odd. I've rolled the word around in my head when thinking about Ryan, but felt so wrong in using it.

I don't know what my future is—whether it includes him or not. I can't get past this suffocating guilt that lives inside of me.

I feel like I'm betraying my husband.

That's a rough thing to move on from, and I certainly haven't been able to do it yet.

But... "I love you too," I whisper against his lips, wondering why those words aren't making me sick.

He stills, his lips hovering over mine, his eyes wide open and unblinking. "Did you really say that, or is the panic-filled adrenaline making me hallucinate?"

Ah, so he does know that we're finally up in the air.

"I said it." I don't know if I can do it again, but the words are out there, and I meant them.

Oh god, I'm so sorry Eric, but I meant them. Fuck, I love them both so much. How is that even possible?

"Did you—" he swallows hard. "Did you just say it because I said it and that's what people do when someone says it?"

I smile. He's so adorable when he's like this. A little psychotic maybe, but adorable. "No. I meant it."

"Who knew those simple words could totally take over the impending sense of doom, and fire, and death; I've been feeling since I saw this fucking airplane you coaxed me onto?"

"Then I guess my work here is done," I smile into his lips, giggling a little when he pinches my side.

"No way. Your sexy ass is going to sit on my lap for this entire nightmare, and when we land—which we better by the way—I'm going to fuck the ever-loving shit out of you. I may even spank you until your beautiful bottom is red." I raise an eyebrow at him. "Don't play coy with me, Mrs. Taylor." *Shit, did he have to use my married name?* Heat rushes through my veins and not the good kind. It's the kind that says I'm a traitorous bitch. "I know you like it like that."

All I can do is nod and offer up a tight smile.

I want out of this airplane. I want off of his lap and out of his arms and away from him this instant. Oh my god, I just told him that I loved him. Why did I do that? I've only ever said those words to Eric.

How could I have done that?

We've reached our cruising altitude and I can feel Ryan relax beneath me, but only a little. His body is still tense and his hands are gripping me like I'm his talisman.

Thank god he's too preoccupied to notice I've completely checked out on him.

What a horrible person I am. On so many levels and to the two men I love most in this world. What am I going to do? I want so many things, and yet I feel like everything I'm doing and everything I want is wrong.

Wrong, wrong, wrong.

"Katie? How much longer?" Ryan's eyes are scrunched shut again and he's sweating. I suddenly feel so bad for suggesting this flight.

"We'll be there soon, baby. Just stay with me," I whisper, kissing along his neck the way I know he likes.

"While I appreciate your stupendous distraction techniques, I'm starting to lose it, so if we could land soon, I'd really be grateful. Even more so if we managed to do it in one piece."

I turn my head to the side and can faintly see the Seattle skyline in the distance. It's a rare clear day—cold, but clear—so I can see the tall skyscrapers.

"We're getting close. Do you want to see the city you're moving to?" His eyes are still shut as he shakes his head.

"Twenty-five until we're on the ground," Steve's voice says on the intercom.

"In one piece," I add, but get no smile.

Ryan is holding onto me firmly, crushing me to his chest, and while I'd like to move so I can buckle up, he's not letting me go.

Something comes over me and I start to sing Love Song by The Cure, as I run my fingers through his hair.

It was what I always did for Maggie when she was hurt or scared.

And just as it worked with Maggie, it's working with Ryan.

He's settling into me, relaxing more and more as the minutes tick by. I don't know if it's the words or the hair thing, or the soothing way I'm trying to sing, but the tension in his jaw and eyes wanes.

As the plane descends into Sea-Tac Airport, Ryan's arms snake around me and he holds onto me for dear life, breathing hard. "Almost there," I whisper.

"Sing again," he pushes out.

So I do.

I start the song all over again and sing just as softly as I was before. He's not melting into me this time. He's a ball of rigid muscle and overwhelming fear.

The plane makes what is quite possibly the smoothest landing I've ever experienced, and once Ryan knows we're safely on the ground, he begins to shake uncontrollably.

"Ryan?" I ask cautiously, running my fingers through his hair and hoping he'll open his eyes to look at me. Maybe I did push him too far. *Shit.*

"Shit," he says, echoing my inner thoughts. "That was so fucking awful. Holy mother of shit that was one of the worst and best hours of my life," he laughs out now, but it sounds a bit hysterical. "Don't ask me to do that again, okay? Only if there's like an emergency and the *only* way I can get where I need to go is by flying."

"I promise. Are you mad at me?" My voice is so small, but he shakes his head, and I can't help but sag into him.

"No. But I am spanking you later."

I laugh, wrapping my arms around his neck and kissing him soundly on the lips.

"I look forward to my punishment, Master," I whisper seductively in his ear, and I can feel his smile against my cheek.

We made it to Seattle.

25

K *ate*

SEATTLE IS BEAUTIFUL. No denying that as we drive in the rental car I reserved—my car won't be here until tonight—toward Ryan's new house. I'm nervous and scared and excited and sick, and everything else a person can feel.

Once we got off the plane, Ryan admitted that he was glad I made him do it, but only because I was with him.

Ugly truth? If he does have to fly again, chances are I won't be with him when he does it.

And yeah, that makes me feel like total and complete crap, because I told Ryan I loved him and I meant it.

I do.

But that doesn't really change the places my mind goes, or how I feel about what I'm doing or my situation. I don't want to leave Ryan, but I don't know if I'm strong enough to stay. If I'm in a healthy enough mental state to fully commit to a man who deserves nothing less than everything.

And yet, every time thoughts of leaving Ryan flit through my mind, my heart aches.

I want our happiness, but the guilt is overwhelming, and until I can figure out how to be with someone other than Eric, it's not fair of me to stay with Ryan.

We pull onto a really nice street that seems to be only a block or two from a main area of shops and restaurants. The houses here are a mixture of good-sized bungalows and craftsman-style. His house is actually the latter and it's big.

Almost too big for one person.

The exterior is a nice, deep gray without being too dark, and the front door is a brick-red, which contrasts nicely. There is a large front porch with two white rocking chairs and a swinging bench off to the right of the door.

We pull into the driveway and the second he turns off the car, I have to get out of it. I can feel the weight of his stare on me, and I don't know what to do with his eyes looking at me like that.

The neighborhood is exclusive. Expensive. And since we're high up on a hill, the views of Puget Sound and the Olympic Mountains in the distance are phenomenal.

Like holy crap, multi-million-dollar view, phenomenal.

He pulls a small keychain that I've never seen before out of his pocket, thumbs through the two keys on it, and inserts one into the front door. He's been silent since we got in the car and right now, the nervous energy is flowing off of him in waves.

Or maybe that's just me—hard to tell, really.

The lock disengages with a satisfying click, and he opens the door to what is quite possibly the most beautiful home I've ever seen.

Gleaming, wide-plank, medium-tone hardwood floors are the first thing you notice, and they seem to stretch throughout the entire house. Off to the left is a massive living room with comfortable looking couches, an intentionally distressed coffee table, two chairs—both the softest looking leather I've ever seen—and a giant flat screen television placed above the mantel of a gorgeous stone fireplace. Behind the living room is an open-concept dining area with a table that can seat at least eight.

On the right side of the room is a large office space that can be closed off by sliding glass doors, and beyond that appears to be another spacious sitting room of sorts, and even farther back is a sizable four season sunroom.

The kitchen is—well, it's my dream kitchen, that's for sure.

It's huge, with the longest center island I've ever seen, topped with Carrara marble above some type of stained wood cabinet that complements the flooring perfectly. The fixtures are all very contemporary and top of the line, including an eight-burner gas stove, double ovens, massive side-by-side refrigerator, and even a wine refrigerator with two separate zones—one for red and one for white.

Yes, I checked it out, how could I not?

Behind the kitchen is an extensive deck with more of those amazing views, and since it's a sunny day, the whole house seems to be filled with warm natural light. Everything is sort of open and cool and modern chic, yet comfortably contemporary. It's all so very Ryan, and I can only imagine how much this place costs him every month.

I don't linger in any room long, desire and curiosity to explore the entire house taking over.

The upstairs is more of the same hardwood floors leading into three bedrooms, all a good size except for the master, which is easily twice the size of the other two bedrooms.

Off to one side are windows with unobstructed views of the Sound and mountains, a ginormous king-size bed with a low-profile fabric headboard, and on the far side of the room is a broad, distressed dresser. The walk-in closet is twice the size of my old bedroom in Boston, and what could only be described as the most fan-fucking-tastic bathroom ever finishes off the space.

Warm, strong arms wrap around my waist as I stare almost blankly out the window at the view I could easily see myself looking at for the rest of my life.

"What do you think?" Ryan asks, his nose gliding shamelessly through my hair to my neck.

"I think it's beautiful."

"I think you're beautiful," he says, nuzzling into me, my body automatically melting into him. "What are you in the mood for, love?"

I shrug a shoulder. "Did you want to go and check out your new neighborhood?"

"Sure. We could find the best places to eat and grocery stores. Crap like that. Or I could take you out to see what the city has to offer? Since we're here an extra day early, we have more time before I have to get back to the real world."

"Whatever you want to do, Ryan. It's your new home."

"It could be your new home as well."

"I know."

He leaves it at that, taking my hand and leading me outside. We end up standing on the sidewalk in front of his house. "Now what?" he asks with a chuckle.

"Dude, you're the computer guy. Look it up," I smirk.

He pokes me in the ribs, and then after punching something into his phone, we set off, heading down the street and to the right. We end up on a main street that is filled with restaurants, shops, and a high-end natural grocery store.

"You hungry, Katie?" he asks as we stop in front of a Thai place.

"Stupid question, my friend. I'm always hungry. Lead on."

"Have I told you that Thai food is my favorite?" he asks after we're seated in the nicer-than-expected restaurant.

"You have not, and I feel a little shortchanged that I'm just finding this out now, after living in a car with you for more than three weeks."

He laughs, taking a sip of his water. "What's yours?"

"Seriously?" I ask, raising an eyebrow at him.

"What? You never said something specific, just that you like everything."

"Fine. I guess if I had to pick a favorite I'd say tapas."

"Really?" he asks, surprised.

"Yeah. There was this restaurant in Boston. Holy hell. The food was amazing. Like straight from Spain amazing. Eric and I used to try and go there on date nights a lot, but it was a tiny place and one could not make reservations, so if you went, you waited. Not the best when you have a toddler at home with a babysitter."

"No," his eyes widen as he thinks about this. "I imagine not."

"But yeah, I love Spanish tapas."

"Would you ever want to go?"

"Where?"

"To Spain?"

I snort. "To Spain?" I repeat, a little surprised by his question. "Sure. I'd love to travel the world a bit. Never really had the chance."

"But you do now." Why does he have to sound so sad when he says that?

I nod in agreement. "I do. And I suppose I also have the means, but I'm not about to do it. It's the sort of thing I've always wanted to do with someone. Not alone."

"So if I said I'd like to travel the world with you, you would say...," he trails off, tilting his head at me.

"I would say you don't like to fly an hour, let alone several, so I'm not sure how feasible that is."

"They have drugs I could take. You're avoiding my question, Katie."

I am. Damn his observant ways. "Of course, I would love to explore the world with you, Ryan. Wanting to be with you isn't the issue here."

"Ah. So you admit there is an issue then?"

I sigh, rubbing my hands up and down my face. I don't want to have this discussion now. I want to enjoy the day with him.

"You want to do this now?" I ask through my hands.

"That depends on how the conversation is going to turn out." He's silent for so long that I drop my hands and look at him. "When do you plan to leave?" He knows. I hate that he knows, and yet I'm a little relieved at the same time.

"Tomorrow?" I sit back in my chair, taking a sip of my water because my mouth is so freaking dry suddenly.

"And where do you think you'll go?"

"I'm not sure exactly."

"Are you still looking for a place you want to move to?" He's so stoic and reserved that I can't read him. I can't tell where this is going.

"No." It's the truth. I'm not. I just need...

"So you've found a place you think you want to move to?" He's leaning back in his chair too, but his arms are folded across his chest, hard and unrelenting in their power and the way they keep us at a distance. Or maybe they're just protective.

"I think so."

"And it's not here? With me?" His tone is growing austere. Angry even.

Don't do this, Ryan. Not yet.

"I didn't say that," I protest quickly. "I didn't. I just need—"

"More time," he finishes for me, annoyed.

I nod. "Yes."

"So was that whole "I love you too" thing bullshit? A way to keep me calm on the plane?"

"No," I say, shocked and indignant that he'd go there. "Of course not."

"So you're saying that you love me, you just can't be with me?"

Fuck. "Not right now, no."

"But you think maybe someday?" He's so pissed. I don't blame him, but still. It's hard to hear and hard to see, and hard to handle.

The waiter interrupts us and we place our orders, though my appetite is almost completely gone. When he leaves, I can see Ryan is waiting for my answer.

So I guess he does want to do this now.

"I love you, Ryan. I do. So much." His harsh expression doesn't alter because he can feel the *but* coming. "But you said it yourself on the plane. *Mrs. Taylor.* In my mind I'm still married to Eric, and I don't know how to shut that off. I don't know how to reconcile loving two men and how that works. How to love you the way you deserve while not betraying Eric or his memory." I'm wringing my fingers in my lap.

"Katie," he leans forward, his features softening, which is not what I expected. "I understand that you still love Eric. I expect you always will. I'm not asking to replace him, sweetheart. I'm just asking for you to give us a chance and see where it goes."

"I know. I know that," I'm nodding.

"But you're still not ready."

I shake my head no.

"Will you ever come back?" he swallows hard and so do I.

"I don't know, Ryan. I'd love to say yes. I'd love to tell you that my world will all make sense again in a matter of weeks and that we'll live happily ever after, but I can't make that promise, and I can't ask you to wait for me while I work out my fucked up mind."

"And if I want to wait for you?"

"Ryan—"

"No, Katie," he snaps, interrupting me. "Don't you think that's my choice? Don't you think I should get to choose who to love and how to do it?"

"No one chooses who they love."

"Ah. So you wish you didn't love me? Is that what you're saying?" He places his forearms on the table, resting his chest on top of them and killing me with his eyes. "I'm an inconvenience to you and this little voyage of emotional discovery you've set yourself on?"

I can't take this anymore. I just fucking can't.

Getting up, I walk around the table, and as I approach him, he leans back in his seat. I don't care that we're in a nice restaurant in the middle of Seattle with people staring at us. I need him to understand.

Climbing onto his lap sideways, I take his face in my hands until he's forced to look into my eyes.

"That's not it at all. You're not an inconvenience, or a regret, or anything else negative. You've reopened my closed-off world. You've given me so much, I can't even begin to tell you how grateful I am, or thank you for it. But I'm not fully there yet. I still have a lot to figure out and work through, and it's not right for me to drag you into that."

He laughs humorlessly, shaking his head like I'm not making sense. His hand comes up, rubbing up and down my spine.

"Okay, Katie," his tone is resigned. "I get it, and I can't argue it with you, because your mind is made up on this. But you should know that I love you. That I'll always love you, and that I want you no matter what. So if you need time, fine. Take time. But you need to understand that I plan on fighting like hell for you."

Shit. I smile huge at that. "You're a fucking rock star, aren't you?"

He laughs, kissing me. "If that's what it takes to eventually make you mine, then sure." If love were easy and played by the rules, I would be his forever. But it's not always that simple. Is it?

26

K *ate*

OUR THAI FOOD IS AWESOME, and I have a feeling that since they deliver, Ryan is going to be eating it often. We didn't talk about anything serious for the rest of the meal. In fact, my new best friend, Luke came and met us.

A little odd? Sure, but what the hell.

Luke is...well, what can I say about Luke?

He's a wiseass in the best sense of the word.

That and he's *hot*. Not quite Ryan hot, but certainly delicious in a very different sort of way. While Ryan does the whole bearded, glasses man-of-mystery thing, Luke does the whole tall, dark, and handsome thing. His hair and eyes are both the same chestnut brown, but the mischief in those eyes is unmistakable.

He's irresistible that way.

Promising all kinds of trouble that you just can't help but say yes to.

Luke made it his personal mission to show us around not only Ryan's new neighborhood, but he also brought us down to the famed Pike Place Market.

Super cool.

Okay, I admit it.

I'm a fan of Seattle.

I mean, come on, flying fish? Who could turn that crap down? No one, that's who. And then there's the beautiful waterfront, and the trees, and the mountains, and the cool shops, and eclectic mix of people.

Yup, I may just love it here.

Ryan held my hand the entire afternoon, laughing and smiling and chatting easily. I was worried. I was even freaking out a bit.

I'm hoping that maybe he understands things finally.

But that whole fighting for me thing? What do I do with that?

Other than eat it up with a spoon? Because as much as I want him to have a real life and not bother wasting it on me, I *want* him to fight for me.

I also love the fact that Ryan has Luke.

They're easy friends, even though the majority of their interactions are ribbing each other. But in all seriousness, I'm having the best day.

"Duchess Kate,"—Luke calls me Duchess Kate— "You seem like a rad adventure girl," he says as we get to the city center. I can't help but laugh, because really?

"Sure I am," I say with a smug grin.

"Then you'll fly up the Space Needle with me?"

"*That's* an adventure? Puh--lease."

He laughs. "Tell that to Mr. Serious over here." He hooks his thumb at Ryan who just rolls his eyes.

"Why do you keep calling him Mr. Serious? Is that meant to be ironic?"

Both guys look at each other, but Luke is giving that smile again. The one he's had all afternoon, and if I weren't in love with Ryan, it would totally make me tingle in the best of places.

It doesn't, though, FYI.

"Because those MIT boys are boring as all fuck," Luke says. "They created lame-ass nicknames for each other. It was like some sort of cult, or initiation into mediocrity or something."

Ryan snorts, pulling me in closer to his side and kissing the top of my head. "And you Caltech assholes really had it going on," he says sarcastically. "Do you know what Luke's handle was when we were in school, Katie?"

"Obviously I don't, Ryan. I was slumming it in high school while you old-ass dudes were busy playing your reindeer games."

"Can I take her, Ryan? Please? Just for a while. I probably won't give her back, though," Luke says, smiling down at me with mock seduction.

Or maybe it's real. So hard to tell with him. *Damn.*

"Try it, motherfucker, and watch what happens."

"Both of you shut up. I want to ride to the top of the Space Needle and you're wasting my time." I look over at Luke. "We doing this shit, or what?"

"Fuck, I'm in love," Luke says, bringing a hand up to his chest over his heart like he's been struck. "You should come with us, man, or I may just stick my tongue down her throat and call it an accident? Or not an accident? Depends on how much she's into it," he shrugs.

I laugh, but Ryan doesn't. He's too busy staring daggers into Luke, who's smiling like the cocky bastard he is.

"Come on, baby, ride up to the top with me." I pull on Ryan's hand and he looks down at me. I think he likes it when I call him baby. In fact, I think it may have superpowers where he's concerned.

He groans, but allows me to drag him along. The ride up is fast and cool, and the views of Seattle, the mountains, and the water, are unbelievable.

Ryan's arms are wrapped around me as we walk along the globe of the observation deck.

"I'm going to miss you," he whispers into me, and I can't help but lean into him. Can't help but want to soak up every single second of my time with him.

"Sometimes what you need is not what you want." It's really all I can offer at this point.

"Maybe. But sometimes what you want is *exactly* what you need. Come here." He drags me over to the glass window and poses us for yet another one of his selfies. He doesn't really strike me as the type of guy who likes taking pictures of himself, or even being in them for that matter, but he takes them of us frequently.

"You guys really do make me sick," Luke says, watching us smile for the phone. "Your cuteness is disturbing."

I shrug. "Probably right, but what can you do?"

"Do you have a twin sister, Duchess?" Luke asks. "An identical cousin, or something like that?"

"Nope. Only child, Luke. So if you like the blonde hair, blue-eyed thing, maybe you should bounce down to California. There was plenty of that when we were in LA."

"Yeah, but I don't really like bleach and plastic. And you forget I lived there once myself. Pasadena is a bitch-slap away from LA."

I laugh. "A bitch-slap? I can't tell if that's ironic or derogatory."

"Could be both, Duchess Kate, could be both." His hand reaches out, touching my waist.

"Luke, I think it's time you get your paws off my girl and get your punk-ass home, before I fire you and find another low-life, mildly talented asshole to take your place."

Luke shakes his head with a half-smile. "Not likely my friend. I'm the best of the best, and the lowest of the low—in that order. It's completely impossible to replace me." He reaches out his hand, and he and Ryan do some sort of bro-shake-hug thing. Luke winks at me, leaning in and giving me a lingering hug and slow kiss on the cheek. "Bye, Duchess Kate. It's really been a pleasure. And if you ever tire of this big guy, come find me. I'm *way* more entertaining."

After Luke leaves us, Ryan and I continue to walk around the top together. I turn to him with a big smile. "I like Luke. I'm glad you have a buddy here."

Ryan gives me his crooked smile. "A buddy? What am I, six?"

"I'm sorry, did you say sex?" I ask, keeping my face impassive.

"Yes. I definitely said sex, so move that *sexy* ass of yours so I can get you home and take advantage of you."

"I believe I am deserving of some spankings."

He groans, dropping his forehead to the top of mine. "Killing me, Katie. Killing me. I never thought of myself as a man who would enjoy spanking a woman, but I am, and I'm dying to turn that round perfect ass a lovely shade of pink."

"Funny, because I never thought of myself as a woman who would *enjoy* being on the receiving end of said spankings, but I am, Mr. Grant, and it's all your fault."

I'm teasing him, but his expression turns serious as he pulls me in, kissing me deeply.

"Then I guess we're meant to be together, Katie."

I swallow hard and don't respond.

How can it feel like what he's saying is right when I always knew I was meant to be with Eric?

By the time we get back to Ryan's, it is late in the evening, almost dinner time. We decide to try out some of the delivery services in the area as we light a fire and curl up in front of it.

Ryan hasn't stopped touching me once.

Not once.

Like he's stockpiling it for when I'm gone.

"The food is ordered, and they assured me it would take at least forty-five minutes to get here."

"Oh," I laugh. "They *assured* you of that, did they?"

He nods, taking off his glasses and setting them down on the coffee table. "They did indeed, love. Now get that bottom over here. I'm not going to tie you up right now, due to time constraints, but I am going to spank you for making me get on an airplane this morning, and then I'm going to fuck you crazy."

Holy hell, I can't help but squirm.

My cheeks are on fire, as is the rest of my body. He walks me over to the edge of the rug between the coffee table and the hearth then strips me down slowly. His eyes rake in every inch of me, memorizing the slopes, and curves, and shades of my skin. I don't think I've ever been so turned on in my life.

He takes off his shirt and jeans, but leaves his black boxer briefs on. Twirling his finger in the air, indicating that he wants me to turn around, I do as I'm told, only to realize that the shades on the window are open.

"Ryan?" I ask nervously. "The window."

"Is facing the water and the mountains. No one can see in, sweetheart. I'd never share this with anyone." His hands run up and down my skin, leaving delicious shivers in their wake. "Bend over," he whispers in my ear, and my breath catches.

My legs threaten to give out on me as I bend forward, placing my hands onto the coffee table and closing my eyes. *Smack!* Ryan's hand hits my ass before rubbing it soothingly to ebb the sting. It doesn't really hurt. He's not hitting me hard. It's just enough to make me feel it.

He does this five more times, and by the time he's done, I'm panting and struggling to hold myself up. Suddenly I feel his mouth kissing and licking and sucking on my sensitive burning flesh, and I can't help but moan loudly. His fingers find me and he releases a moan of his own, before his mouth replaces them.

I wouldn't say I'm sexually innocent, but I've never had someone go down on me from this angle, or been this exposed while experiencing it. It takes me no time at all to reach my climax, and when he slides inside of me, it's the ultimate connection.

"Katie," he moans my name over and over. "I'll never get enough," he groans.

I know the feeling.

We come together in the most spectacular way and just as we finally manage to catch our breaths, the doorbell rings, making us both burst out into laughter.

"I hope he didn't hear us," I giggle.

"If he did, he can't be anything but jealous, because that was earth-shatteringly good." He kisses the tip of my nose before getting up, throwing on his jeans—sans boxers—and going to the door.

I dress quickly because even though I'm off to the side and am blocked from view, I don't exactly feel comfortable lying here naked on the carpet with the delivery guy only a few feet away.

Ryan and I eat penne in vodka sauce and chicken parmesan in front of the fire and the television, watching the new Star Wars movie on the huge flat screen. It's heaven, so fucking ideal I want it to last forever.

But I feel the clock chiming inside of me.

The ever-present tickle of guilt.

The hint of betrayal, and the sting of longing, turn my insides out and cause my chest to clench in the worst way. I cling to Ryan, unable to stand even an inch of space between us, and he's only too happy to hold me just as close.

I want to beg him to never let me go.

To fight the way he said he would.

To be patient and give me time to figure everything out. But I don't. Instead, I silently sit here and watch the movie, breathing in his scent, which is starting to feel like my home, and enjoying this suspended moment in time.

Because it won't last.

In fact, it's just about up.

27

R *yan*

I KNOW before I open my eyes and reach out my hand that she's gone. My bed is cold. My house quiet. My heart is aching.

Dammit, Katie, how could you run out in the middle of the night?

I should have known she'd want to avoid a big goodbye. I should have expected this.

But I didn't.

I didn't, and now I'm crippled with it.

I could go out and try to find her. Try to bring her back and make her stay with me forever, but I won't. There is no point. She wanted to go.

"Fuck!" I yell out, slamming my fist into the rumpled sheets on her side of the bed. Moving my body over, I bury my face in her pillow, inhaling her smell. The best fucking scent in the world. Katie.

I miss her. It's only been a couple of hours since she left, and I already can't stand how much I miss her. The doorbell rings and it takes me less than a second to fly out of bed, throw on my glasses, and run down the stairs in only my boxer briefs. Maybe she went out to get me coffee and a Diet Coke for herself. Maybe she didn't leave me.

I fling the door open and want to punch the shit out of the face on the other side. Fucking Luke. Why is he here?

And why is he not Katie?

"Why do you look like you're about to pull out a knife and stab me to death on your front porch? And why are you answering the door mostly naked? Even though I think you're good looking, you're just not my type," he winks. I'm not in the mood for his shit right now.

"What do you want, Luke?" I snap, hoping he'll just go away and leave me to search the house for Katie before breaking something large and heavy when I convince myself that she's actually gone.

"Breakfast, man. We talked about it yesterday, remember? Duchess Kate invited me." He's scrutinizing me closely before his eyes wander past me into the house. "Where is Duchess Kate?" He can sense that something is off, and I don't think I can bring myself to say the words out loud.

"No breakfast today. Just go." I start to close the door when his hand reaches out to stop it.

His eyes flash with confusion before transforming to realization. "She left you, didn't she?"

Does he have to sound so sympathetic about it? It just makes me want to punch his face in all the more. When I don't respond, he runs a hand through his short brown hair that he probably spends a small fortune to have cut.

"Fuck, man, I'm sorry. Are you okay?"

"What the fuck do you think?" I yell at him, unable to contain my fury any longer and taking it out fully on him.

"I think you love her."

"Go away, Luke," I point toward the street behind him. "Please. I can't deal with you and the shitstorm that's going on inside my head."

"Do you want to go out and get drunk? Or laid maybe?" His hands fly up when he sees the rage creeping up my face. "Okay, not either of those things. But I don't want to leave you alone right now. Have you tried calling her?"

I shake my head, sighing out in frustration because he's not going to fucking leave. "No, asshole. I knew she was going to take off. It's not like she didn't tell me before doing it."

"I don't understand. Why would she go and tell you about it beforehand?" Luke walks past me into my house, ignoring the death look I'm throwing him. Heading into the kitchen, he plops down on one of the black leather barstools.

"Because she's been through a lot of shit and isn't ready for a relationship, or anything like it for that matter."

"But she loves you," he states firmly and clearly, like there isn't a doubt in his mind. "I freaking saw it, man; otherwise I wouldn't have messed with her or you so hard."

Luke is also getting upset now. He liked Katie. I know he did. For me, he liked her. Maybe for himself a little too, but I'll ignore that.

I shrug, walking over to make myself some coffee. My head is throbbing so bad it feels like it's going to explode.

"You know we could always hack her phone or her credit cards? Find out where she went, and then you can show up and do the whole big romantic gesture." I throw him a look that says *shut the fuck up now*. "Okay, fine. No hacking or grand gestures of love. So you're just giving up?" He can't believe it, and neither can I.

But I'm not giving up.

I'm just giving her what she asked for.

Time.

Once I get the coffee going, I turn around to face him, but the look in his eyes is not one I want to see, so I move my attention to the window instead.

"I'm not giving up. I love her. I'm just giving her some space and time."

"Fine. You know the situation better than I do, but all I'm going to say is don't wait too long. You two were good together, and I only spent a couple of hours with you."

Does he have to be such a good friend? It's odd, but right now, I don't want comfort or platitudes, or brilliant words of wisdom and advice. I just want to deal with this by myself and wallow in my own self-pity.

I have nothing to say back to that, so I pour myself a cup of the black stuff, hoping it's the cure for the pounding in my head. It's not. Only one thing can make me feel better, and she's off somewhere without me.

Somewhere unknown.

Dammit, Katie.

"Let's go eat. I'm hungry. And I don't think you sitting in this house is the best idea." Luke stands up to his full height—which is an inch or two shorter than me—and waits, his eyes locking onto me like a vise. "I'm telling you, man, when things went to hell with Ronnie, I only got into trouble when I was home alone."

"I'll be fine, Luke. Really." I run a hand through my hair as I sip my coffee. "And I'm not hungry."

"Fine. No food. Do you want to work?"

Do I? I don't know. It's certainly a distraction, and I could use one of those about now.

"What kind of work?" I ask, moving to the large island and setting my plain black mug on top of the marble with a clink.

Luke smiles like the devil himself. "Pen testing?"

"Pen testing what, Luke?" I have zero patience right now.

His smile grows wider. "Tommy's shit?"

I laugh, and oddly, it feels good despite the vacuous hole where my stupid, pathetic, traitorous heart should be. "Sure, man. Let's fuck up Tommy's shit and see if we can nail his balls to the wall."

He laughs too, but the gleam in his eyes tells me he's excited. "A grand says I get in before you."

"You're on, motherfucker."

I run upstairs and change into some clothes. As comfortable as Luke and I are around each other, I'm not going to sit around him in my boxers. My cell phone is still on my nightstand and I can't help but look.

Nothing. No call. No text. No nothing.

Dammit, Katie.

I thumb through the pictures that I took along the way—sort of like I knew I'd lose her and would need them—and scroll all the way back to the beginning, to our first night in DC when I got Tommy to take a picture of us.

I didn't even know her then.

She was just the girl I had dreamed of my entire life—the girl from my memories, and fantasies, and wildest imagination. I select the picture and text it to Katie.

This was my plan. I told her I'd fight for her, and I intend to.

So I'm going to send her a new picture everyday—maybe more than once a day—of our trip. Of our time together.

Of us.

Katie is nostalgic as hell. She lives in her memories. I intend to implant myself firmly into them. She'll see me and feel me every day. She'll know that I'm thinking about her. Missing her.

And I will make damn sure she's doing the same about me.

Luke is right. I could hack her without much energy or effort. But I'm not going to—though it is tempting as hell. She doesn't even know this, but I've already linked our phones so I could just press that pesky app and find her right now. I did it after that asshole in Charleston tried shit with her. I did it as a precaution. As a safety measure.

But now? Now I could use it to find my girl.

My girl who doesn't want to be found.

Nope. I'm not going to give in like that. I'll give her what she wants with a caveat of my own. If she doesn't like it, she can change her number.

She won't.

She loves me. She wants me. She's just scared of what that means for her and her past.

The text goes through and I smile, tucking my phone into the back pocket of my jeans since I don't expect her to text back. No, my girl is far too stubborn for that.

"You better not have started without me, dickhead," I say once I get into my office and find Luke sitting with his computer already set up on his lap, comfortably lounging on the small couch behind the desk against the window.

"Nope." He looks up at me as I sit in the plush leather office chair, opening my own laptop. "Are we going to tell Tommy about this little infiltration, or just let him sweat about it?"

"As much as I'd love to let him get his panties in a twist, I think after we crack his shit wide open, we should tell him it was us." Tommy is a mediocre programmer at best. His real talent is having good ideas, but he often relies on others to make them happen.

"You're the boss, but if you don't get your ass in motion, I'm going to smoke you in a matter of minutes."

"Sure you are." My arrogance is usually well-founded. I'm very good at what I do. It's why companies from all over the world come to me. Why I never got caught when I did something worthy of getting caught for.

I'm cautious. Quiet and controlled.

And even though companies do come to me, they don't actually know who I am. I'm a faceless name. And ever since my fuckwit cousin tried to dox me to the cops and the Feds—oh, and blackmail me for my money, can't forget that—I try to fly even more under the radar.

But my new software is going to change that, and I have to accept it. Get used to it. Maybe even embrace it.

"I'm in," I exclaim, only to hear Luke hiss out a slew of curses. That distraction lasted all of five minutes.

Great.

But today is the first day in almost a month that I didn't wake up and see Katie. That I didn't get to look at her smile and hear her laugh, and see her blue eyes sparkle and light up.

I miss her. I fucking *miss* her.

It's amazing how fast it happened.

She became my world overnight, and within a matter of days, it was impossible for me to imagine living without her. But here I am, living that nightmare and not knowing what to do with it.

Empathy can be a real rude awakening, and for the first time, I understand her. Not exactly. I mean, I didn't lose her completely. She's not dead, and there is a chance I could see her again. Have her again.

But I can empathize with her inability to let her family go. To believe that they were her entire world and that she can't go on fully without them.

I get it now, Katie.

I only had her a few weeks.

She'd had Eric for almost fifteen years. Maggie aside, because that's a pain I pray I never experience, and no one can fully heal from that. But Eric? Yeah, I may be starting to get that a little.

I want my girl back.

I want her to walk into my house and hold her small, curvy body on my lap and kiss the hell out of me until I'm convinced she's never going to leave me again.

Loss sucks.

Life without Katie sucks.

It's like all the color that surrounded me these past three weeks has been obliterated. Zapped out, leaving me stuck in varying shades of gray.

Luke and I dick around with Tommy's stuff for a while, working silently side by side. It's good. We haven't done this in years. Not since right after we graduated.

Well, I should say after *I* graduated.

Luke got kicked out of school, and I hired him once he was let off with a small slap on the wrist. He's got his own things going on the side, which is fine as long as he doesn't get nailed for it. I don't ask and he doesn't tell, except to swear to me that it's not illegal.

I'm not sure if I fully believe that, but whatever.

I wonder where she could be, where she decided to go.

Back to San Francisco? I know she loved it there, could see herself living in the city. Maybe she went back to Portland since we skipped over all of that stuff. Maybe she said *fuck the West Coast* and headed back east.

I really have no clue.

She never mentioned her plans, except to say she wasn't sure.

The notion that she's gone forever is more than I can handle. It's like a sucker punch to the big, gaping hole in my gut. How am I going to sleep without her warm softness beside me tonight?

I can't believe how much I miss this girl. Every small thing about her.

Dammit, Katie.

That seems to be my new theme. Dammit, Katie.

I knew she'd wreck me, and yet I let her in, so maybe I should be damning myself.

"You're zoning out." My head snaps up to see Luke, sipping on a soda that I do not remember him getting, giving me that concerned look. "Stop thinking about her; it's not going to help. If it's meant to be she'll come back to you."

"Thanks, Dr. Phil, but I don't remember asking you." I lean back in my seat, the back of the chair reclining with my weight. "You may think you know what this is like, but that doesn't really make me feel better, so I'd rather not hear your insights, or commiserate on how we had it perfect once."

"I don't remember you being this much of a dick after Francesca kicked you in the balls."

"That's because I wasn't," I sigh, running a hand through my hair and rubbing my eyes under my glasses. I'm so freaking tempted to hit that button on my phone and see where she is, but I feel like that's wrong. Like it will only make it worse if I see where she is, accepting that she's physically somewhere else and not with me.

"I'm going to go heat up some leftovers. You want some?" But the second the words are out of my mouth, I know I cannot eat that food. Katie's food. "Forget that, I'm going to order a pizza."

"I'm down for that," Luke nods, his eyes trained back on his laptop. "Holy shit," he laughs out loud and hard. "You're not going to fucking *believe* this."

"What?" I ask, walking over to him, adjusting my glasses so they're pushed back up my face. "Get the fuck out." We both look at each other, blinking with our mouths agape.

"Looks like Tommy could be in a lot of trouble."

I nod. "Looks like it. Do you think he knows this is here?"

"I doubt it. There is no way he'd allow a backdoor in his system."

"Right. But the real question is, who put it there and who's accessing it?"

Luke shrugs with a *fuck if I know* expression. "You need to call his ass, like this second, and *I'm* going to order the pizza. This could take a while."

28

K *ate*

THE BEACH IS as gorgeous as I remember it being. The hotel, just as beautiful. Do I care? Not in the slightest.

I'm miserable.

So miserable I find my pathetic ass waking up crying. I haven't done this since the months following the accident.

The night I left Ryan, I hadn't gone to sleep.

After we watched Star Wars, we went to bed, made love, and then he passed out with me wrapped in his arms. It felt like it was exactly how it would be every night for the rest of our lives. But that niggling feeling in the back of my mind, twisting my insides, was still there.

I was restless, and when I got up at four, my instinct was to pack up all of my stuff and go.

So I kissed Ryan goodbye, told him that I loved him, and left.

Dick move? Without a doubt.

But I couldn't say goodbye to him. I just...couldn't.

It would have been impossible to look into his eyes and tell him I was leaving. It would have broken me, and I needed this escape. Despite my misery, I know this is how it's supposed to be. I drove straight to the airport, parked my car in long-term parking, went right into the terminal and bought a one-way ticket to Hawaii. Short of going home—which was not an option for me—this was the closest place I knew I'd be able to feel Eric.

See him again.

That was all I could think about doing.

So I wake up crying—thank you for that, Ryan—go for a run, eat something, and then sit on the beach, watching the waves while thinking.

I do a lot of that.

The first day I was gone, Ryan sent me the picture Tommy took of us in DC in that restaurant we went to. Yesterday it was a picture of us on the beach in North Carolina. He's sent them at the same time every day, which means I should get it soon while I watch the sun come up.

I have no intention of living in Hawaii, or even staying here particularly long.

I just needed an escape, and the thought of driving south or east just didn't appeal.

The thought of *driving* didn't appeal.

I just couldn't start over again. It felt like fate, a good omen maybe, that Hawaii was the first flight out. Like somehow Eric was directing me.

But today Eric isn't really who's occupying my thoughts.

It's Maggie.

My fingers clasp my pendant, a place they've been visiting more and more frequently in the last couple of days. We only took her to the beach once, and that was on the north shore of Massachusetts. She would have loved it here, would have been non-stop action. Dragging both Eric and me into the ocean, and fishing, and jumping in the pool.

If I close my eyes, I can almost picture it.

I hate this feeling, yet I somehow revel in it.

But if I'm honest with myself, I haven't felt this low in a while.

Not since that night in the car with Ryan, and even then it wasn't this bad because I had him there to hold me through it. Ryan. Yeah, he seemed to make all of this ugliness better. Seemed to make it easier to carry and walk through, knowing he was with me on the other side.

My phone pings from the pocket of my shorts, and for a moment, I hesitate, knowing what it's going to be. But then my curiosity gets the better of me, so I slide it out of my shorts, swipe the screen to unlock it, and stare at the image.

It's of me on the beach in Charleston, staring at the sunrise— much the way I am now—but this is a candid shot. I didn't know he was taking it and it's obvious. My eyes are distant, my hair blowing out behind me, and a small grateful smile is pulling at the corner of my lips. I can't see my entire face, it's a profile shot, but I get the point.

I wonder how many pictures he took without me noticing.

There's a message with the picture, which is new for him.

This was the moment I knew I was in trouble.

I'm not really sure what he means by the word *trouble*. Did he know that I would hurt him? Is that what he's trying to say? That he knew I'd be no good for him? I can't stand that thought. I can't sit here anymore; it's making me nuts.

I need to go find something to do.

Lucky for me, this island has no shortage of activities to occupy my time.

I find a lot of things to do.

I end up going for a really long walk and then hiking around a remote part of the island. By the time I make it back, it's late and I'm hungry and tired, but my mind is quiet, and I sleep.

My early morning run consists of pounding rain.

Not exactly fun and it definitely knocks out sitting on the beach, because this rain is supposed to keep up all day.

I miss Ryan. I miss Eric, and I miss Maggie.

Not in that order. Maggie is first, and always will be. But I've been putting off thinking about Ryan. I see the pictures he sends me, and then I tuck them away.

Eric, on the other hand, is everywhere—just as I intended him to be. I see his smiles and feel his touches and hear his laughter. Hear his words. And it breaks me all over again.

I know this is bad.

I know what I'm doing is counterproductive, and detrimental to my mental health and all that bullshit, but I can't seem to stop it either. I long for those memories. I want to drown in them and never come up for air again. Immerse myself in the pain of it.

My phone pings right on schedule, but this time, I set my phone face down on the nightstand and crawl back under the covers.

It's raining anyway.

Two hours later when I wake up, the first thing I do is go for the damn phone that has been waiting for me. Another candid picture of me. This time I'm driving, my mouth slightly open like I'm saying something or singing, I can't tell which.

Another message.

This was the first time I heard you sing—it was on the way to the show we went to.

I remember that night. I remember the dancing and jumping around, and the fun we had together—until that creepy guy came along of course. Another text comes in while I'm still looking at the picture, which surprises me. Ryan usually only sends one a day.

It's of us at that show, all red-cheeked and smiling.

I would do anything to keep you safe— I would slay dragons for you.

Damn him. *Dammit, Ryan.*

I toss my phone back on the nightstand and cover myself with my blankets again. I'm done for the day and it isn't even lunchtime.

I slept through the rest of the day and night. I haven't done that in almost two years. I should be concerned about this, and maybe I am a little, but I can't seem to stop it either. This downward spiral has got me firmly in its grasp and I'm allowing it to hold on tight.

Why? I really don't know, actually.

I just don't have any fight in me right now.

It doesn't help that I dreamt of Eric all night. He was smiling and happy and holding my hand, but then he kissed it before letting go with that adoring smile of his. I kept reaching for him, but it was like he was gone and I was left all alone again.

The sky is still dark as I crawl out of bed and throw on some running stuff. At least I'm still running. That's a positive thing, but it's really not enough.

Certainly doesn't feel like it is.

The rain is gone and the predawn sky is clear and calm.

So is the ocean. The waves are hardly making themselves known, the tide silently sliding up and down across the sand. I run farther than I have since I've been here. I can't seem to stop. I feel like I'm chasing after something I know I'll never reach.

I decide to shower at the spa instead of in my room, and after eating something, I venture into town. It's a busy island, and the streets and shops are filled with locals and tourists who stayed away during yesterday's rain. As I'm walking down one of the main drags, something catches my eye and I stop instantly.

A kickboxing studio.

I open the door and walk into the heavily air-conditioned building without conscious thought.

"Aloha, may I help you?" a friendly woman with long, straight black hair and dark skin asks. My eyes travel around the room, only seeing two other people. One is punching a bag, the other coaching. The smell of rubber and cleaning products surrounds me, and it's as familiar as it is new.

Taking two large steps forward, I reach the woman with a fake smile plastered on my face. "I'd like to work out for a while. Is that okay?"

Her eyes travel over me, but whatever she's thinking is well-concealed. "Do you have any gloves?" I shake my head. "Normally we require sneakers in the gym."

Right. I'm an idiot. My eyes roam down to my black flip flops. "I can come back." I don't even look up at her as I say it.

"No," she says with unexpected force. "You can stay. But if you come back after today, you'll need to be better equipped."

My eyes fly up to hers, and I can't help the smile I feel spreading across my face. My first genuine smile since I've been on this island.

"Thank you."

She hooks me up with black gloves and brings me over to a trainer named Tiger. Whatever, I'm not judging the guy's name. He's a house of a man with a military-style crew cut, black hair, and skin equally as dark as the receptionist.

"Why are you here today, Kate?" he asks.

"I have a lot of crap I need to work out, Tiger, and I can't seem to make that happen on my own."

"Fair enough, let's get started."

He lines me up, gives me some instruction, and then lets me have at it.

My fists fly through the air repeatedly. My hands and knuckles burn, despite the protection of my gloves. My arms are sore and tired.

But I don't care.

It's a high, and I find I'm smiling big through my sweat and tears. Yes, there are some tears involved.

"Can I come back again tomorrow?" I ask Tiger when I'm too exhausted to continue. I don't think doing this after an exceptionally long run was the way to go.

"I'll be here at ten tomorrow morning, waiting for you." His accent is so thick that it takes me a moment to understand him, but when I do, I smile wide, thank him and then leave.

I feel better.

Much the way I did in Dallas the last time I boxed. I think I could get addicted to this high.

My first thought is that I want to call Ryan and tell him, which just sucks.

I mean I miss him as my lover, but I really miss him as my friend.

Miss being able to talk to him and joke with him and tell him anything, knowing he'd never think less of me. That's so rare, right? Other than Eric, very few of my friends were like that. Women can be quick to condemn, at least that was the situation with many of my friends.

They judged me on my relationship with Eric, judged me on getting pregnant so fast with Maggie, judged me when I didn't get over losing them within six months of their deaths. Not all of them, but most, and it made me closed off and afraid to open up.

Until Ryan.

I didn't even have to think about it with him, it just happened.

I wonder how he's holding up, if he's okay and getting into his new life the way he should. His work is a big part of him and I know having Luke there will help.

I intentionally didn't bring my phone with me, but I sort of can't wait to get back to my room and see if he texted me a picture and message. I live for those messages. Picturing the way he says the words. How his green eyes light up with humor and mischief. His crooked smile that totally nails me every time.

The text is there waiting and when I see it, it makes my heart stop.

It's two pictures again. The first one is a candid of me at the pool in Miami, lounging in my white bikini.

I have never wanted a woman as badly as I want you.

The second picture is a selfie we took inside the club.

I miss holding your sexy body while we dance—something I never enjoyed before you.

I had been all over him that night. Couldn't get enough, and even though I convinced myself over and over again that our interactions that night were harmless and simple flirting, deep down I knew better.

By day five on the island, my routine had changed again. I wake up, go for a shorter run, eat breakfast, and then hit up the kickboxing gym for two hours.

After that, I obsessively check my phone for more pictures and messages. Some are simple and don't have a lot of deep meaning.

Some throw me totally off balance. Like the one he sent me of our night in New Orleans.

This was the worst night of our entire trip for me, but it made me realize you're the only woman I'll ever want.

I don't know why it was the worst night of the trip for him, but I do remember that his clothes smelled of perfume when I packed them up and there was an empty condom wrapper in the pocket of the jeans he had worn out that night. He had been with a woman. I was certain of it, and though I tried not to let it hurt me, it did. I ignored that feeling, though, told myself he was allowed to be with other women.

I wonder if he regrets being with her, whoever she is?

The rest of my week gets better day by day.

I've stopped crying, stopped wallowing in my own misery and taken action. In addition to the kickboxing, I've started going to yoga. I've never been a big fan of all that breathing and meditation, but what the hell? It can't hurt, and I swear I've never been in better shape in my life.

I miss him. I miss Ryan so much; all I can think about now is going back to Seattle. But I still feel like something is holding me back and I can't get a firm grip on it.

Or how to change it.

While I'm staring at the picture Ryan sent of me in Dallas after I boxed for the first time, the message reading, *this was the moment I realized I was in love you,* my phone rings in my hand. It's my mother-in-law, Rebecca.

I haven't spoken to her since before I left Boston.

I hit the green phone symbol and answer the call. "Hi, Rebecca." I'm trying for upbeat here, but I doubt she'll be so easily fooled.

"Kate, honey," her affectionate timbre hits me hard, warming the blood flowing through my veins in the best possible way. "It's so good to hear your voice. How are you?"

"I'm okay, how are you?" I sit back on my bed, knees bent, staring out at the ocean that's only a hundred feet from me.

"Hanging in there. Where are you?"

I hesitate. "Hawaii." My fingers twirl in my hair over and over again.

Rebecca is silent for so long, I'm about to see if the call discon-
nected when I hear her huff out some air into the phone. "Why are
you in Hawaii, Kate?"

"I just needed to come back. To..." Christ, how do I say this to her?
I'm closer with Rebecca than I am with my own mother. But she's
Eric's mom, which means the last thing I want to do is hurt her.

"Your mother said you were traveling with someone," she interrupts. "A man. Did that not go well? She was hoping it would lead to
something."

"What?" That's news to me. And why on earth would she tell
Rebecca that? "Rebecca, the man I was traveling with, he's..." He's
what? Just a friend? I can't say that about Ryan and be honest. Shit.

"Did it turn into something more? Your mother was sure it would.
Said he was your childhood prince or something." Her tone is even,
maybe a little hopeful, which I don't get.

Or maybe I'm just hearing what I want to hear.

"Why would Mom say that to you?" I'm so pissed off right now.

"Don't be upset with her. I wasn't."

That totally confuses me.

"He... I—" I run a hand through my hair, covering my eyes. I can't
handle this conversation. I don't want to hurt her.

"Honey," her tone is soft. "I'm hoping it *did* turn into more. If he's
a good man, worthy of a woman like you, then it would make me so
very happy to hear that you're with him now."

"How?" I can barely get the word out. I'm totally flabbergasted.

"What?" she half-laughs. "Did you think I'd want you to be alone
and miserable for the rest of your life?"

"Um..." I really don't have a response to that.

"Kate," she says my name all motherly, with a stern intonation.
"What I want is for you to be happy. That's all Eric ever wanted too. It
would kill him all over again to know that you've been suffering the
way you have, for as long as you have. He loved you with all his heart,
and he would *want* you to find someone and start again. Have more
babies. *Be happy*," she emphasizes.

Fuck, I'm crying so hard I can barely breathe.

"Did something happen with this new man?"

"Yes," I sob out, curling into myself. "I'm so sorry. I never meant for it to happen."

"Stop that. I'm happy for you if he's what you want. You're doing nothing wrong by being with another man. It's a *good* thing. A *healthy* thing."

"No," I shake my head even though she can't see it. "I feel like I'm betraying Eric's memory. Our marriage. My love for him."

"You listen to me, now," her tone is unyielding, leaving no room for argument or interpretation. "You are doing no such thing. You loved Eric and he loved you. No one is questioning that. Eric never *once* questioned it. You *should* love another man. You *should* get married again and have more children."

"I don't know how, Rebecca," I admit, feeling so...lost. "I do love Ryan. He's the person I was traveling with, and he's so incredible. But I just can't cross this bridge. I still feel like I'm married to Eric." My head rolls back against the wood headboard and I stare up at the rattan ceiling fan that's going around and around.

"Honey. You're not moving on from Eric's memory, from your marriage to him. You're not *forgetting* him. You're moving *forward*. You will always love Eric. You will always have the wonderful happy memories of your life with him. But that was your old life, Kate. You hear me?" she says forcefully. "Your *old* life. Did you ever consider that Eric is the love of your old life, and this man could be the love of your new one?"

No. No, I did not, because I never considered my marriage to Eric, my life before, as an old life and this as a new one. "I don't know what to do," I confess, feeling so defeated and broken all over again.

"You're going to get the hell out of Hawaii for starters." Damn, I love this woman. "You're going to go back and get your life together. Get a job, make some friends, start again. And if you want to include this Ryan in that, all the better."

"Shit," I laugh out. "What did I do to deserve you as my mother-in-law?"

"Knock that crap off. You're my daughter forever, and that means

I'll always want what's best for you. Now, hang up with me and go out and find yourself again. You've been missing for far too long."

I do hang up with her shortly after that, and take the longest shower ever—mostly because I'm so lost in thought—then I pack my bags and do as I was told.

I leave Hawaii.

29

R *yan*

"THE AGENT for the homeowner is calling again," my assistant Claire calls out to me from my home office. "Do you want me to pick up or let it go to voicemail?"

"Let it go to voicemail," I yell back from the kitchen. "I already told them I haven't decided about purchasing. I've still got three more months left on my lease, for fuck's sake," I snap, like their constant pestering is Claire's fault. Why is there no food in my house?

"Don't bitch at me, Ryan," she hollers back. "I don't take that crap and you know it." We're getting a little stir crazy in my house. The snow outside is out of control, and since Seattle is known for rain and not snow, the city doesn't know how to handle it and shuts down.

Pussies.

They should try spending a winter in Philly or Boston.

I walk back from the kitchen into the office, where I find Claire sitting on the couch with her phone next to her, along with my cell phone, and her tablet perched on her lap.

"Sorry. I just wish the building were open." I purchased space in a building downtown about two months back, but with the damn snow, it's closed, and there isn't anything I can do about it.

"I know. Grow up and get over it. Just be thankful that your brilliant assistant lives within walking distance, or you'd be on your own."

Is it wrong that I love how unprofessional Claire is with me?

I mean, who the hell talks to their boss like that?

Freaking millennials.

"The four people Luke hired to run the new contracts start tomorrow, and I have to get their paperwork in order before they can."

"That's why I pay you the big bucks, Claire. Did you want to stay for dinner? I'm starving and praying that the Thai place is both open and delivering." I sit in my desk chair after snatching my phone off the couch.

I have their number programmed into my phone already, which some may consider sad, but I consider a necessity.

Especially since I have zero food in my house at the moment.

"No. I have a date tonight, and I need to go home to shower and shave for him."

I cover my ears with my hands. "Jesus, Claire. Would it kill you to have a *little* professional decorum? I don't fucking want to hear about you shaving for anyone."

She smiles brightly as she winks one of her dark-blue eyes at me. "Professional is not really my style, and definitely not why you pay me the "big bucks," as you old people call it," she puts air quotes around the words. Tucking her tablet into her messenger bag, along with her phone, she stands up, her dark-red hair straggling under her bright-green beanie.

"Later, skater," she throws me a wave and heads for the front door.

I shake my head just a little indulgently before calling in my dinner, and the gods are smiling on me because they're not only open, they'll be here in less than an hour.

Awesome.

Claire's voice catches my attention, and it takes me a moment to realize that she's actually talking to another person. Why is she still here? I get up and walk to the door, wondering if it's something for me that explains her lingering, when I freeze mid-step.

She's not on the phone. She's talking to someone who is at my front door.

What the hell?

Claire's formal intonation reaches my ears. "Yes, he's here." Huh? Who could be looking for me? Judging by her tone, it's not good. I can't hear who she's speaking to, though. Maybe it's a neighbor or something. "Do you want me to get him, or are you just going to stand there soaking wet and freezing?"

I take another few steps in the direction of the door, but still hold back in case it's someone I don't want to deal with.

Claire isn't being a bitch, though her words aren't exactly kind.

"No." It's a woman's voice, but it's faint and difficult to hear. "I should go."

I halt mid-stride once again.

It can't be.

I'm hearing the voice I've imagined in my head too many times.

"I don't mean to intrude."

Holy shit.

My heart starts to pound in my chest, and my pace quickens to the door without conscious thought. I fling the partially ajar door that Claire is blocking all the way open, startling everyone. It's far too late to play it cool, but I don't care. I need to know if it's really her. It's been three months since she left me in the middle of the night. Three months of unanswered texts.

Three months of fucking misery.

I can feel Claire's scrutiny on me, but I can't remove my gaze away from Katie.

Her pale-blue eyes are staring up at me, wide as saucers. Her cheeks are the color of roses, as is her nose for that matter. She's wearing a black winter coat that is soaked through, along with her jeans and boots. Her long blonde hair is sticking out from under her New England Patriots—fucking Katie—stocking hat and is so saturated with moisture that rivers of frozen water are running from it down her shoulders and chest.

She's stunning.

So fucking beautiful that my breath is caught in my chest.

"Hi," she offers timidly, shifting her weight and biting her lip. "I didn't mean to interrupt your company." She looks at Claire quickly before turning back to me. "I'll just come back another time." She looks like she's about to run again, but I can't think clearly enough to do anything other than stare at her like a deer in headlights.

"Katie," it's all I can manage, and I feel like a prize idiot for the way I'm behaving, but I had started to convince myself that I would never see her again, so excuse me for being shocked as shit right now.

Claire snorts, waving her hand, drawing Katie's eyes away from mine. "I'm not company, but it's nice to finally meet you, Kate. This miserable bastard has told me a lot about you." Claire points her thumb in my direction. "I was just leaving. You should come in, though. You look like you're about to freeze to death."

Claire stares at me as though I should take over at this point, like any sane, normal person would do. I can't seem to be able to form words.

Katie's eyes widen further, maybe a little panicked. "Um. No. I..." She looks behind her at the street, like she's second-guessing her decision to show up here.

Finally, my brain catches up. "Katie. Come in, please. Claire, I'll see you on Monday. Go, before you run out of time and your date shows up early."

"Shit. Totally forgot." Claire steps out of my doorway into the dark, snowy, early evening, stopping in front of Katie. "You understand," she winks at Katie. "I can't exactly have my date come over when my legs aren't shaved, right?" She grabs Katie, pulling her in for a hug and whispering something I can't hear into her ear. Katie laughs, hugging her back like they're old friends.

They pull apart and Claire pats Katie on the shoulder before shoving her toward the door. I step back, and Katie reluctantly enters the house, looking around like it might be different than it was three months ago. It's not, so her inspection is short.

"I, um. Shit," Katie laughs self-consciously as I shut the door behind her. "I'm dripping water all over your house."

She's standing still on the entry rug, and this is getting awkward.

Awkward and wrong.

"Let me take your coat and then you can go over to the fireplace and warm up." I'm so glad I lit that thing in anticipation of watching a movie tonight and eating by the fire.

She turns on her heels and smiles up at me. "Thanks, if you're sure I'm not imposing," she spews out. "I know I should have called or—"

"You never have to call, and you're not imposing," I rush, cutting her off mid-sentence. I need to find my inner, composed, confident self, and quick.

I take her coat, shoving it into the closet by the front door. Her dark-green sweater isn't wet, but her jeans definitely are.

"Do you want to change into something dry?" *Please say yes. Please say yes.*

"I'm sure the fire will dry me off in no time." She looks up at me from under her lashes as she takes off her boots and walks with socked feet over to the hearth. Sinking down on the edge of the carpet, she reaches her hands out, hoping to catch the warmth in her fingers, which are no doubt frozen through.

I pad over to the sofa, sinking down into it slowly, unable to take my eyes off of her.

"What are you doing here?" I don't mean it to come out the way it does, but she shows up at my door after *months* of radio silence?

I have no idea what this means, or what she's even doing in Seattle. I guess I'm angry. Yeah, that's one emotion going through me right now. Ecstatic joy and thrilled beyond belief are there too. Oh, and then there's dread and anxiety. Can't forget those.

Her cheeks become even redder if that's possible, and I feel like a shit for asking her like that.

"I meant, what are you doing in Seattle?" I clarify in a softer tone.

Her small body turns towards me and her eyes fill with...regret? Apology?

"I live in Seattle," she says so quietly, I have to strain to hear her, and even then it takes me a moment to understand her words.

"What? Since when?" I wasn't expecting that answer at all, and it's definitely throwing me through a loop. I lean forward, placing my forearms on my spread thighs.

"For the last two and a half months."

I shoot up off the couch, pacing toward the dining area with my hand running through my hair. I have no idea where I'm going, but there is no way I can sit right now.

She's been in Seattle for two and a half *months*?

That's practically since she left me.

What. The. Fuck?

"And you're just showing up now?" I turn to her, resentful, hurt, incredulous, and full of unanswered questions.

She stands up, walking to me and suddenly the last thing I want is her close proximity.

"Please sit down, Ryan. I have a lot to tell you. A lot to explain."

Her tone is confident, and now that I'm looking at her, *really* looking at her, I see her eyes are lighter somehow. Not the color necessarily, but they're lacking the weight that used to surround them.

"Please," she says again when I don't move.

Walking back over to the couch, I reluctantly sit down, rubbing my hands up and down my face.

Katie strides over, sitting down next to me, but leaving enough space to maintain my sanity. She smells like the cold and snow—and Katie. I hate the power she has over me. Hate how I still love her as if the months of absence never happened.

"After I left here," she starts quietly, calmly, her hands folded neatly in her lap. "I hopped on the first flight out, which just so happened to be to Hawaii. I was a mess," she chuckles lightly, but there is no humor in it. "For so many reasons, really." She tilts her knees in my direction, her eyes locked on mine. "You see, I left because I felt like I was betraying Eric by loving you. By wanting to be with you. I missed Eric terribly, and I thought that if I still missed him like that, then there was no possible way I could ever be with you fully."

"Katie, that's not what I was asking for."

She holds up a hand, stopping me. "Please just let me talk. I know you have a lot to say as well, but if I don't do this, I'll never get it out."

I wave a hand in the air, giving her the floor, though I just want to grab her and pull her into my arms and not bother with the rest. I also want to shove her out the front door and slam it in her face. I don't think I've ever felt such conflicting emotions in my entire life.

"At first, it was all about Eric and Maggie. I stayed at the place where we honeymooned, with the sole intention of seeing him in my mind. Of feeling him everywhere I went. And Maggie is a natural extension of everything I do, and always will be, so she was there too. Then you started sending me those texts." I can't help but grin, even though it feels funny on my lips and small in purpose. "I loved those texts, Ryan. Counted down the seconds until I got another. I rarely let my phone out of my sight for fear that I'd miss it. I was indignant and depressed and grief-stricken, and fucking heartbroken for so many reasons, and just...emotionally spent."

Katie shifts closer to me, but I don't dare move. I can't let her touch me. She's going to leave again the second this conversation is done, and if she touches me, it'll ruin me for good.

And then what?

Then I'm fucked, that's what.

"Then one day, out on a walk, I found a boxing studio. My trainer, Tiger—" I raise an eyebrow at the name that she ignores. "—was so amazing. And Ryan?" I look at her fully as my name passes over her lips. "It helped. Something about beating those bags just does it for me," she smirks, tilting her head down, her wet, blonde hair clinging to her cheek.

The urge to brush it behind her ear is real, but I hold myself back.

"Anyway, I was still so conflicted about everything, and then a friend called," her smile widens. "My mother-in-law. Long story short, she set me straight on a lot of things, and that afternoon, I flew back here, to Seattle."

I stand up, needing to move, and end up pacing around the coffee table in front of the fire, but the heat coming off of it is too much, so I head to the kitchen, needing a fucking drink.

Katie gets up, following me in.

Grabbing a glass from the cabinet, I pour myself three fingers of whiskey, downing half of it in one gulp.

"You got some for me?" she asks, and I smile into my drink as I down the rest of it. I grab another glass and pour her some, before refilling mine.

"So you've been here since you came back from Hawaii?" I question and prompt. I need her to keep talking.

She nods, taking a small sip of her whiskey and licking her lips the way she always does after she drinks alcohol. Fuck, I love that.

"I'm sorry I didn't come to you sooner."

I hate the sincerity in her voice. Unable to even look at her right now, I turn, facing the sink and the window with my back to her.

"I wanted to. Believe me when I tell you that I did, but I still wasn't ready. I needed more time. I needed to find myself."

"What the fuck does that mean, Katie?" I spin around to glare her. "What kind of crap is that? You couldn't even let me know that you were safe? That you were in town and doing okay? I would have given you space if you had asked, but to never even contact me..." I shake my head, unable to finish my thought.

She looks down, setting her glass on the marble. "I'm sorry, Ryan. I really didn't think of it like that. I was afraid that if I came to you too soon, I would mess everything up worse than I already had. I've never been alone. Not since the age of twelve."

She does that nervous laugh thing again before pulling her attention back up to me.

"I mean, I was alone for those two plus years after they died, but that didn't really count. I've never been alone, living a real life. So I got a small apartment close to the hospital, transferred my nursing license here, and I joined a mixed martial arts studio to help channel my anger. I do yoga twice a week to try and Zen out all of that anger, and I go to a support group once a week for people who have lost spouses and children. I finally feel like I've gotten myself together," she spits out as fast as she can before her shoulders sag slightly, like just saying all of that was exhausting.

Slowly, she moves around the island, stopping in front of me and locking her eyes with mine.

"I know I've been gone a while. That you've been living your life without me and that I don't deserve your forgiveness, let alone another chance, but I want it. Both of them. I want to be with you, Ryan, and all that entails."

30

R *yan*

I WANT to say yes to her instantly. To grab her small perfect body that I love so much and kiss her into tomorrow, but I'm not moving. I'm just staring at her, wondering if she's going to cut me to shreds again. Wondering how long this new Katie will last before the old wounds come out and take her from me.

"I'm ready, Ryan," she says as if reading my thoughts. Stepping forward, she reaches out, placing a hand on my arm. Her touch is like the best sort of fire on my skin. "I wouldn't be here if I wasn't. It's why I stayed away so long. I'm ready and I love you, and I'll never hurt you again," she promises.

Lowering my head, our foreheads touch and a heavy, shaky breath leaves her lungs as her eyes close. "I missed you," I whisper, staring down at her.

My world begins and ends with her.

"I've missed you too. So much. I'm so sorry," she says as sweet tears cascade down her reddened cheeks.

My thumbs come up to wipe them away, caressing her silken cheeks and cupping her jaw.

"Don't cry, sweetheart. Everything is going to be okay."

Her eyes open, blinking a few times to clear her tears before focusing on me. "Really?"

"Yes. I love you too much to send your adorable ass packing."

She laughs through her crying, and I can't help but return her glowing smile.

"Good. I was worried you would be over me by now."

"Never, Katie. I already told you that. Haven't my pictures and texts been enough of an indicator of my feelings for you?"

She shrugs a shoulder. "You could just have a penchant for sending pictures and texts. It's hard to say what kind of kink you're into."

I laugh and brush my lips against hers, unable to hold back any longer. She tastes like minty toothpaste and whiskey, and Katie.

She tastes like my Katie and I can't get enough of her.

Just as I'm about to part her lips and get a real taste, the mother-fucking doorbell rings.

"Expecting company?" she asks, quirking an eyebrow up at me.

I nod. "You hungry?"

She nods back. "I'm always hungry."

"Then I'll go get our dinner and you can sit your ass down in front of the fireplace, but only after you go upstairs and find yourself something warm to wear. I don't want you getting my couch all wet." I pull back with a devilish smile. "At least not yet."

She laughs, shaking her head and pushing me toward the door like the last three months of separation never happened. Like we've been playing this game all along. Like we'll be doing it with each other for the rest of our lives.

I pay the guy, and when I turn around after shutting the door, Katie is walking down the stairs in one of my shirts and nothing else.

She looks crazy sexy.

She may have something on underneath, or not. There is definitely only one way to find out, though.

"That smells good. I'm starving."

Me too, I think, but definitely not for food. I set the bag down on the coffee table before crooking a finger at her. "Come here."

She smiles playfully, knowing where my mind is and fully intending to mess with me. "Mr. Grant, I believe I was promised dinner. Is this how you treat all your dates? With seduction *before* the meal?"

"Well, madam—" No way in fucking hell am I calling her Mrs. Taylor again, *ever*. "Most of my dates don't show up in only a t-shirt after a three-month absence." I take a step into her, like a tiger stalking its prey. "And they certainly aren't nearly as sexy as you are right now."

The hands folded against her stomach are shaking, but it's not in fear. It's in anticipation. I can see it in her eyes as they darken the closer I get to her.

I haven't been with anyone since Katie.

Couldn't stand the thought of it, really.

So now, I'm going to fucking devour her and we might not come up for air until I have to go to work on Monday. First, I have to clarify something.

"Are you working this weekend?" She mentioned she has a job and I know nurses work odd hours.

She shakes her head, sinking her white teeth into her plump lower lip.

"Do you plan on going anywhere anytime soon?"

Another shake of her head, the damp ends of her hair making rings of water on the cotton of the shirt she's wearing.

"What if I never let you leave again, Katie? What if I demand you stay here with me forever?"

Her eyes widen at the thought, and I wonder just how ready she really is. But then a smile spreads across her face, lighting up her eyes, and it's the most beautiful thing I've ever seen. She steps into me, gliding her small hands up my chest, her eyes watching the motion until they find mine. Holy hell that's hot.

"Then I guess I'm your prisoner, Master." *Fuck.* She crooks a finger at me, asking for me to bend down so she can whisper in my ear. "I'd very much like to be yours forever." Her sweet breath brushes against the shell of my ear. "I love you, and I'm yours if you'll have me."

My arms wrap around her in an instant, and I pull her tightly against me, taking her mouth like a starving man who's found the best tasting food in the world.

Dammit, I've missed her lips, her taste, her smell, her touch.

I'm dizzy. I'm lost. I'm never coming up for air again. Everything I need to survive is in my arms right now, and I'm never letting go. Ever.

"Katie," I breathe, and she shudders.

"I've missed you so much, Ryan. I'm so sorry for everything I put you through."

"I've missed you too, and you have the rest of the night to make it up to me," I wink. Scooping her up in my arms, her legs wrap around my waist as I carry her upstairs to *our* bedroom. I'm going to need time with her. Hours and hours, and days and days, and months and months, and years and years.

Forever. That's what I need.

I set Katie down on the bed gently. Despite how rough I want to be with her, I'm holding myself back. I can be rough with her later, but the first time we're together again, I want it to be everything she wants it to be.

"Ryan. I need you. Now." She reaches for me, grabbing my shirt and pulling me on top of her.

Well, on second thought. *Fuck gentle.*

I ravage her. Taking her mouth hard, I rip my shirt off her small curvy body, only to find that I was right about nothing being underneath, other than her panties. A guttural groan comes from my chest and I can't get enough. Can't touch her enough, taste her enough, kiss her enough. I need more.

"More," she moans, reading my thoughts exactly as she arches her back, her lips parted. So fucking hot. "Oh god, Ryan. More."

And that's exactly what I give her.

Because she's more.

She's so much more than anything I've ever experienced. Nothing will ever feel as good as being inside Katie. All of my fantasies and memories and thoughts about being with her have not done the real thing justice. She's incredible. We come together, her nails raking down my back, only adding to the pleasure of it.

Katie is wrapped up in my arms, her back to my chest, my nose buried in her hair. It's hard to believe that this is real. That she's back and in my arms without any plans to leave.

"I've missed you so much, Katie." I feel like a broken record saying that, but I can't seem to stop.

She nuzzles against me. "Me too, baby. Me too." We lie like this for a few more moments, our breathing evening out again when she says, "Ryan? I'm really hungry."

I laugh. She's always hungry.

It's one of my favorite things about her. "Then let me feed you." We get dressed again—she's only wearing my shirt, which I love—and I reheat the now cold Thai takeout. "Thai food?" she smiles as she crunches on a spring roll. "I should have known."

I pause, food suspended in midair. We're sitting on the floor eating in front of the fireplace with our backs against the coffee table. "Is that a problem? Because if it is, I may have to rethink this whole loving-you-forever thing."

She laughs, slapping my arm playfully. "I have no problems with Thai, but I can't live on takeout, Mr. Grant."

I frown at her. "Then how will we eat?"

She blinks at me. "Cook?" Her eyebrows raise up like she doesn't understand how I didn't automatically draw that conclusion.

"I don't cook." I'm not being an ass or anything. I really do suck at it, and beyond that, I have zero interest in learning when there is someone who will do it for me, like a restaurant.

"Well, I do, and since I enjoy it and am rather good at it, I guess it's going to fall on me to sustain us."

"You cook?" I can't handle this. "And not only do you *like* doing it, but you're *good* at it?"

She laughs at my expression. "Yes."

"How did I not know this?" I ask more to myself than to her. "If it's possible, Katie, I may love you more now than I did moments ago."

"Pathetic," she shakes her head, feigning dismay. "I was a wife and a mother, cooking sort of came with that."

I cannot believe how casually she just said that. The flash of pain still flies through her eyes—I suspect it will always be there—but she's not letting it control her anymore. It's not running her life, she is, and she's kicking ass at it.

I'm feeling brave, or stupid, or both. "Do you want that again?" She knows I'm not asking about the cooking.

She just stares at me for a long beat, my heart rate increasing with each second that ticks by. I'm suddenly wondering if I've pushed her too far. But I have to know. Finally, she nods once, but no words come with it. I don't know if I had asked her that question months ago if she would have given me the same answer.

"Do you?" Her voice is so soft it takes me a moment to realize what she asked.

I look over at her, her sweet face shining up at me, so vulnerable and beautiful. "Yes, Katie. With you, I want everything," I tell her, leaving no doubt as to what I'm saying, because as much as I need to know, so does she. "But first I want you to move in with me." There, I said it.

"But you don't know me that well."

She's kidding me, right? "Katie, I lived with you in a car for almost a month. I'd say I know you pretty well, and we can learn the small stuff as we go."

She smiles softly, her shy smile. "Are you sure that's what you want? I mean, it's been so long since we've been actually together. Longer than we were together."

I put down the container of noodles and reach for her, laying her ly on the floor and hovering my long body over her short one. I love how she feels beneath me. I love how perfectly she molds to me, how she feels like she was made to be in my arms.

"I don't care about any of that, Katie. I want what we had in that car. I want the excitement and the laughing, the teasing and the fun, the lust and the love." Her heart is hammering against my chest. "I want our adventure."

Her smile is dazzling. "Okay, Ryan. I'm in."

EPILOGUE

Two and a half years later

"CAN'T YOU DRIVE ANY FASTER?" Katie yells at me as I try to get us around midday traffic in Seattle. The fact that it's also the last day of Bumbershoot—which is where we were when this happened—is only making it worse. I'm freaking the fuck out. My heart is racing a mile a goddamn minute and I'm sweating like a fat man running up a mountain.

"I'm trying, sweetheart." Fuck, I can't even sound calm. "I'm going as fast as I can."

"Ryan, love, I'm not delivering your children in my Prius."

I look over at her, feeling my eyes turning as wide as saucers.

She's beet red, her brow slick with sweat, and her eyes are...in control. "How close are you?"

"My contractions are three minutes apart and I'm having twins. None of this is good. I should be in the hospital by now." She's talking so fast I can hardly keep up. "My fluid was clear, so that's good. But these babies weren't supposed to be delivered for three weeks, and even that was early, so you need to get me there *now*."

"Just breathe, sweetheart. Breathe." Isn't that what you're supposed to say when your wife is in labor? That's what they always say in the movies, but she's shooting me a look that says she's about to pummel me. Out of freaking nowhere, she folds into herself, grabbing her round, tensing belly and yelling so loudly that the windows shake.

"Fuck," I hiss out.

"Ahhhh. Ryan, drive this car to the goddamn hospital!"

"I am!" I shout back over her screaming, but I realize I slowed during her last onslaught of pain.

Shit. Crap. Shit.

The navigation pops on telling me to take a left, and I do that at the speed of light. The Prius can really corner; I'll give it that.

"You doing okay? Hanging in there?" God, everything I'm saying feels wrong.

"They're early, Ryan. Early even by twin standards." Shit. She's crying. "What am I going to do if they're not okay?"

I reach out and grab her hand to squeeze, but I quickly have to put it back on the wheel since I'm weaving like a bastard around cars.

"It's going to be fine. Our babies are going to be perfect, just like their mother, you'll see." She's right, though; she's only thirty-four weeks. "The last ultrasound looked good, baby. Remember that."

"Ryan, if something happens to me, you'll protect our babies with your life, right?"

"What the fuck?" Yeah, I said that out loud, but seriously?

"Promise me," she snaps back with a force I didn't know she possessed. "I need you to promise me. Not only am I a nurse who's seen the worst of the worst, but I've lived it too."

She's thinking about Maggie and Eric.

Of course, she is.

I soften my outrage. "I promise, Katie. I will always protect my family. You included."

She doesn't say anything, but her eyes close and she begins to hum as her hands run rhythmically over her large belly.

We got engaged about a year after Katie moved in with me, and we married a few months later in a small ceremony. Nothing fancy.

Katie said she didn't want to do that again, and I didn't care either way. I only cared about making her mine forever, so I went along with whatever she needed to get through it.

That included taking off her precious pendant.

It was her therapist's idea and I supported her no matter what she chose.

Small fact I did not know: that pendant contained some of both Maggie and Eric's ashes, which is why she clung to it. Even though that did creep me out a little—sorry, I'm only human—I understood her desire to have it. The pendant didn't go far, though; it sits in a fire-proof case in her nightstand.

We also flew to Boston—with me heavily sedated—after the engagement, so she could tell Eric in person and talk with him about it.

It was emotional as hell, and even I got in on the action by asking his permission to take his wife as my own. I half-expected him to reach out from beyond the grave and grip my balls in a vise, but he didn't.

He was very understanding.

At least that's what Katie said when I told her my concerns.

So I married her and we ended up buying the house I was renting because it's an awesome house with a good-sized backyard and has three bedrooms, which we're going to need very, very soon.

My software hit the market and my company has grown exponentially. I put Luke in charge of its release, including dealing with the press. When our company makes a public statement, it comes from him. We have some of the biggest corporations in the world as our clients, and I've even had to occupy an entire building since we now have over two thousand employees and are still growing with a shit-ton of hardware to house.

Luke and I also single-handedly saved Tommy's company.

He had been hacked hard and didn't even notice it.

Loser.

We still don't know who was behind it, and that's a bit of a concern. But we fixed it and locked his shit down with my new, very expensive software, and since then, he's been good. So good in fact, that the measly twenty percent he gave Luke and me is now worth a quarter of a billion dollars.

And that's not even cracking the shell of what my company is pulling in.

But none of that means anything without Katie and our family that's about to begin.

She's my world, they're my world, and I've never been happier or felt more complete in my life.

Adding to that, my brother Kyle, my newest corporate lawyer, moved out here around the time Katie and I found out we were expecting twins. Unfortunately, I think he's got a thing for my little redheaded assistant, but I'm not going there right now.

I pull into the emergency room turnaround, slam the car to a stop and press that stupid parking button. Racing around to the other side, I yank open the door. Katie can barely walk or move, that's how much pain she's in.

Thankfully, a doctor taking a smoke break outside—really?—comes to our aid and grabs a wheelchair. The security guard runs over, yelling at me to move my car, but I toss him the keys and tell him that either he can have it towed or I'll give him a hundred dollars right now to park it for me.

He shuts up and gets in the car.

Like there was any chance I was leaving my wife right now.

"Take me upstairs," Katie is yelling and crying. "I don't want to deliver where I work."

"Kate, you're delivering these babies now," Dr. Clarkson, her boss and chief of the ED, says. "You're fully dilated, and I'm afraid if I try to bring you up, you'll deliver in the elevator."

"This is so humiliating," Katie covers her face in between contractions as she props herself up on the gurney in the trauma room. "Everyone I work with is going to not only know what my vagina looks like, but what the inside of it looks like as well."

"Then they'll all be jealous it's not theirs," I add, running a hand down her sweaty blonde head.

She looks up at me with wide, tired eyes. "They will, won't they?" God, I love her.

"Okay, Kate, I feel a contraction coming." Dr. Clarkson is shielded head to toe in protective gear like she's going into a hazmat situation, and is poised at the foot of the gurney between Katie's open legs. We've also got two nurses in here who are friends of Katie's, so it's all good. "Get ready to push, Kate, we've only got a small window to get these babies out. I've got the NICU on standby and Peds is on their way down."

Katie nods, looking up to me quickly with tears glassing-over her beautiful eyes.

"It's going to be fine, sweetheart." I lean down to kiss her forehead.

Katie cries out, and Clarkson yells *push,* and then everything goes into fast motion. More doctors and nurses come rolling in with machines and incubators, all wearing masks and hats.

I'm suddenly terrified.

I need my babies to be okay. I need my Katie to be okay.

I position my body behind hers, helping her to sit up to better improve her pushing angle or some bullshit like that, and I hold her to me, vowing never to let go.

Katie screams and yells, and seconds later, the smallest slimiest human being I've ever seen is pulled from her. The baby is a gray-bluish color, and before I know what's happening, everyone is rushing around again. The baby—whose gender I couldn't even see —was passed off to the doctors in masks with machines.

"Is it breathing? Oh god, I can't hear it," Katie cries out.

"It's a boy, Kate. You have a son," Dr. Clarkson says calmly, looking both of us in the eye in turn.

I sob and so does Katie, my body covering hers as we embrace. I'm shaking and crying like I never have before, so completely overwhelmed by everything. We whisper words of love to each other.

I have a son, but the fact that he's not crying and has six people working on him is not good.

"What's going on?" Katie yells out, trying to see around the doctors. So am I, but I'm being held back by someone who tells me I have to let them work. I'm about to pummel the rather large woman when a small pissed off wail pierces the chaos, and everyone freezes before they sigh in relief.

"Five minute Apgar is seven, Kate," one of the doctors says to her. "He looks good. His weight is excellent for a thirty-four weeker."

"That's because he's got a large penis like his father," I whisper to Katie, but apparently not quietly enough because others around us laugh. She smacks at me playfully before arching her back and crying out in another contraction.

"You're at ten centimeters again, Kate. You ready to push out baby number two?" Clarkson asks.

She nods as tears stream down her face.

"You're doing so well, baby. I'm so proud of you. I love you so much," I whisper into her ear, watching the doctors continue to work on our son.

"Push, Kate. Now," Clarkson demands and Kate complies, but the baby doesn't come out as quickly as the last one did. It takes her three more contractions and three pushes with each one before our little girl comes out.

Unlike with our son, she cries instantly, and so does Katie as she whispers something about giving Maggie siblings. I can't begin to imagine just how emotional this moment is for her.

Both an extreme high and extreme low.

A few minutes later, our perfect babies are placed on Katie's chest, and both immediately latch onto her beautiful full breasts—who can blame them really?

The staff gives us privacy for a few minutes now that our son seems to be out of the woods, but they're still taking both of them up to the NICU for a few days at least.

Fine. Whatever, I won't fight it.

"You did so well, sweetheart. They're perfect," I kiss her sweet lips, looking down at our instant family. I never knew happiness could feel this way. Never realized that things could actually get better. But they have.

"You were part of this too, you know?" She looks up at me with the most contented expression I've ever seen.

"Love, all I did was orgasm inside of you. Not exactly a hardship for me. In fact, when they give us the go-ahead, I'd like to do that again."

Her eyes widen in horror. "Make more babies?"

"No." I shake my head. "Orgasm inside of you." She really should have gotten that point. I'll blame it on the fatigue and hormones. "I think we'll start with the two babies we have and see where we end up in a few years."

"Thank Christ. I was worried there for a minute." She looks down at our little bundles that are happily sucking away.

"We have to name them."

"You don't like the names we came up with?"

We had two of each gender since all we knew was that we were having twins. We decided to be surprised on the rest.

"Yes, but which ones, love?"

"Oh. Right." She sinks her teeth into her lip, worrying it back and forth. "I think I like Will."

"I assume that's for our son?" She looks up at me like I'm an idiot. "Just making sure." I hold my hands up in surrender. "Will, it is. I think I like Leah for our girl."

She nods. "Will and Leah. Perfect."

"Just like you. And them, of course." I lean down and kiss her lips again, brushing my fingers across their tiny soft heads and kissing them. I've heard babies smell good, but I never realized just how amazing it really is.

All of it. Every single thing about this is just…perfect.

"We're perfect, Ryan," Katie says, echoing my thoughts as she always seems to do. "And thank god we didn't have them in the car."

The End

LIKE RYAN and Kate's story? Get the entire series HERE on SALE Sign up for my Newsletter and get a free copy of one of my books. Keep reading for a sneak peek of Start Over.

ALSO BY J. SAMAN

Wild Love Series:

Reckless to Love You

Love to Hate Her

Crazy to Love You

Love to Tempt You

Promise to Love You

The Edge Series:

The Edge of Temptation

The Edge of Forever

The Edge of Reason

The Edge of Chaos

Boston's Billionaire Bachelors Series:

Doctor Scandalous

Doctor Mistake

Doctor Heartless

Start Again Series:

Start Again

Start Over

Start With Me

Las Vegas Sin Series:

Touching Sin

Catching Sin

Darkest Sin

END OF BOOK NOTE

Hi everyone, and thank you for reading Ryan and Kate's story. This book seemed to just fly out of me, and I have to admit, it was as emotional as it was fun to write.

I guess it begs he question, can you fall in love like that twice? I like to think so. I like to think that Kate's story isn't unique. The road trip in this story is once of my favorite aspects. I've done much of that trip before, but I still have so much of this country, this world to explore.

Kate and Ryan just clicked together in my head. I quickly fell in love with both characters separately, as well as together. I hope you enjoyed it as much as I did. I want to thank my family for always being loving and supportive of me, even when you don't realize you're being so.

Subscribe to my newsletter that has my newest releases, cover reveals, sales, giveaways and so much more. SUBSCRIBE or check out my website: http://jsamanbooks.com

Love you all!!!!

Oh yeah, please leave a review. I'm an indie and need all the help I can get.

Keep reading for Chapters 1 & 2 from Start Over!!!

START OVER

Ivy

"No one drinks like that unless they're in love," the woman next to me says. I've been drinking in the pub for the past hour, and though I had noticed the nice pair of legs dangling out of the tiny skirt when she'd sat down next to me half an hour ago, I didn't do further research.

I ignore her as I take a sip of my Manhattan, which I only drink during dire situations.

"Oh, come on," she continues, clearly not taking my not-so-subtle hint. "It can't be that bad."

I turn my head to her. She's pretty. Red hair and dark blue eyes, at least that's how they appear in the dim lighting, attached to petite yet soft features.

I shrug a shoulder, turning back to the mahogany of the bar, hoping the heavy bass beat will serve as enough of a buffer between us.

I've never been in this pub before. I guess that really shouldn't surprise me since I've never been much of a boozer—not even in college when you're supposed to hit the turps.

I only live a few blocks away. Staggering distance. That's what they call it, isn't it?

Yes, that's exactly what they call it. I plan on getting good and drunk tonight. I'm sure I'll regret it in the morning, but for now, it seems like an ace of an idea.

My drinking neighbor says it can't be that bad, but she's wrong.

I lost someone today. Not me per se, and it wasn't my fault or anything, but still. It's a life gone. A family devastated. You'd think by this point I'd be used to it and no longer take it personally, but I'm not, and I do.

So I'm getting pissed.

I take a sip of my second Manhattan of the night, admiring the fact that the bourbon and sweet vermouth are now flavorless.

"Breakup or unrequited love?" the girl on my right asks again.

"Neither."

And it's the truth. I'm not in love and I'm not going through a breakup. Sometimes, life just requires a night of drinking in solitude. I don't share these moments of somber contemplation with anyone. Not my colleagues or staff. No one. Which is probably why I don't have a ton of friends. They're all big on commiserating together. I'm not.

Why does everyone always assume that everything has to do with the opposite sex?

"Okay, fine," she says a little dramatically as she sips her . . . whatever the hell that is. "If you don't want to talk about it, I get it."

"Sorry, it's not you."

"Oh right, the whole *it's not you, it's me* line," she laughs. "Your ex must have been a real bitch."

I can't help but laugh with her because this woman is actually a nice distraction—one I could use.

"A bitch?" I turn to face her.

"Yeah, to make you so bitter. Was she whoring around?"

"Whoring around?" I feel like we're playing dirty Mad Libs here, but I can't quite get the punchline. And now I'm mixing metaphors, which tells me I should have eaten dinner before I took to the booze.

Wait, did she say *she*?

Ginger here looks at me equally confused. "The woman you broke up with," the redhead enunciates each word like I'm a child.

"I'm not gay." I tilt my head, wondering why she automatically assumes I am. She should meet my sister, Sophia, then her gaydar would be off the charts. "And I didn't break up with anyone."

She bites her lip, amused as hell. "If you're not gay, what are you doing in a gay bar?"

Her question catches me completely off guard, and I spin on my stool to survey the crowd.

Sure as rain, she's right.

Judging by all the female couples, this is very much a lesbian bar. "Oh." At least I have a good place to take Soph when she comes to visit next month. The drinks are ripper.

She laughs out loud, head tilted back, smacking the bar twice for effect. "It's fine; I'm not gay either. Well, not really anyway."

I swivel back, reaching for the stem of my fancy glass.

"Then why are you here?"

She shrugs a shoulder, "They have the best mojitos in town."

I eye her drink quickly before turning back to my own and finishing it down. "I'm Ivy."

"Claire."

"Nice to meet you."

"Ditto."

Claire downs the rest of her drink in one impressive slurp of the straw before slamming it on the counter and wiping her mouth with the back of her hand. She stands up slowly, adjusting her tiny skirt before slapping a twenty on the bar.

"You ready?"

I furrow my eyebrows. "For what?"

"To get out of here."

"I thought we already established that we're not gay?"

She snorts, "I'm not going to screw you, Ivy, though I do think you're rather babealicious—in a serious, brooding sort of way. I'm

headed to a party at a friend's house, and I want you to come
with me."

"A party?" I deadpan. "You don't even know me."

"True, but that doesn't mean we can't be friends. Now come on,
I'm borderline bitchy late instead of fashionably late."

What the hell.

I toss down some money and follow my new friend, Claire, out
into the cool misty night. She turns right, immediately setting off at a
good clip and crossing her arms over her chest to stave off the cold.

"I like your accent. Australian?"

I nod. "Yes, but I've lived in the States for nearly sixteen years
now."

"That explains why you have a slight accent, but don't sound over
the top Aussi."

I snicker. "Over the top Aussi?"

"Yup. I would know. I lived in Australia for six months when I was
a kid."

I turn to her, taken a back. "Oh, yeah? Where abouts?"

"Sydney. Army brat. My dad was there for training or something."

I can't imagine moving around like that for short stints at a time.
Probably explains why she's so affable and outgoing. How else do you
meet people or make friends in that sort of situation?

"What about you?"

"Just outside of Melbourne."

"Is your family still there?"

I shake my head, stepping around a couple who decided that the
middle of the sidewalk was the perfect place to make out. "My mum
and dad are here in Seattle now, and my sister lives in California."

"Nice." Claire stops at the foot of a large craftsman-style home.
"This is us."

I angle to her, my eyebrows raised, because the house is
completely dark.

There are no lights on and no cars on the street or in the
driveway.

"It's a surprise engagement party for my boss and my best friend," she explains, climbing the few cement steps up to the door. "They're getting married in a couple of months, but the ceremony is going to be super small, so one of Kate's work friends set this up so they could celebrate with her."

"Oh, that's a lovely thing to do."

"It is." She looks at me as she opens the front door like she lives here. "But if you say lovely again, we can't hang out."

I snicker, grinning for the first time all day as I wearily follow her in.

"Don't worry, it's just me," Claire calls out, clearly not wanting a houseful of people to yell surprise at her.

"About damn time, Claire," an enticing male voice bellows out from the dark.

"Suck it, Luke," Claire says as she grabs hold of my wrist, seeming to know the way. I allow her to lead me, wondering what the hell I'm doing in a strange house with a strange girl. Around us, people are giggling and shushing one another.

Stumbling over someone, I mutter out an apology as Claire jerks me down to the ground behind a heavy, solid piece of furniture that can only be a sofa or chair.

"If you had gotten here on time, I wouldn't have to give you shit," the same male voice whispers in my ear.

"Sorry?" I whisper back, a little unsettled by his proximity. Our hands are essentially touching as the warmth of his body cascades over mine, his breath brushing my face. He smells like the rain, fabric softener, and some woodsy cologne. It's fantastic, and I practically breathe him in before I can stop myself. It's the sort of scent that women all over the world fantasize about because it's just that good.

"You're not Claire," he says, and I feel his fingers skimming my own in what can only be a purposeful motion. I jerk my hand back to my lap.

"No, I'm not." I don't offer more of an explanation than that. Suddenly I'm embarrassed to be here, practically sitting against a strange man in the dark. His body and face somehow seem closer, though all I can make out are shadows without specific features.

"That's a good thing," he whispers. His breath blowing at a wisp of hair near my neck, sending chills across my skin.

What the bloody hell was that?

It's the alcohol. It's making me dizzy and not myself.

He must not realize how close he is to me, so I shift to the other side, abutting Claire's small frame.

As I look around, squinting my eyes against the black, I realize that this isn't just a house party—it's an intimate gathering of friends, and I met the only person I know here twenty minutes ago.

I've never done anything like this, and I have no excuse for my behavior now except that it was a real bastard of a day and I needed the mental diversion.

"Luke," Claire whispers, leaning across me.

She must have bloody night vision goggles or cat eyes or something because she seems to have no difficulty seeing in the dark.

"This is Ivy. I picked her up at Cello's, even though she's straight. Ironic, huh? I meet the only other non-lesbian there and talk her into leaving with me."

"That's fucking hilarious," Luke deadpans. "Now can you shut up so we don't blow the lame-ass surprise? They just pulled in the driveway."

I'm about to ask how he even knows that when I hear car doors slamming shut and a man and a woman talking and laughing.

Keys jiggle in the lock, and I can feel Claire—at least I hope it's her—grab my hand in excited anticipation. The door flies open and someone flips the switch on the lights, and suddenly everyone jumps up, including me, and yells surprise.

I'm temporarily blinded by the sudden transition in lighting, and as my pupils constrict and accommodate, I'm being pulled into the rushing crowd of well-wishers.

Somehow I manage to pry myself away from Claire's ninja grip and maneuver myself to the back of the heap.

The group of about thirty people is laughing and talking animatedly with a woman I cannot see, but her fiancé is towering over the rest with dark, nearly black hair, a thick beard, and glasses.

Not a bad-looking bloke.

My eyes scan the room, debating if I should make a run for it out the back when a small blonde woman with an angelic face and light blue eyes approaches me. She looks familiar, but for the life of me I can't place her.

"Ivy Green?"

"Um . . . Yes?" Why does that sound like a question?

"Welcome," she says warmly, and I smile, feeling horrible for not knowing her name when she clearly knows mine. "I'm Kate Taylor. I work at the hospital with you. I'm a nurse in the ICU, but float to the ED sometimes."

And then it all clicks into place.

"Yes, of course," I beam, relieved that I know a second person here, again, sort of. "I apologize for not realizing who you were straight off."

She waves me away like it's nothing. "Claire said you were her date for the night. She's my maid of honor."

That relief from moments ago crashes to the floor, shattering into a million pieces. I'm mortified, because this is clearly *her* engagement party that I'm crashing, and I didn't even know her name.

"Yes, sorry. I hope that's all right?" I look around helplessly. "I realize I'm intruding."

"Not at all. I'm glad you're here. The more people I know at the hospital, the better."

I can relate to that.

Though I've been working there since the start of my residency, I haven't really clicked with many people. But that's all on me. I've been consumed with work and thought of little else.

Scanning around, I see a slew of other familiar faces, including Craig Stanton, who mercifully has yet to notice me.

"It's a bit unexpected that I'm crashing the surprise party of a work colleague."

"I know, right?" Kate laughs out loud.

"What's so funny?" Claire hops over to us. Literally, she's hopping across the room. "You macking my date?"

"No, but I definitely knew her before you did."

"No way," Claire half-yells, pouting with a disappointed jut of her lip.

"It's true, mate," I say, patting her shoulder like she's a small child. "I work at the hospital with her."

"Figgity fuck, Kate. How is it you've met everyone I know before me?"

"Not Luke. You definitely knew him first."

"True, but that dickwad doesn't count."

"Get over it," Kate laughs, before giving a pouting Claire a kiss on the cheek. "I have to mingle, but I'm glad you came, Ivy. I hope we can talk more later."

"Thanks. Me too." I mean that as well. Kate is as sweet as her face.

"Come on, Ivy, let's go hit up the bar and look for unattached men. Something tells me it's slim pickings in that department."

Claire leads me toward the back of the house and into a gorgeous gigantic kitchen where there is a bar set up on the center island and a few people I don't recognize, milling about.

"What's your poison? Another Manhattan?" Claire asks, pulling two red plastic cups off the stack.

"Uh, sure. Why not? I don't have to be on shift until ten tomorrow."

"Atta girl." She pours a lot of whiskey and a splash of sweet vermouth into the cup and hands it to me. No ice. Not even slightly chilled. Just straight up alcohol.

"You're joking, right?" I ask, eyeing the warm, no doubt overly strong, beverage.

"Not at all. This party is lame. We need to get our drink on if we're going to last."

"I can't drink like this. You'll be holding my hair above the toilet in no time."

"Don't tell me I picked up a pussy of a drinker?" she snorts. "Get it? Pussy of a drinker? I picked you up at a *gay* bar."

I really have no words for that one.

I shrug, "Sorry, mate, but yeah."

"At least have a few sips." She drops a couple of ice cubes from the bucket into my cup with a splash. "There, better now?"

"Fine, but if I get sick and make a total mess of myself, you better not think less of me."

"Never. Cross my wicked, black heart." She makes an X over her heart with her finger.

"I'm not sure if that lends itself to trust, but I'll go with it for now."

"Good." She smiles brightly, holding up her own cup filled with some crazy concoction. "To new friends."

"To new friends," I repeat as we crash our plastic cups against each other with a crinkling sound before I take far too large a sip. The liquid burns as it slides down my throat, but for the first time in days, I'm relaxed and happy. Hoping it lasts longer than just this drink. Wondering what else this night has in store for me.

Wait till Ivy runs into Luke, the man she had a one-night stand with ten years ago. Will their chemistry be all that it was that night? Find out in Start Over!

Made in the USA
Middletown, DE
29 February 2024

50565985R00172